KU-614-927

SEE NAPLES AND DIE

SEE NAPLES AND DIE

by

John Davies

Dales Large Print Books
Long Preston, North Yorkshire,
England.

British Library Cataloguing in Publication Data.

Davies, John
    See Naples and die.

    A catalogue record for this book is
    available from the British Library

    ISBN 1-85389-979-8 pbk

Copyright © 1961 by John Davies

Cover photography © J. Allan Cash Ltd.

The moral right of the author has been asserted

Published in Large Print 1999 by arrangement with Rupert
Crew Ltd.

All rights reserved. No part of this publication may be
reproduced, stored in a retrieval system, or transmitted
in any form or by any means, electronic, mechanical,
photocopying, recording or otherwise, without the prior
permission of the Copyright owner.

LINCOLNSHIRE
COUNTY COUNCIL

Dales Large Print is an imprint of
Library Magna Books Ltd.
Printed and bound in Great Britain by
T.J. International Ltd., Cornwall, PL28 8RW.

1

Blair splashed more whisky into his glass. He set the bottle back on the table, turning his mouth down at the sight of the label on it. Haig. That bottle might have held Haig once, but only a very long time ago.

It was all part of the great, sprawling racket that was North Africa. He was part of it himself. And to-night he was more than usually sick of his own role.

He picked up the glass and swallowed half the stuff in it. He looked around him with a jaundiced eye and decided that the Hotel Oasis was at its most stinking to-night. The basket chair that rather uncertainly supported his weight creaked as he shifted impatiently, resolving to give Leclerc another ten minutes to come through. If the Frenchman hadn't called by then, he was going to get up and go.

Blair was sitting at a small bamboo table in the Hotel Oasis's dirty, flyblown foyer. On the wall above it there was a smeared

7

mirror in a tarnished gilt frame which gave him a view of the desk and the greasy young Tunisian clerk behind it. Business at the Oasis wasn't exactly brisk and the clerk was bored. Right now he was picking his nose.

Blair emptied his glass and reached for the bottle again. As he did so, the phone rang at the desk. The clerk picked it up. 'Hotel Oasis.' He listened briefly and then held out the receiver. 'For you, M'sieur Blair.'

Blair got up and went over to the desk. He was big, broad-shouldered, slim-hipped, with a strong, weather-beaten face and crisp, wiry black hair. He was dressed in a rumpled white linen suit.

He took the phone. 'Yes?'

'Monsieur Blair?'

It wasn't Leclerc. The Frenchman's voice was dry and pedantic. He sounded like a university don, which he wasn't. This was a very different voice; soft, silky, wheedling.

'Who is it?' Blair asked curtly. There were a lot of voices like that in North Africa, and he didn't like any of them.

'It is Mifsoudis, Monsieur Blair. Constantine Mifsoudis. Perhaps you do not remember me?'

Blair remembered Mifsoudis. The man was a small-time Tunis travel agent— 'travel agent' being a courtesy term. Like so many others, Mifsoudis used his so-called agency as a cover for his real business. He was just another of the numberless contact men who lived on the contraband and illegal entry trade between Tunis and the countries on the northern shores of the western Mediterranean.

He said, 'I remember you. What do you want?' He was frowning now, and not only with distaste. He was conscious of the sharp sense of danger that he seemed to be more aware of now with every day that passed.

Not that Mifsoudis was dangerous. He and his sort were of little account in themselves. What disquieted Blair was how this little rat should have come to know that he was at the Hotel Oasis that night. It wasn't a place that Europeans frequented—which was why he was there. He himself used it simply as a contact point with Leclerc. And he certainly never advertised his visits there, any more than he advertised his connection with the Frenchman himself.

Mifsoudis said, 'You are returning to

9

Naples to-night, *capitano?*'

Blair said shortly, 'Yes.' There was no point in not admitting that. The charter trips he did with the launch were well enough known. In fact they had been deliberately very much publicised. Blair had to have his own cover, just like everybody else.

The wheedling voice came over the phone again. 'You could perhaps take another passenger, *capitano?*'

'Hardly. My boat is full.'

'But you could find room for one more?'

'Who?'

'A lady. Very beautiful.'

Blair grunted with disgust. He was sick to death of very beautiful ladies. He said, 'Who is she?'

'A very special passenger, *capitano*. She will pay you well.'

'In kind, I suppose?'

'What is that, please?'

'Skip it. Will she pay money?'

'But of course. American dollars ... That is all right?'

Blair didn't answer at once. If it was what it sounded like—illegal exit and/or entry the other end—he wouldn't touch it. He was pretty sure he wasn't going to

10

touch it anyway. He was asking questions only to try to find out what was in the wind. You had to know what the score was, all the time.

He said, 'Is she hot?'

'Oh, a lady, *capitano*—but most sexual, I am sure.' Mifsoudis gave a high-pitched giggle. He sounded like a pimp.

Blair said, 'For God's sake—is she on the lam? In trouble with her husband—or the police?'

'She is not married,' Mifsoudis said. 'Her passport describes her as *femme-sole*. More than that, and the other details given there, I do not know.' The little tout was primly, absurdly on his dignity now. 'I am a travel agent, *capitano*, not a policeman. But I am sure she is a perfectly legitimate lady. Otherwise I would not be arranging her passage.'

Blair said, 'Come off it.'

'But I assure you—'

'She just wants to go across to Naples?'

'Yes. That is all.'

'What's wrong with a plane, or the regular boat? Why the hell should she want to come with me?'

Mifsoudis giggled again. 'Plenty ladies want to come with you, *capitano*—or so I hear. Now, please—you will take her?'

Blair paused again. 'How much?'

'How much do you want?'

'I'll take her for five hundred bucks. If her passport's in order.'

The price shook Mifsoudis, as Blair intended it should do. He said, 'Five hundred dollars? That is a very great deal of money for a short sea trip!'

'It includes danger money.'

'But I have assured you she is not dangerous!'

Blair smiled tightly. It was a smile with no humour in it. He said, 'You also told me she was beautiful. And apparently you know what a sucker I am for beautiful women.'

Mifsoudis said doggedly, 'It is too much money. Very much too much.'

Blair said, 'All right—I'm not bothered. If the trip's worth five hundred dollars to her, okay. If not, it's still okay with me. I don't give a damn whether she comes or not.'

There was a brief silence at the other end of the phone. Then Mifsoudis said, 'Very well.'

'You mean she'll pay it?'

Mifsoudis said stiffly, 'Yes. If it is necessary.'

Blair said, 'She must be pretty set on this stunt. I don't get it.'

Mifsoudis said, still more stiffly, 'I can only tell you I don't know anything about that. My client's private affairs—'

'Forget it,' Blair said. 'You've got her there?'

'I can reach her by telephone. She is waiting to hear.'

Blair said, 'Okay. Her name?'

'She is Mademoiselle Meya Nordstrom.'

'Danish—Swedish?'

'Swedish, m'sieur.'

Blair turned the name over in his head. Meya Nordstrom. He had never heard of her—or had he? Just very faintly it rang a bell. But he couldn't put any sort of dossier to it. Probably he'd seen it in the papers. She was probably just one more of the dubious ornaments of the shifting, cosmopolitan socialite set that idled their lives away in the fashionable resorts of the Bay of Naples; in Naples itself, and Sorrento, and Capri.

One of the film crowd, he reckoned. Not very successful, or he would have been able to place her, would almost certainly have met her. Maybe she had 'retired' from the screen. There were a

13

lot of beautiful Scandinavian women in Italy. Most of them had started off by trying their luck in the Roman studios, and most of them, as a simple matter of arithmetic, had fallen by the wayside. A lot of those had settled for being kept by some wealthy man or other in some villa or apartment, either in Rome, or one of the *chic* and moneyed play-places of the south.

He remembered that Mifsoudis was still waiting at the other end of the phone. He said, 'One other thing.'

'Please?'

'I told you just now I've got a full complement of passengers already. This Nordstrom woman will have to put up with any berth I can find her.'

'Very well.'

'Right. You know where the launch is? I bet you do.'

Mifsoudis said, 'In harbour, of course. I do not know precisely where.'

'She's alongside the north jetty here in La Goulette. And we're sailing at midnight. If she wants to come with me, she'd better be aboard by then. I won't wait for her.'

Mifsoudis said wearily, 'I will tell her.'

'And I want cash on the nail, when she embarks. Dollars, as arranged. Otherwise I still don't take her. Your customer will be left on the quay.'

Mifsoudis sighed. 'You are a very hard man, *capitano*. But I will tell her that too.'

The phone clicked. Blair hung up at his end. He smiled grimly to himself again as he replaced the receiver. No doubt Mifsoudis had hoped to take a big cut for himself out of the passage money this woman was prepared to pay, but he wasn't likely to get much out of it now, since Blair had put the price so high. No wonder the little squirt had sounded more and more depressed.

He stood for several moments with his hand still on the instrument, asking himself once more the question he had asked Mifsoudis: Why did this woman want to take passage with him when she could do the trip much more comfortably by air or the steamer at a fraction of the price? Was she just another of the idle, over-sexed, spoiled rich women who plagued his life? Or was there something more to it than that?

He turned irritably away, telling himself

15

that he was getting as nervous as an old woman who thinks she's got a man under the bed. This Nordstrom creature was no doubt just another of the kind he suspected her to be: a woman with too much money, and nothing to do except think up little whimsies like this. Maybe she thought that by this kind of antic she would make an impression on him and be able to jump the queue of other women bidding for the attentions of the glamorous Captain Blair!

That was all it was. But—what the hell? He didn't care what she was. As far as he was concerned, she would simply be handing him five hundred good American dollars for a short ride across to Italy. Why refuse it? He would be a fool to pass up that sort of money if it was even half-way honest.

It was the other sort of money that had begun to worry him. Badly.

He went back to the table across the foyer. He sat down again in the rickety cane chair, poured himself another shot of the stuff in the bottle. There was nothing else to do.

It was half an hour later when the phone rang again. The clerk answered it and held

16

out the receiver. Blair took it, and this time it was Leclerc. He heard the precise, dry-as-dust voice he was beginning to hate.

'Bruce?'

'Yes.'

'How are you?'

Blair said sourly, 'Pretty drunk. And you're damned late.'

'I am very sorry.'

'Forget it. What's on your mind?'

'Very little, to-night—of any immediacy, that is.' Leclerc paused. 'Perhaps you will be interested to hear that the last little venture went through very smoothly.'

'Don't they always?'

'Indeed they do ... at least, they do when you are on the job.' Leclerc paused again. 'One might be inclined to say that you are getting almost too good at the game.'

'Meaning?' Blair said. A sort of subtle menace had crept into the Frenchman's tone.

'Oh, nothing.' Blair could almost see Leclerc waving a hand airily. 'Or only that our competitors appear to be coming rather interested in you.'

Blair said shortly, 'Well, I'm not interested in them.'

'I'm glad to hear it. But they have

17

perhaps—made approaches?'

'No.'

'They will do—and very soon, if my information is correct. You had better watch your step, my friend.'

A pulse of anger began to beat in Blair's head. He said, 'Is that a warning? Or a threat?'

'A threat, my dear boy? Why should I threaten you?'

'I tell you I'm not interested in them,' Blair repeated. He paused, then added deliberately, 'And maybe I'm losing interest in you too.'

'Why should you do that?'

'Maybe I want to pull out of the whole rotten racket.'

'Really? That might not be very wise.'

'I see. You're threatening me now, all right, aren't you?'

Leclerc didn't answer for a while. When he did, his tone was a lot sharper. He said, 'This is nonsense. I think you are not quite yourself to-night. Let us forget it and return to business.'

Blair hesitated too. Then he said, 'Okay. Go ahead. I'm listening.'

'Good,' Leclerc coughed his dry, fussy little cough. 'The situation at the moment

18

is that there will be nothing for at least three weeks. Then, if I anticipate correctly, there will be something big. I will let you know the details later in the usual way. In the meantime you will keep in touch. Is that understood?'

'Okay.'

'You are returning to Naples to-night?'

'Yes.'

'Then all that remains is for me to wish you *bon voyage*. It is a calm night. You should have a very pleasant crossing. Good night, my friend.'

Blair hesitated again, debating briefly with himself whether or not to mention the Nordstrom woman. Leclerc, who knew most things that were going on, and most people at any rate of the shadier kind, might just possibly have some knowledge of her. But he was still out of temper with the Frenchman. He decided that what passengers he carried aboard the launch on her charter trips concerned nobody except himself and the 'legitimate' side of the outfit he worked for. Certainly not Leclerc.

He said good night curtly and hung up. He slipped the clerk behind the desk the usual note to keep his mouth shut, and turned away to the street door. The clerk called after him to know whether he wanted a cab. Blair gestured his refusal and went out into the night.

The Hotel Oasis was one of the dreariest of the poor hotels in La Goulette, which lies across the lake from the city of Tunis. Blair walked back to the launch through the dark and narrow streets of the town. La Goulette was a dismal place altogether, not much more than a system of docks and quays at the entrance to the dredged channel leading in from the Mediterranean across the Lac de Tunis to Tunis itself. It was at its best at night, when you couldn't see it.

Tonight the streets and alleys were a little less fetid than the Hotel Oasis, but not much. Blair sweated as he walked. His clothes were sticking to him, and his head was thick with the cheap spirit he had drunk. He felt suddenly that he would willingly give everything he had for a breath of his own sharp, native Scottish air. It was a moment of nostalgia such as he had not experienced for a long while past, and it took him painfully by surprise.

He came out after a while on a wide

20

stretch of waterfront. The lights of Tunis winked across the lake. A faint breath of a breeze coming off the water brought some slight relief from the heat and stink. He walked on along the waterfront to where the launch was lying. She was at the extreme outer end of the north jetty, under the light tower. Blair always berthed her there. The light shone stark on the uneven stones of the quay. And it was because of the light that he chose that particular berth. In his game, it was always wise to take a look at visitors before they got too close.

Vittorio Massena—Blair called him Vic— was lounging on deck, leaning against the deck-house smoking one of his interminable and foul cheap Italian cigarettes. Down below Blair could hear the two Maltese clattering dishes in the galley. They were chattering together as they worked, and suddenly a gust of their easy, uninhibited laughter came up the companionway. All at once Blair envied them their hard-working but innocent, carefree life.

He scowled. What the devil was the matter with him to-night? He must be getting soft in the head.

He went up the gangway and on board

the launch. He joined Vic in the lee of the deck-house. Vic said, *'Sei in ritardo, capitano.'*

'Leclerc was late coming through,' Blair said. 'The mob's not back yet?'

'Not yet.'

'They'd better hurry. I told them we would be sailing at midnight.'

'They will come.'

'They'd better make it snappy,' Blair repeated. 'I want to get out of this dump.' He took his pipe and tobacco pouch from his pocket. He began to fill the pipe. 'By the way, we've got an extra passenger going back.'

Vic glanced at him sharply. 'Who?'

'A woman. Some Scandinavian job called Nordstrom. That slug Mifsoudis called me while I was waiting for Leclerc and asked me if I would take her.'

Vic took the cigarette out of his mouth. With a jerk of his shoulders he pushed himself off the deck-house. He wasn't lounging any more. Vic was twenty-five, slimly built but wiry, with black hair and a narrow, intelligent face. He was a typical young Neapolitan. A deceptive air of laziness cloaked an alertness and resource which had served both himself and his skipper well in the time that they had been together. It manifested itself now in both his attitude and his voice as he said, sharply, 'Mifsoudis telephoned you up there at the Oasis?'

Blair nodded. 'I know—how did he know I was there?' He lit a match and drew at his pipe. The bowl glowed red and he shook out the match. 'I don't think there's anything to worry about, though. We're in the clear this trip.'

'You told him you'd take her?'

'Yes. At a price.'

'Why does she want to come with us?'

'I don't know, but she's going to pay five hundred bucks for the privilege.'

Vic whistled softly through his teeth. 'Five hundred dollars? This is something that smells a bit? eh?'

Blair nodded. 'A bit, perhaps—but I wasn't going to pass up that sort of money. Best to take her anyway, if only to try to get a line on what she's up to.' He smoked thoughtfully for a while. 'As I say, whatever it is, there can't be much harm in her coming across with us, as long as her papers are in order. We're not carrying anything this trip.'

Vic said, 'It still has a bad smell.'

23

'Forget it,' Blair said shortly. 'We've got bigger things than that to worry about.'

Vic leaned back against the deck-house again. 'Where are we going to put her? The cabins are full.'

'I told Mifsoudis we were full. I said she'd have to take any berth we could find her—and apparently she doesn't mind that either.' He paused. 'She'd better have my cabin. Nip down and tell the Malts to clean the place up a bit and put fresh linen on the bunk.'

'What about you?'

'I'll take the spare forepeak berth. It won't kill me for once. I'll be on the wheel most of the night anyway.'

'Okay.'

'Tell them to shove my things up forward.'

Vic went below. He was back on deck again a couple of minutes later. He rejoined Blair and lit another cigarette from the stub of the one he had been smoking. They both stood and smoked in silence, waiting.

The charter party got back ten minutes later. Two cabs turned out on to the waterfront and rattled along it towards the launch. They stopped with a squealing of brakes at the gangway.

Blair knocked out his pipe on his heel. He said, 'Here they are. The flower of your nobility.'

'The flower of my backside.' Vic spat over the rail.

The cabs disgorged their passengers. There were eight of them, four men and four women. They were all young, and all of them tipsy or worse. They came straggling up the gangway, laughing and calling to each other.

Blair went to meet them at the head of the gangway, without any enthusiasm at all. This was the twentieth such party he had brought across to Africa from Italy. Twenty batches of rich young dissolutes. The advertised purpose of the trips was to visit the ruins of the ancient city of Carthage, which lay some four miles outside La Goulette, but this was just a laugh. The crowd he brought over never got farther than the modern quarter of the legendary old city and spent all their time ashore in the night spots and big tourist hotels.

That wasn't what they really came for either. Blair knew, and it was a humiliating thing to know, that he himself was the real attraction; that they came because it was, for the moment at any rate, *chic, e alla moda,* to make a fast trip on the launch run by *Il Capitano Blair,* the bold, bad British buccaneer.

All this nonsense dated from the time, nearly six months back now, when the Italian authorities had picked Blair up on a charge of suspected smuggling. He'd got away with it, but the case had received quite a bit of publicity, and the sharp characters who ran the charter firm he was working for as a cover had been quick to exploit the situation.

Make a trip with *Il Capitano Blair,* the big, bold, handsome British smuggler, was the line they had come up with. And it had certainly paid off. It was naïve, perhaps, even childish, but it had worked very effectively particularly with the idle Italian socialite set who would do anything for a new thrill, however phony it might be. Soon there had been so many people of that kind wanting to sail with him, and the rates had soared so high, that no one else got a look in.

At first Blair hadn't given a damn. If the wealthy morons he ferried back and forth across the Mediterranean liked to think that, when they did a trip with him, there were also a couple of million American cigarettes tucked away somewhere aboard, that was no concern of his. He got his cut, and they deserved something more than just the ride, if only for the sort of money they paid. But very soon the silly racket had begun to irk him badly. He got very tired of the kind of people his passengers were. The men all seemed to be degenerates of one sort or another, and all the spoiled, expensive women were empty-headed and over-sexed.

The women were the biggest headache. Somehow, in addition to his reputation as a smuggler, Blair had got a name for being a devil with the girls—the complete corsair. The result was that on every trip the main object of most of the female passengers seemed to be to share his bunk with him.

Now, six months later, he felt about all the passengers he carried just about the same way that Vic did. They made him want to spit. And the present mob were no better than any of the others. He'd had enough trouble with them already, on the way over from Naples.

He waited impatiently as they straggled on board. The girl Rosetta was ahead of the rest. She was weaving. She saw him standing there, stumbled over the lip of the gangway and ran towards him. *'Capitano!'* she cried. She threw her arms round his neck and pressed her soft full breasts against him. *'Caro capitano,* I need a man to-night—not those!' She tossed her head back in scorn of the rest of the party, then looked up at him again. 'I need a big strong man like you to hold me.'

Blair reached up and took the girl's wrists. He broke her grip, not over-gently, and put her away from him. He said, 'I'm a working man, *contessa.* I've got my boat to run.'

The girl stood pouting. The others were on deck now, milling round. Vic came forward to deal with them. He said, 'There is a meal ready in the saloon. And drink. Plenty of drink.'

Blair said, 'I want the decks clear while we get ready for sea. You can come up later, if you want.'

They cheered him raggedly and went drifting below. All except the girl Rosetta.

'You too,' Blair told her.

'I will wait for you in your cabin,' she said.

Blair said, 'My cabin is occupied. We

28

have another passenger on the way back.'

'A woman?'

'That's right. A woman.'

She looked at him in sulky reproach. Then she smiled. Perhaps it was enough for her to have her estimate of him confirmed. She turned away and followed the rest.

The deck was quiet again, the waterfront as deserted as it had been before. There was laughter and talk in the saloon, but it came muted up the companionway. Blair looked at his watch. It was nearly midnight.

Vic said, 'You should let yourself go a little, *caro capitano.*'

Blair saw, by the light from the tower, that the boy was grinning at him. He said irritably, 'With that lot?'

'Why not? Some of the girls are pretty.'

'They may be.'

'That Rosetta—you truly would not like her?'

'Don't be a bloody fool.'

'Because you have the middle watch?' Vic laughed, a true Neapolitan laugh, gay, infectious, earthy. 'I will gladly do it for you.'

Blair said, 'Vic, for Christ's sake—'

Vic said more seriously, 'But you should

have a woman. It is not good for a man to live like a monk.'

'I can do very nicely without that kind,' Blair said shortly. 'If it comes to that, I could do very nicely without any more of these bloody stupid trips. I'm sick to death of them.'

Vic shrugged. 'But they are useful. They give us good cover.'

'Cover be damned,' Blair said. 'I'm tired of having to have cover.' He glanced at his watch again. 'Where's that other confounded woman?'

Vic said, 'I think perhaps she is coming now.'

A car had just turned out on to the waterfront from the direction of the town. It rolled smoothly towards the launch and stopped abreast of the gangway. The driver got out and hurried to open the rear door.

A woman got out. She was alone. She was dressed in white and the light from the tower at the end of the jetty shone pale gold on her hair. She walked unhurriedly to the gangway and up it on to the launch's deck. The driver of the car followed her carrying a small overnight bag.

Blair said sourly, 'Royalty this time.'

She stepped on deck. She was tall and long-legged. She was wearing a white coat of some light silken material, and Blair caught a delicate drift of perfume. She looked fresh and cool even in the hot night.

'Captain Blair?'

'Yes.'

'You were expecting me.'

She spoke in English that was only very slightly accented. Her voice was as calm and cool as the rest of her, and the words she used were a statement rather than a question. Her easy, well-bred assurance annoyed Blair, and so did the sudden feeling he had that he ought to have changed his suit. Somehow this woman made him feel decidedly scruffy.

He said ungraciously, 'You've left it pretty late.'

'Pardon?' She looked at him politely. 'I was told only that you would be sailing at midnight, not that I was required to be on board earlier.'

Blair's irritation increased when he found himself at a loss for an answer. He said lamely, 'you ought to know there are formalities—'

'Ah, yes, the formalities.' She was

laughing at him now. She opened her handbag she carried on her arm and took out a long envelope from it. 'I imagine this is the most important of them.' She held out the envelope and when Blair took it she said, 'You wish to count it now? I am sure you will find it correct.'

Blair said stiffly, 'You have your papers?'

'But of course.'

She took a passport out of her bag and gave it to him. He glanced at it perfunctorily and handed it back. 'The other passengers are in the saloon. There is supper there, if you want it.'

'I would rather go straight to my cabin.'

'As you wish.' He hesitated. 'I'm afraid I've had to give you mine—I hope the agency explained that we had no spare passenger space.' His sense of annoyance and general discomfiture grew still stronger at having to make apologies.

Meya Nordstrom smiled at him. She was perfectly, effortlessly in command of the situation. She said, 'They explained. Please do not excuse yourself. It is good of you to put yourself to so much trouble.'

Vic came forward. He took the bag from the driver of the car. He said, 'This way, *signorina.*'

'*Grazie* ... Good night, Captain Blair.'

She followed Vic below. Blair watched her disappear down the companionway. Then he turned abruptly on his heel. He went aft and down to the engine-room to start up for the trip ....

The launch left a few minutes later. Vic came on deck again and cast off. Blair took the wheel. With her engines throttled right down to a muted throb, the launch's high, flaring bows cut smoothly through the calm, velvet-black water of the narrow channel which led out from La Goulette to the open sea.

The channel was some two miles long. The seaward end of it was marked by a green-occulting light buoy. A quarter of an hour after leaving the jetty, the launch slid past the buoy. Ahead of her now, under a clear sky brilliant with stars, lay the wide expanse of the central Mediterranean.

As soon as she was in the open sea, Blair shoved both throttle levers forward. The throb of the launch's exhausts rose to a full-throated roar. She sat up on her step and tucked her stern well down. A wide V angled out from her bows and her wake boiled white astern.

Blair was driving her fast, though still

well below her top speed. Her two big Daimler-Benz engines could push her along at thirty-five knots in calm weather, but she burned up fuel at such an alarming rate, when she was flat out, that she would never have made the crossing. He settled her at twenty-five, which he reckoned would get her back with just a drop left in her tanks. He was glad the weather was so quiet. He badly wanted to get this trip over.

She was a big boat, a hundred and twenty feet over all, but she was easily managed by two men. The engine controls were close beside the wheel. In fact one man could handle her comfortably once she was under way, and a crew-hand was needed only for oiling and running maintenance, and for handling her lines when she left or entered harbour. Often, on her less publicised trips, Blair and Vic were her sole complement.

To-night's crossing looked like being uneventful. The sea was as calm as a pond, and the launch sped smoothly across it. The wheel was rock-steady under Blair's big hands. The compass needle never deviated a fraction of a degree from the course. And he could steer a straight course this trip. There was no need to worry about the preventive boys.

He began to feel in a better humour. The frustrated irritation he had felt most of the evening died away. Just for the moment, as he smoked his pipe in the darkness of the wheel-house, he was at peace with the world. There was nothing more satisfying to his mind than to have the wheel of a good boat under his hands.

But the peace didn't last. When the launch was about ten miles out, the charter party came up from below and began dancing in the dark on the deck forward of the wheel-house. They had two portable radios blaring out dance music from two different stations. The effect was cacophonic.

Vic came up to join Blair. He stood at the open starboard window of the wheel-house, smoking and staring idly out.

Blair said, 'I thought you were going to turn in.'

Vic jerked his head at the deck where the tourists were. 'With that noise?'

'What about the Nordstrom woman?'

'She shut herself in your cabin when she came aboard. There has been no sign or sound of her since.'

Blair grunted. 'The sooner we land the

whole damn' bunch, the better.'

'In this weather we shall make good time.'

'We should be in to-morrow afternoon.'

'*Bene.*'

'You'll be able to spend the evening with Gina.'

'*Si.* And then?'

'We're getting a lay-off, at any rate as far as Leclerc is concerned. There won't be anything else, he says, for the next three weeks.'

'So.'

'You don't like that?'

Vic flicked the butt of his cigarette out of the window. The wind of the launch's passage caught it and whipped it astern. He lit another. The flame of his lighter showed up the dark lines of his thin, good-looking face.

He said, 'You know how it is. The more trips—'

'The sooner the wedding bells, eh?'

'Yes,' Vic said softly. 'The sooner the wedding bells.'

The launch rushed on, and they were silent for a while.

'That seems a good thought to sleep on,' Blair said. 'You'd better get some rest.'

'*Si.* A good thought,' Vic agreed. He walked across to the wheel-house door. '*Buona notte, capitano.*'

★ ★ ★ ★

Blair had the rest of the middle watch to himself. Vic was due to relieve him at 4 a.m. After a while the passengers went below, and all was quiet. The wheel-house was dark, except for the dim illumination of the compass and instrument panel. The sea was empty. The launch needed only a very occasional touch of the wheel to keep her on her heading.

It was a very different trip from the last one they had done in this direction. That time they'd run into some real dirt on their way back from the African side. It had been only a brief summer gale, but it was a bad one while it lasted. They'd had a hell of a time bashing through it to the rendezvous off the coast west of Naples, and a worse one transferring the cargo to the fishing boat that was to land it.

But Blair had welcomed the storm, bad though it was. Bad weather was the best cover of all. It had been a safe run, and the load a big one.

37

He smiled to himself now, in the darkness, as he recalled Vic's delight at the size of his cut that time. It must have put the boy quite a bit nearer marrying his Gina.

Then the smile died, because he'd had a strong feeling lately that they were pushing their luck. And he felt more worried on Vic's account than he did on his own ...

Staring out through the wheel-house window he spotted a ruffle on the water ahead. A breeze was getting up. It was a perfect night for sailing. He found himself wishing he was back aboard his old ketch *Fortune,* feeling her heel to the light air, hearing the quiet creak of her gear. No power vessel in the world could compare with a sailing craft for bringing a man peace and contentment.

His thoughts drifted back to the day he had left Southampton in the ketch. A wet, cold day it had been. He felt a quick surge of nostalgia for the steep, short green seas and the boisterous, keen breezes of the bleak grey Channel.

He'd come a long way since then. A very long way from any real sort of peace and contentment.

He jerked himself back to the present.

The launch had swung a couple of degrees off course while he was dreaming. He put the wheel over to starboard a spoke or two and then back the other way to check her.

Suddenly he tensed a little, then relaxed again. He waited a while, and then said, 'Can't sleep, mademoiselle?'

Meya Nordstrom came a step into the wheel-house from the door. She said, 'It is very hot below deck.'

It was a trace of her perfume on the air that had told Blair she was there. And her voice, he noted now, was perceptibly warmer than it had been earlier.

He was not surprised at her appearance. Just a little disappointed. She had so obviously contrived this meeting, and it seemed certain now that she was, after all, just another spoiled, idle, hungry woman looking for something new in men, like so many of the others he had carried aboard the launch.

He didn't say anything. A trifle grimly, he left it to her to make the running.

'It is a beautiful night. I felt I must come up on deck.' She hesitated. She seemed unsure of herself now. 'I do not want to intrude, but I felt that, at this hour, I

39

should tell whoever was in command of the boat that I was wandering about.'

Blair said evenly, 'That was very considerate of you. Thank you.'

'You do not mind?'

'Help yourself. You're the customer ... cigarette?' Blair suddenly felt that this was as good a time as any to talk to her. He fished in his pocket, offered her his case.

'Thank you.'

He lit the cigarette for her with his old brass storm lighter. Their eyes met over the flame, but hers told him nothing. She straightened up, drawing in the smoke. The tip of the cigarette glowed red in the darkness.

'American?' she asked.

'That's right. Luckies.'

'You are running a cargo to-night?' She put the question lightly.

Blair said, 'A cargo of what?'

'American cigarettes, of course. People do, don't they?'

'I believe they do.'

'With fast motor launches—like this?'

'This is a charter boat.'

'Of course.'

Blair couldn't be bothered to play games any longer. He said, 'Look, lady—will you please tell me just why you are aboard my boat?'

The cigarette glowed in the darkness again. 'Why shouldn't I be?'

'Because there are easier ways of getting from Tunis to Naples.'

'Perhaps.'

'Quicker ways. And much cheaper, at the rate you're paying.'

'But not so—romantic.'

Blair said heavily, 'Miss Nordstromn, I don't think we are either of us interested in the romantic angle.' He had a sudden conviction that this was true. 'I should be glad if you would tell me the real reason.'

'Does there have to be a real reason?'

'Doesn't there?'

'Couldn't it be just—a whim?'

Blair laughed shortly. 'A damned expensive one.'

She laughed too, as lightly as she had spoken. She said, 'I can afford to indulge my whims, even if they are expensive.' She paused, then went on, seemingly serious for the first time. 'Do you know what I think, Captain Blair?'

'What?'

'I think you are too suspicious. You look

41

over your shoulder at people.'

That was so true that Blair had no answer to it. And before he could find anything to say, she had gone.

He saw her a minute later, up in the bows of the launch. She stood there, a pale, ethereal figure with her white coat blowing about her. Then she turned and walked slowly aft along the starboard side. She passed out of sight of the wheel-house windows and he didn't see her again ....

His spell on the wheel drew to an end. At four in the morning Vic came up, yawning and coughing over his inevitable cigarette. Blair gave him the course and estimated position and went below and turned in.

The forepeak berth was unfamiliar and he was restless. He found it impossible to sleep. He was up and about again a couple of hours later. He spent half an hour down in the engine-room, then washed and shaved. He needed a clean suit of whites, but that damned woman was in his cabin.

His stomach was sour from the poison he'd drunk at the Oasis the night before, and he felt thoroughly out of humour with the world. He went through into the saloon, but couldn't face breakfast. He waved the steward away, poured himself a large Scotch, and felt a trifle better after it. He went up to the wheel-house again.

There was little sign of the passengers during the forenoon. The charter party were sleeping off their hangover. They were the sort of people that rarely got out of bed before noon anyway. Meya Nordstrom made a brief appearance on deck, and Blair seized the opportunity to send one of the stewards into his cabin for a clean suit.

When Vic came up to relieve the wheel at noon, Blair said, 'What's happening down there?'

'The Swedish woman is in the saloon,' Vic said. 'The others are still sleeping.'

Blair handed over and went down. The saloon was empty. The Nordstrom woman must have gone back to the cabin. Lunch was laid for him on the saloon table. He ate without much enthusiasm, took a good deal more whisky with it, then went forward to the forepeak berth and slept for a couple of hours. When he roused out again, in mid-afternoon, he put on the clean white linen suit, picked up his cap and binoculars and went on deck.

All the passengers were there now. The charter party was gathered at the starboard rail, looking across the silken blue sea at the steep, vivid shores of Isola di Capri. The launch was running up the west coast of the island, on the last leg of her usual round trip. Outward bound from Naples, she went through the Bocca Piccola, between the eastern shore of Capri and the Italian mainland. She returned via the Bocca Grande, the much wider approach to the Bay of Naples between Capri and Isola D'Ischia some thirty miles to the eastward. Both times the launch passed close to Capri, to give her passengers an all-round view of the island.

Blair put on his cap as he stepped on deck, pulling the peak well down against the high glare of the sun. His eyes ranged quickly over the passengers. Meya Nordstrom was standing up in the bows of the boat, where he had seen her the night before. She was some distance away from the others, who were gathered in a group abreast of the wheel-house. Her manner generally suggested that she was holding herself aloof from them, and he approved her good taste in that at any rate.

He walked forward to speak to her, he didn't quite know why. She, too, was gazing across at Capri. She turned her head as he came up, and smiled at him.

'The island is so clear to-day,' she said.

Blair nodded. 'Visibility is good.'

It was the first time he had seen her in daylight and at close quarters, and it was almost a shock to him to realise how beautiful she was. She was tall, with the figure of an *haute couture* model. The false breeze made by the launch's swift passage pressed her thin white dress against her, limning her high breasts and the long, clean line of her thighs. Her eyes were a clear, deep blue, her hair fine-spun and naturally blonde, not artificially, almost brassily golden, as it had looked to him under the La Goulette light the night before.

She was lovely. If there was anything at all that marred her beauty, it was something about her eyes. They were almost the colour of the sea to-day, but there were shadows under them; the shadows of illness, worry, some distress?

Blair rested his hands on the rail beside her. He said, 'Almost back.'

45

She looked up at him again. 'How much longer?'

'A bit over an hour.'

The launch was running close in. The steep shores of Capri rose from the calm, deep azure sea not more than half a mile away, in sharp-etched, vivid detail.

Blair said, 'Often, in weather like this, there is a haze over the island.'

Meya Nordstrom stood gazing across at the verdure-clad, deeply fissured cliffs. 'May I look through your binoculars?'

Blair was carrying the binoculars slung on his chest. He slipped the lanyard off over his head and handed them to her. 'Wait a moment,' he told her as she was putting them up to her eyes. He put the lanyard round her neck. She looked up at him as he did so, and for a moment they seemed very close and intimate. It caused a curious disturbance in him, and made his tone almost brusque as he explained, 'To stop you dropping them over the side. Good glasses cost money.'

'I am sure they do.' She seemed quite composed. She raised the binoculars and trained them on the island.

She kept them trained on one particular spot for a long time. She seemed to be examining something intently.

'Something interesting?' Blair ventured.

'I am looking at my villa.' She took the lanyard from round her neck and handed the binoculars back. 'You are right—the visibility is extremely good to-day. I can see everything so clearly.'

Blair said, 'You live on Capri?'

'In the white villa there above the town, just over the shoulder of the cliff to the left. The one which is by itself.'

Blair raised the glasses and scanned the section of cliff she indicated. The villa jumped suddenly into view among the luxuriant green which covered the cliff. It stood high and solitary, bone-white in the sun.

He said, 'It looks a wonderful place.'

She nodded. 'It is enchanting.' She glanced at him quickly. 'One day ... perhaps you would care to come and visit me there, Captain?'

Blair said, 'That would be very pleasant.'

'Perhaps soon?' Meya Nordstrom said. 'Between this trip and your next—if you have time?'

'I would very much like to, if I can,' Blair said.

'Then I will look forward to it.'

47

Blair didn't answer this time. He still had the glasses to his eyes and he was looking at something he had never noticed before, although he had done this run past the island many times. Immediately below the villa there was a miniature bay, not much more than a wrinkle in the cliff, with a finger-nail paring of beach and a short stone jetty running out on its southern side. The jetty was obviously a private landing for the villa, though it puzzled him how anyone could get up the cliff to the house above, at least without an extremely steep and arduous climb.

He lowered the binoculars. He said, 'You are on your way back there now?'

'Yes.'

'How will you go?'

'I can get the island boat from Naples.'

'Will you be in time to get one to-day?'

She shrugged. 'I don't know. If not I can stay the night in Naples.'

'You really are doing this trip the hard way, aren't you?'

She did not answer him. Blair asked the question flippantly enough, but she did not take it the same way. Her face looked troubled.

48

Blair said, on a sudden impulse, 'I can put you off now if you like. We can run into Marina Grande.'

'But—' She seemed very uncertain. 'But that would delay you.'

'Not very much.'

She hesitated again. 'Then, perhaps—if you would be so good ... it would be a great convenience.'

Blair nodded. 'I'd better go up to the bridge. We'll be altering course shortly to go in. If you would care to go below and collect your things—we'll be there in a very few minutes.'

She did not go at once. She turned to him, as though there was something she wanted to say to him. But in the end all she did say was 'Thank you.' Then she turned abruptly on her heel and left him.

Blair followed her aft as far as amidships, and then went up to the wheel-house. Vic was humming quietly to himself at the wheel. He grinned when Blair came in and said, 'So you are taking my advice, eh, after all? You have found a woman you like?'

Blair said, 'We're going to run in to Marina Grande and put her ashore—she lives on Capri.' He spoke shortly, because

49

he felt puzzled and uncertain. He was trying to work out why he wanted, and yet didn't want, to get rid of this woman. He had to admit that he was strongly attracted to her. But at the same time she disturbed him. He also couldn't help feeling that, in some obscure way, she was dangerous.

'I'll take the wheel,' he said.

He took over from Vic, and brought the launch round until she was heading for the entrance to Marina Grande. A few minutes later she was running in between the two moles which formed the harbour entrance. As she entered the harbour, Blair sounded her siren, and Vic hoisted the 'foreign' flag at the cross-trees of the launch's short mast. Blair was always very careful not to infringe the law where his charter parties were concerned, and he wasn't going to land the Nordstrom girl without some sort of immigration clearance.

The inner part of the harbour was crowded with pleasure craft. Blair ran up alongside a launch of about the same size as his own which was lying alongside the quay. A harbour official was waiting on the quay and, as Vic made temporarily fast he came clambering over the intervening vessel and jumped aboard.

Meya Nordstron was standing on deck near the wheel-house with her small bag in her hand and her coat over her arm. Blair explained the circumstances of the launch's call to the official, and he nodded. No, he did not require to see the lady's papers. He knew Signorina Nordstrom well. Her disembarking would be quite in order.

Vic had opened the gate in the guardrail and was standing ready to hand the girl across on to the other vessel. She turned to Blair.

'*Grazie.* You have been very kind.'

'All part of the service.' Blair held out his hand. 'Good-bye, Miss Nordstrom. Nice to have had you aboard.'

'Not good-bye.' She smiled at him. '*A la rivederci,* Captain Blair. Don't forget you are coming to visit me.'

She stepped across on to the other launch. The little, fat harbour official followed and helped her ashore. She walked away along the quay. Blair watched her until she was out of sight. She didn't look back.

The launch cast off and headed out again, running on up the north coast of Capri, then altering course for Naples. She entered harbour at four o'clock, and Blair lost no time in putting the charter party ashore. They were willing enough to go, bored by the trip by now, and feeling a bit let down because there had been no excitement. As soon as Blair had got rid of them, he took the launch on across the harbour and moored her alongside in her usual berth in the small pleasure-craft basin near the root of the San Vincenzo mole.

The two Maltese stewards left as soon as they had finished squaring up below. Blair carried them aboard only on the actual charter trips. A little later Vic, all slicked up and full of exuberant good humour, went ashore to catch a bus out to Porto Sannazzaro and his Giannina.

It was stuffy below, and Blair was smoking a pipe on deck when Vic left. He watched the boy walk jauntily away along the quay, and then he went below. He poured himself a whisky and sat down at the saloon table with it. But he forgot it. For a long time it stood untouched in front of him.

The mood of depression which had come upon him the previous evening in La Goulette was still with him. He couldn't get the Nordstrom woman out of his head.

And he was worried about Vic.

It was Sam Everett who had found the boy for Blair some six months back. Blair, being a one-boat operator and a foreigner, needed an Italian to crew for him, preferably a local man, someone who really knew his way around. Sam, who, it seemed, knew everybody on the Naples waterfront, had told him he could put him in touch with a useful lad who was anxious to make some big money fast.

The boy was Vittorio Massena, and Blair soon found out why he needed money. Young Massena was quite open with him. He needed it to get married. He was a hard-up tunny fisherman, and the girl he was in love with was out of his class, at least as far as money was concerned. Her name was Giannina Pieroni, and her father owned a small but prosperous hotel at Porto Sannazzaro, some twenty miles round the bay northwards from Naples.

Vittorio and his Giannina were desperately in love, but that, of course, their families being Italian, was not enough reason for them to marry. Little Papa Pieroni got apoplectic at the thought of his daughter, his only, cherished daughter, throwing herself away on a ragged, disreputable *pescatore*. At the same time he liked the boy and, again in the practical Italian way, put forward a proposition. If and when young Massena could prove himself worthy of marrying into the Pieroni family by raising enough capital to buy a modest share in the Albergo Italia, he would be welcome as a son-in-law. And when the boy asked blankly how, in the name of the Holy Mother, he could be expected to do that, Papa merely shrugged. Enterprise! For a really smart young man there must be ways and means.

So young Massena needed money, and needed it quickly. He couldn't expect Giannina to wait for ever. She would get tired of waiting, and she was very pretty. There were even now plenty of others hanging around her. And so it was no wonder that he jumped at the chance of a job with Blair. Running contraband was a lot more profitable than fishing for tunny. And it would be more exciting too.

Blair swallowed half his drink and shook his head impatiently, as though to dismiss his thoughts. He was getting to be a proper old woman about the boy. Why worry about him? Vic was in his element. He took the whole thing very lightly. He enjoyed the element of risk. And he was tough and self-reliant, well able to look after himself.

Not only that—at least he had an end in view that made sense of what he was doing, the chances he was taking.

Blair finished off the whisky and sat staring into the empty glass in his hand. What end or object had he himself got? The answer to that was simple—none at all. The money he was making was big enough, but that didn't mean anything. It never had done, not even when he'd started in the racket. Money didn't mean a thing in itself. You had to want it for something, to buy something, the way Vic wanted it to buy happiness with his Gina. And there was nothing he wanted that money could buy.

What else? There was the excitement, but that was a hollow, empty thing too. It would be better to say there had once been excitement in it for him. That was what had tempted him into the game in the first place, when he had craved any kind of drug or stimulant that would help him forget the past. But that seemed a long time ago now. He didn't get any kick out of it any more.

It was high time he gave the whole thing up. It was crazy to go on sticking his neck out, especially as the game was getting more and more dangerous every day.

Very much more dangerous for the one-boat operator like himself.

The law wasn't the trouble. That was a known hazard, and one he could cope with without much difficulty. He had proved that over and over again. The real danger, and one that was growing all the time, was that the whole contraband racket in the Naples area was falling more and more into the hands of one big, ruthless organisation. It was an organisation that was obviously determined to get the whole thing sewn up, which meant rubbing out the smaller outfits, including the single boats.

There was one man behind the organis-ation. Volpi. Leonardo Volpi. Italian-American, and a throw-back in a way, a gangster of the old Chicago school. Deported from the States a year ago. They'd got too smart for him there. But they didn't seem to be too smart for him in Naples. Volpi had brought a fortune back with him to his native land, and he was establishing himself there fast, by bribery and terror. He had hired a formidable bunch of thugs to work for him.

Blair knew all this, and so did everyone else in the smuggling racket. So did the police and the Italian preventive service. But knowing it and proving it were very different things. Volpi ruled by fear, the old-style fear of the sub-machine-gun's deadly chatter sounding for anyone who talked.

And so no one talked. From time to time one or perhaps two or three of Volpi's men were picked up, but they kept their mouths tight shut. They knew they would be shut for good if they didn't. And so there was no evidence at all against the big man at the top.

Volpi had taken in one or two of the small men who had been operating when he first moved in on the territory. Others, the awkward ones, and those he didn't consider would be useful to him, had turned up from time to time as bullet-riddled corpses floating in the sea. Blair was surprised that, so far, he hadn't himself come up against the big boy. Perhaps it wouldn't be long now before he did—Leclerc had hinted at it, this last time they had talked together. One thing he did know, and that was that something of the sort must come soon. And he wondered whether when it did come, he would be considered worth using, or strictly expendable.

A show-down with the Volpi outfit would have to come, that was to say, if he stayed in the game much longer. He knew that, if he'd had any sense, he would have got out of it long ago. Or at least he ought to get out of it now. If he didn't, both he and Vic stood a first-rate chance of being found floating face-down, the same as the others.

Even if he avoided that, there were equally unattractive possibilities. He knew that he was beginning to drink a lot too much. Beginning? He'd been drinking too much for a long time now. The bottle was beginning to get a terrible hold on him. If he let himself go and gave in to it, he could see himself turning into another Sam Everett.

Blair frowned at the thought. Sam Everett was as grim an object lesson as anyone could want in what could happen to a man who had had a raw deal from life and had tried to forget it in liquor, and who had gone down the slide all the way.

Not so long ago Sam Everett had been a brilliant young egg-head, holding down an important professorship in archaeology in Harvard. Then he had come over to Italy, to the university of Rome, as a guest lecturer on an exchange arrangement.

A terrific break, that had seemed to him, an assignment nothing short of a dream come true. Sam had flung himself into his teaching in Rome with tremendous enthusiasm—it still flared up sometimes even now, when he talked about it. He'd taught with a sort of inspired passion, and he'd bought himself a boat. He'd always had a mania for boats and the sea.

At that time Sam had been a very happy man. He had the ideal job and, in his vacations, he'd combined his two ruling passions to go looking for the treasures of antiquity that had long been lost under the sea. He'd gone prospecting along the Italian coast with his boat and a deep trawl.

And he'd found a lot that was of value. He'd made quite a name for himself. Among other things, somewhere off the Sorrentino Peninsula he'd dredged up half a statue of Apollo that had caused a considerable stir in his own particular world, and which was now a prized possession of the Museo Nazionale in Rome.

But then something had gone wrong. Sam never disclosed what it was, not even in his most drunkenly confidential moods. Blair suspected that, as in his own case, it had been a woman. Sam was certainly very bitter about women.

Anyway, whatever the reason, the smart and up-and-coming young Professor Everett had turned with astonishing rapidity into a seedy drunk. He'd drifted down to Naples, and soon was no better than any of the other bums and dead-beats who hung around the waterfront.

He still had his boat, and he still went around fishing for treasure, in a fuddled sort of way. He also, in his early days in Naples at any rate, got involved in the smuggling racket and ran a cargo when he could. But he wasn't reliable enough to get much business. As time passed, he hovered more and more on the brink of things, picking up trifles here and there, a jackal of the game.

Sam wasn't likely to get shot or knifed.

He was too harmless, too ineffective to bother about. But to come down to Sam's level, Blair thought, would be the worst fate of all. He would rather be dead.

He got up, went into his cabin and stretched out on the bunk. He decided he'd go ashore later, if only to get away from the close confines of the boat. But it was too early yet. The boat was better than the seething, sun-soaked clamour of the streets. The city would be more tolerable after dark.

He needed sleep. He'd had little enough in the past twenty-four hours. But he was too restless, his mind too active, even to relax.

After a short while he sat up and swung his legs to the floor. He lit a cigarette and, as he sat frowning through the smoke, his eyes caught sight of Ann's photograph on the bulkhead. He stared at it, but it wasn't of Ann that he was thinking, but of another, very different woman. A woman called Meya Nordstrom.

He felt a sudden shock of surprise, almost of disbelief. It was the first time in two years that he'd given a thought to any woman except Ann. He felt, too, a queer sense of disloyalty that disturbed him

61

strangely. That was crazy—to feel disloyal to a woman who hadn't any use for him. But he felt it just the same.

He stubbed the cigarette out angrily. What in God's name was the matter with him? He was through with women. He didn't want any more to do with them, any of them.

He heaved himself up off the bunk and went prowling out into the saloon again. The bottle was waiting for him there, but with an effort he left it alone. He sat down on the settee on the starboard side. He could hear voices and movement outside along the waterfront, but the sounds were muted and seemed very far away.

He felt very much alone, very cut off from normal people and the ordinary ways of life. He was getting more and more depressed. This was the bad time, when there was nothing to do but think. This was the time when men of the sort he had become let go their hold on normality and decency a little more and slid a bit farther down the hill ....

He went ashore as soon as it was dark and headed for the Bar Marina. He badly wanted someone to talk to, someone who spoke his own language, or something like it. He knew Sam Everett would be in the Marina, if his boat was in harbour—and he didn't go to sea much these days. And it was just possible that Sam wouldn't be too drunk yet to talk to.

Blair told himself wryly that it was a pretty poor state of affairs when Sam Everett was the best company he could find, but he had to admit that that was about the size of it.

He reached the bar and went in. The place was a dump, a sordid little dive, a haunt of the riff-raff of the waterfront. It was hot and airless, and it stank of a mixture of fish, stale garlic and cheap liquor.

He noticed as soon as he got inside the door that the little hole was a lot more crowded than it usually was at that rather slack hour of the evening; and also that things were a lot quieter than normal. He knew at once that something had happened, and he didn't need two guesses as to what it was. Someone had been picked up by the police or the preventives, or had been found floating in the harbour. Whenever that happened, the chill wind of it had a sobering effect on the habitués of the Bar Marina. Most of them lived outside the law, in one way or another, many of them on a fine edge of danger. They were strictly expendable, and they knew it.

And whenever something happened to one of them, there was always a sort of suspicious, waiting stillness among the rest. As there was now.

Every head had turned to the door as he came in through it. Everyone was looking at him now, as he crossed to the bar. He lifted his hand in a casual, general greeting but, although he was well known in the place, no one spoke or made any sort of response at all.

Salvatore was lounging behind the bar, his fat arms on the dirty zinc top. He seemed to look at Blair almost fearfully. When Blair gestured to him, he nodded nervously.

'Whisky, signor?'

'Thanks,' Blair said. 'Sam been in?'

Salvatore shook his head. He splashed whisky into a glass and put it in front of Blair.

'Out on a trip?'

'No.'

Blair picked up his glass and drank. He put it down again. No one said anything.

He could feel the eyes of everyone in the place still on him.

He glanced round. 'Talkative lot to-night, aren't you?' he said. Then he turned back to Salvatore. 'What is this—a funeral?'

Salvatore's fat jowls quivered. 'You might call it that, signor' he said. 'Signor Everett is dead.'

Blair had taken up his glass again. He put it down slowly, without drinking.

'Dead?'

'*Si.*'

'How?'

Salvatore shook his head again. 'On his boat. I do not know ...' He looked past Blair. 'Giorgio ... Benno ... they bring the news.'

Blair picked up his drink and swallowed it. He said, 'Give me another—fill it up.' He waited until Salvatore had poured the drink, then took it across to the bare, rough wooden table in the corner where Giorgio and Benno Partici were sitting.

He knew the Partici brothers. They were partners in a fishing boat. They did a certain amount of fishing—for cover; that blasted word he was so sick of. Their real business was taking hot cargoes off the deep-sea launches, such as his own, and running them ashore. He had worked with them himself more than once, and knew they were tough and reliable.

The two brothers were hunched over a bottle of rough red *vino*. Blair put his glass down on the stained table top. He sat down on the wooden bench beside Giorgio. He said, 'This is true about Sam?' Instinctively he kept his voice low.

'*Si*. It is true,' Giorgio said briefly.

'How did it happen?'

Benno Partici picked up the bottle in his big, calloused fisherman's hand and splashed wine into his thick glass. He said sullenly, 'We cannot tell you. We do not know.'

'Tell me what you do know.'

Giorgio was the more forthcoming of the two. He said, 'We saw his boat, when we were out in ours. It was drifting. We knew something was wrong. We ran alongside and went aboard. We found them both dead.'

'Both?'

'The boy who worked for him. Alessandro Leoni. He was dead too.'

Alessandro Leoni. Blair drank thoughtfully. The boy Sam had called Leo. Leoni had crewed for Sam, the way Vic did for him. Both of them dead.

There had been a third. Sam always carried another hand too. Tomaso. Little Tommy. Though Tommy had been more a cabin boy than a hand. He couldn't have been more than ten years old.

Tomaso was the only name he had. He was one of the swarming *scugnizzi*, one of the myriad homeless children of Naples, a parentless waif of the waterfront. Sam, a sucker for kids, had taken pity on him and given him a job and a home on his boat ....

Blair said, 'There was another one—a kid. You found him too?'

'No,' Giorgio said.

'He wasn't on board?'

'He was not on board when we found the boat. We do not know if he was there when it happened.' Giorgio drank deeply and wiped his mouth with the back of his hand. 'We do not know anything about him, except that he has not been seen since. We looked for him, of course, to see if he could tell us what had happened, but he has disappeared.' Giorgio shrugged, and both the shrug and the tone in which he had spoken were casual, as though the

67

fate of a ragged little orphan was of no account.

Blair came reluctantly to the vital question. He said grimly, 'How did they die?' He felt he knew the answer already.

Benno stirred. He said, 'They were shot. They both had many bullets in them. It must have been an automatic weapon.'

Blair frowned. A drifting boat. Two bodies aboard, riddled with bullets, and no attempt made to dispose of them, although it would have been simple to have dumped them over the side. It was another act of terror; a warning and a threat. A gang killing. A Volpi job. It bore all the marks of it.

But Sam? Why should they have killed poor, harmless, befuddled Sam Everett? How could he possibly have mattered to them?

Giorgio at that very moment echoed the thought. He said, 'But who would want to kill Signor Everett? He was the friend of everyone.'

Blair said curtly, 'Don't be stupid.' He was annoyed, but more with himself than anyone else, because he had been thinking much the same way as Giorgio only an hour or two back. Sam was in no danger, because he didn't matter, he didn't cut any ice in the game. But he had mattered, in some way or other.

He went on, more reasonably, 'You ought to know you can't be the friend of everyone when you lead the sort of life he led, even if he was more of a drunk than anything else.' He drew a deep breath. The real shock of it was just getting home to him. He said, 'When did it happen?'

Giorgio said, 'Three days ago. At least that is when we found the boat. We do not know how long they had been dead. Not long, I think. Perhaps the night before. The boat could not have drifted far in daylight without being seen.'

'Three days,' Blair said. 'That means you found them on Tuesday?'

'*Si*. It was that day.'

It was also on Tuesday that Blair had left for North Africa with the last charter party. The launch had left after a quick turn round. He had brought her back from Africa on Monday night with a cargo of cigarettes, had transferred the stuff in the small hours to the inshore boats, berthed at dawn, and she had been away again with her passengers by noon. It was his habit to work fast like that, if he could.

69

It was confusing to the customs boys. It made it difficult for them to be quite sure whether he was making a legitimate trip or not.

He said, 'What did you do when you found them?'

'We towed the boat in,' Giorgio said. 'It was slow. We did not get in to Naples until night. We looked for you to tell you then, but your boat had left.'

Blair nodded. He said, 'Where did you find the boat?'

'In the Bocca Grande. A long way out, and almost half-way between Isola d'Ischia and Isola di Capri.'

'And when you got in—you told the police?'

'Si.' Giorgio shifted uncomfortably. 'It seemed the wisest thing to do.'

There was a pause. Blair lifted a hand and beckoned to Salvatore, who had been watching the threesome in the corner anxiously. Salvatore waddled over from the bar with the whisky bottle and filled Blair's glass again.

Blair said, 'When was Signor Everett in here last?'

Salvatore said, 'It was on Sunday. I remember that because Signor Everett said

70

it was a good day to get drunk on. A good day for a good act, he said. He was a very strange man.'

The better the day, the better the deed. Blair could hear Sam saying it, with that wry, defeated humour of his. It brought the slight, fair-haired, essentially decent and gentle American back vividly to his mind. And now Sam was dead. Murdered. Shot down in cold blood.

He felt anger mounting in him. With an effort he kept it down. He looked round the low-ceilinged, smoky bar, and then at the other three with him. He said, 'Do you know if he was on to anything special?'

There was a silence. Then Salvatore said slowly, with obvious reluctance, 'He told us that he would be going out in his boat the next day.'

'What sort of trip was it? Did he seem worried—afraid of anything?'

There was another silence. To Blair it seemed to weigh heavily, ominously upon the whole room.

Then Salvatore spoke again. He said, 'He told us he was going out again with the net he fished for his treasurers with.' The fat bar-keeper hesitated, then turned suddenly and called, 'Nicolo, come here a moment.'

A young man got up from another table and came across the room.

'What?' he said. 'What is it?'

'Tell Signor Blair about Signor Everett. What he was talking to you about, and what he showed you.'

'Last Sunday,' Blair said.

Nicolo was a thin, sallow, tubercular young Neapolitan. He worked as a deck-hand on one of the island boats. He had a sharp, sensitive, intelligent face, and it was because he spoke better English than any of the other habitués of the Bar Marina that Sam had liked to talk to him.

'Signor Everett is dead—you know that?' Blair said. And when Nicolo nodded, he went on, 'You must have been one of the last to talk to him before he was killed. Tell me what he said.'

Nicolo nodded. He said, 'Signor Everett was here all the evening. He got very drunk, even for him. Not quietly drunk, as he usually was, but excited. Very excited.'

'What about?'

'About'—Nicolo lowered his voice—'about this thing which he showed me.'

'What was it?'

'It was a—little pot.' Nicolo shaped it with his hands. 'It was something he said he had found.' He stopped abruptly and looked about him. There were secretly listening ears everywhere, perhaps even here in the Bar Marina. It could be very bad for anyone who talked too much about certain things.

Blair said impatiently, 'Come on, let's have the rest of it.'

Nicolo drew a deep breath. It made him cough. When the racking spasm was over, the silence seemed deeper than before.

Then Nicolo said, 'I will tell you, signor, because we were both his friends.' He gestured nervously. 'This little thing—for a long time he talked very strangely about it, saying how much money it was worth. And also how evil it was.'

Blair said curtly, 'What was it?'

'It was what was in it,' Nicolo said. 'For a long time he talked about it without opening it, but then he did, and showed what was in it to me, and some of the others who were here that night. By that time he was too drunk to care what happened to him.'

Blair said, 'For God's sake—what was in the thing?'

73

Nicolo said, 'It was full of a white powder.' He added curtly, 'That is all I know.'

He turned away and lit a cigarette. The scratch of the match was loud in the stillness of the bar. Nicolo coughed again, agonisedly, as he drew the smoke down into his sick lungs. Then the silence came back again, even more heavy, more ominous than before.

Blair sat motionless at the table, staring in front of him. His face was grim. He didn't ask any more questions. He didn't need to. He knew, as everyone else there in the Bar Marina knew, what it was that Sam Everett had found.

The atmosphere was heavy with fear. There was nobody in that sleazy little place who wasn't living more or less in the shadows, and most of them were involved somehow or other in the contraband game.

But none of them wanted anything to do with the racket in drugs.

2

It was Blair himself who finally broke the tension. He said to Nicolo, 'That's all?' He wasn't really asking for any further information. He put the question simply for the sake of hearing a voice, even his own.

Nicolo nodded briefly. '*Si.*'

Salvatore said, 'It is enough, signor.'

Blair looked at the fat bar-keeper. He said, 'It's more than enough.' He got up heavily off the bench.

'Go carefully, friend,' Giorgio Partici said.

Blair laughed shortly. 'Don't worry. That sort of thing's not in my line.'

He paid for his drinks and left the bar. He needed to be on his own. He badly wanted to think. Not that there was any real problem facing him, now that this had happened to Sam.

This was the writing on the wall. He knew now that he'd got to get out of the smuggling racket before it was finally too late. If it wasn't too late already. He wasn't in as deep as Sam apparently had been—or was he? *Don't worry,* he'd said just now, *that sort of thing's not in my line.* But you could be in deeper than you knew. This business about Sam was a case in point. He couldn't believe that Sam had been in the drug-running game, not from choice at any rate. If he'd got involved in it, it must have been more or less involuntarily. And that was something that could happen to anyone.

In the smuggling game—or in any kind of racket, he supposed, if it came to that—you could only too easily get more involved than you ever wanted or intended. He'd known that, really, all along the line, but it had never been brought home to him so vividly or with such brutal force as it had been to-night. Take the very instance of the drug racket itself. You might hate it like hell and be firmly resolved never to touch it. But it needed only a packet or parcel of the stuff—or, say, a little pot of white powder—to be planted on your boat, and then you were a cocaine or a *khif* runner whether you liked it or not, and you were liable to find yourself in just as much trouble as if you had been running the evil muck by design.

He walked slowly towards the launch. He was so absorbed in his thoughts that he was virtually unaware of his surroundings. Though had he been as alert as he usually was, he still couldn't possibly have known that he was being trailed. The figure that crept and ran after him, flitting from one black alley mouth or patch of darkness to the next, had no more substance than a shadow, and made no more sound.

He got back to the launch and went on board. It was still quite early and the boat was in darkness. Vic hadn't come back yet. He switched on the lights and sat down in the saloon to wait for the boy. He'd got to tell him as soon as he could that they were chucking their hand in.

It was midnight when Vic came aboard, in an exuberantly cheerful mood after the evening he had spent with his Gina. He sprawled at the saloon table, eating bread and salami and drinking from the bottle of wine he had brought back with him.

He wanted Blair to drink with him, but Blair refused. Vic tried to insist.

'Cheer you up, *capitano*,' he said. 'You don't look too good to-night.'

'I'm all right,' Blair said.

77

He felt reluctant to bring the boy down to earth, but it had to be done. He let him chatter away for a while longer. Then he made an effort.

'It looks like you had a good evening,' he said.

'Molto bene!' Vic made a delicate circle with his thumb and forefinger and sat back against the padded back of the settee, closing his eyes blissfully. He was still chewing hard. Then he sat up again, very eager and wide awake. He tore off another chunk of bread and stuffed it into his mouth. He said, 'You know what I was thinking on my way back in the bus? You want to know what I was thinking?'

Blair said, 'Give me one guess. About Gina.'

'Si,' Vic said. 'About Gina, and about myself. I was thinking that another five or six trips will be enough, if they are good ones.' Then his face clouded a little. 'There is only one thing—this other thing I was thinking too.' He looked earnestly across the table at Blair. 'It is that I shall have enough money then to get married, and that of course will make me very happy. But I shall not be happy when I have to leave the boat.' He gestured and

78

ended, simply and sincerely, 'I so much like working for you, *capitano.*'

Blair said curtly, 'You won't be much longer.'

'*Come?*'

'Your problem's just solved itself.'

'But I do not understand ...'

'It's simple enough. There won't be five or six more trips. There won't be any more trips at all.'

It took something drastic to stop Vic eating. He stopped now, abruptly.

'What is this? What has happened?'

'Sam Everett's been killed.'

Vic's mouth fell open. 'Signor Everett? Killed? You mean—'

'I mean murdered, liquidated, rubbed out. And it's not hard to guess who did it—or at any rate who gave the orders.'

Tersely he told Vic the details, while the boy listened, frowning and intent, his food and his thoughts of Gina forgotten. At the end of the brief recital of the facts, he stared at Blair in blank astonishment.

'*Santa Maria!* he exclaimed. The astonishment held a moment longer, and then his expression changed and he looked troubled. 'And this that you say about no more trips ...?'

79

Blair said shortly, 'We're through. It's getting too tough. We don't want to end up like Sam—or I don't, anyway.' He got up from where he was sitting and, walking round the table, put a hand on the boy's shoulder. He said, forcing a cheerfulness he didn't feel, 'You needn't be too gloomy about it. This is really our lucky break.'

Vic looked up at him. 'Lucky?'

'If you look at it the right way,' Blair said. 'The truth of the matter is we've been sticking our necks out for a long time. A lot too far, and a lot too often. Maybe we needed something like this to happen to bring us to our senses.'

Vic hunched his shoulders and stared sombrely in front of him. He said, 'If you say so. But it is hard for me to look at it that way.'

Blair said, 'You don't have to worry about the money you still need. I can find that.'

He shook the boy's shoulder affectionately, then turned abruptly away and went aft to his cabin ....

The figure that had trailed Blair along the waterfront stood in the blackness under a warehouse wall, directly across the quay from the launch. He had been watching the

80

launch ever since Blair got back to her.

He saw Vittorio Massena return. He waited until the lights aboard the launch went out. Only then did he turn and slip away into the labyrinthine alleys of the city.

3

Breakfast on the launch next morning was a subdued business. Both Blair and Vic had a lot to think about.

Vic was usually full of talk, but to-day he sat at the table in glum silence, until at last he said hesitantly, *'Capitano—'*

'Eh?' Blair jerked himself out of his own private worries.

Vic said, 'Gina is coming to the city to-day. I thought that if you did not need me aboard—'

Blair gestured briefly. 'Go ahead.'

'She is coming down to the boat to call for me—but things are different now. I can tell her that I am not free to-day. She will understand.'

'No need for that—no need to change your plans.' Blair drank some of his coffee and grimaced over it. He said brutally, 'I told you we're through anyway.'

'But I do not like to go until we have talked more—'

'We've talked enough,' Blair said. Then

he looked across at Vic and went on more gently. 'Go off and enjoy yourself. If there is anything more to discuss, it can wait till you get back.'

Gina arrived an hour later, vivid, gay, and full of eager expectation of a day in the city with her *amico del cuore*. Vic was plainly just as eager to spend the day in her company, but he was still reluctant to leave Blair.

'Go on—clear out,' Blair told him. He smiled at the girl. 'Enjoy yourselves.'

Gina's white teeth flashed in a warm smile for Blair. She said, 'You are kind to let me have him. We shall have a wonderful day.'

They left the launch a few minutes later. Blair was alone.

It was another day of great heat. There was no breeze at all, and the stale air that hung over the inner harbour was stifling. Blair prowled about the boat, stripped to the waist and still sweating freely. He was as restless as a cat. He started a small repair on the port engine, but the atmosphere in the engine-room was unbearable, and he gave it up.

He sat down in the saloon with a bottle of Scotch, poured himself a drink, and swallowed it. Then he got up again. He was growing more restless every moment. He felt he'd got to get away from the close confines of the boat. Anywhere, so long as he had a bit of space and air around him.

He went through to his cabin and sat down on his bunk. After a few minutes he got restlessly to his feet once more. Without quite knowing why he was doing it, he washed and changed into a fresh suit of whites.

A few minutes later he left the boat. He didn't know where he was going, except that he wanted to get away from the harbour.

He walked up into the town. He still had no real objective, and he tried to idle away the time by having a couple of drinks in a bar. But in the crowded, narrow streets he felt more stifled and shut in than ever. The city was noisy and stinking. He told himself once more that what he needed was space and a breath of clean air to breathe.

By noon he was back down at the harbour, drifting aimlessly along the quays. He reached the pier the island steamers went from and saw a Capri boat getting ready to cast off. He stood to watch her go, and he remembered Meya Nordstrom's invitation to visit her. Suddenly he had an overwhelming desire to see her again.

He strode quickly down the pier towards the steamer. He caught her with half a minute to spare, and stood at the stern rail as she thumped her way out over the oily waters of the harbour.

The steamer headed south along the shores of the bay. Off her starboard bow Capri lay almost lost in a pale mauve haze. The little boat made her routine calls, the last of them, on the mainland, at Sorrento. From Sorrento she steamed out round Capo di Sorrento and then headed for the island.

Blair made his way up to the bows as she steadied on this last leg of the trip. He stood there watching Capri grow gradually more distinct in colour and detail. The haze lay lower on the water as the steamer approached. Soon he could see the scattering of villas on the higher slopes, chalk-white against a background of lush green.

He found himself looking for the villa where Meya Nordstrom lived, and reached for his binoculars before realising that he hadn't got them with him to-day. In the act of doing so, he had a sharp mental picture of Meya looking up at him as he slipped the lanyard of the glasses over her head.

Meya. She'd never, since he met her, really been out of his mind. All along, and in spite of all that had happened since then, the memory of her had persisted in his inmost thoughts; insidiously, like the perfume she wore. He'd kept remembering her as he'd first seen her at La Goulette ... then standing up in the bows of the launch in the soft night ... then at his side as she looked at the villa through his glasses. He could still hear her voice.

The steamer closed the island and altered course a little to run into harbour. She steamed slowly into the Marina Grande and tied up alongside the quay. The passengers crowded ashore. Blair let them go, then he followed them over the gangway.

He saw a woman a little farther along the quay. It was Meya.

He stood and watched her. She did not appear to have seen him. She was standing some twenty yards farther along the quay, to shoreward of the point where the steamer had berthed. She was looking out across the harbour. She was wearing white again, and the sun was bright on her hair. She looked exactly as he remembered her best: cool and elegant; very lovely; and a little unhappy.

He walked quietly up behind her. He said, 'You must be a witch.'

She turned with a start that didn't seem wholly natural. She said, 'Oh ... you!'

'A white witch. How did you know I was coming to Capri to-day, when I didn't know it myself until an hour or so ago?'

She looked at him, her blue eyes puzzled. She said, 'But of course I did not know—'

Blair grinned at her. He couldn't help it. He felt suddenly and quite ridiculously pleased with life. He said, 'You must have done. You're here to meet me.'

She smiled at him. She said, 'I'm afraid I am not as clever as that.' She turned to look out over the harbour again. 'It is just that I often come here to watch the boats come in. Many people do. It is a favourite pastime on the island.'

Blair said, 'I know.'

'You know Capri?'

'A little. I've been here quite a few times.'

'With your tourists?'

'Yes. Once or twice.'

'But you are not with them to-day?'

'No. I came on the steamer—letting someone else do the driving.' He took a deep breath. 'I came to see you.'

She turned to him again. She seemed oddly disconcerted. She said uncertainly, 'That is very nice.'

'You invited me, remember?'

'Yes. I remember.' She seemed to avoid his gaze. 'And how fortunate it is, our meeting like this! You might have gone all the way up to the villa and I would not have been there.'

'I should have been very disappointed.'

There was a silence. They looked at each other. Then she shrugged slightly. 'And now?' she said. 'How shall I entertain you, Captain?' She gestured a quick little apology. 'I do not know—you have taken me by surprise.' She hesitated. 'It is a very hot day. If we went back to our beach, it would be nice, perhaps, to swim?'

'An inspired idea,' Blair said.

'Then—we will go?'

'Just lead the way.'

She looked up at him, then turned away. She still seemed hesitant and unsure, and somehow troubled. She walked slowly shorewards along the quay and Blair fell into step beside her.

He expected her to walk on to the harbour front, where perhaps a car was waiting for her, but she came to a stop again after a few yards. Blair saw a trim white motorboat lying alongside the quay. The boatman in her stood up when he saw them, ready to help them down.

'We go by boat?' he said.

'Yes. It is so much more convenient. If you remember, the villa is only just round the headland.'

She took the boatman's proffered hand and stepped down into the little launch. Blair jumped down after her. They sat together on the padded crimson leather seat in the sternsheets. The boatman, a grizzled, elderly, silent man, cast off and took the wheel.

The boat drew away from the quay and headed out of the harbour. She was fast and almost silent, a beautiful little job. There was obviously a great deal of money here, and Blair found himself wondering just what the set-up was. A wealthy husband? The girl sitting beside him wore no wedding ring.

The launch sped smoothly out of the harbour and rounded the eastern headland. Beyond it there opened the little bay Meya had brought to Blair's attention the day before. The villa, perched high on the cliff, came into view first, and then the little beach and the jetty at the foot of the steep ascent.

Meya turned to him. 'You see—we are already there.'

The launch landed them on the jetty. The boatman stood deferentially until they were both on the quay, then settled himself in the stern, obviously to sleep in the sun until he was needed again.

They walked together the short distance to the shore. As they started across the soft volcanic sand of the beach, Blair said, 'It occurs to me that I haven't anything to swim in.'

'That is no trouble. I am sure we can provide something for you.'

About half-way round the little crescent of the beach, set back against the myrtle-covered cliff, there was a small pavilion. It was built of wood, and was obviously a large and rather elaborate bathing hut. In front of it on the sand there stood a gaily striped beach umbrella

Meya led the way towards the pavilion. She went inside and Blair followed her. She pointed to a door opening to the left. She said, 'That is the room the men use. I think you will be able to find what you need.'

She pointed to a closet before she left him. In it Blair found a wide assortment of beach gowns and bathing trunks. Most of the trunks were exotic, flowered or figured creations in bright colours. As he searched through them, he scowled at them in obstinate Scottish revolt at such effeminacy, and was relieved when he unearthed a relatively subdued fawn-coloured pair which looked big enough to fit him.

He was ready first. He stood waiting a few yards outside the pavilion, feeling the sun hot on his body; feeling, too, a strange excitement growing in him at the thought of being there alone with Meya.

She came out to join him a minute later. She was wearing a severely plain one-piece white bathing suit. By contrast with it, her long limbs were a clear honey gold. She had shaken her hair free, and her eyes seemed to Blair to be bluer than ever.

He felt his pulse beat faster at the sight

of her. He wondered what was happening to him. He said, 'You always seem to wear white,' and it seemed to him just about the lamest remark he had ever made.

Meya looked down at herself, and then at him. She said, 'It is perhaps a little boring?'

'Not in the least. You should never wear anything else.'

She smiled at him. 'Thank you, Captain. You are very gallant.'

She ran down to the sea and plunged in. Blair was close at her heels. They swam together, far out and back again. The water was cool and invigorating.

They returned to the beach. Laughing and breathless, they walked up to the umbrella. They threw themselves down on the sand under it, and as they did so a boy in a white jacket came across to them from the foot of the jetty carrying a tray.

Meya said, 'I am sure you would like a drink.'

Blair stared at the boy. Everything seemed to be laid on. Almost too well laid on, a faint voice warned him. But he ignored it. The voice was very faint, and he was in a queerly reckless mood.

He said, 'You can't tell me now that you're not a witch. How did you conjure him up?'

Meya laughed. 'It is still not witchcraft. It is simply that there is a telephone in the pavilion. I telephoned while I was changing and asked them to send a tray down.' She smiled at the boy as he came up. '*Grazie*, Paolo. Please put it down at my side here.'

The boy put the tray down on the sand. There was an assortment of bottles and glasses on it, and a covered bowl which obviously contained ice. Meya turned to Blair and said, with a gaiety which now seemed just a little forced, 'What will you have, Captain? Something long and cool, I imagine, on a day like this? A Campari-soda—or perhaps a mint julep? That is a very good drink for a hot day, I think—and I can make it very well.'

Blair had already noticed the bunch of fresh mint on the tray. He had thought how strange it was that the sight of those few green leaves could cause him such sudden and unexpected pain. Even after two years.

He was half-absorbed in his thoughts. He came abruptly back to the present and

93

said, 'Thank you—not a mint julep.'

Meya said, 'It is not a drink you like—or perhaps not one you know?'

There was a silver cigarette box on the tray. She opened it and took a cigarette and then offered the box to Blair. He took a cigarette himself and lit them both.

He sat back, leaning on his hands, drawing in the smoke and staring out to sea. But he was a long way away from the little beach where he was sitting, a long way away from Capri, or Naples, a long way even from the Mediterranean. He was sitting on an immaculate, smooth-shaven lawn, under a heavy-scented magnolia, in front of a rambling and gracious old house in South Carolina.

He became aware of Meya again. He said, 'I used to drink mint juleps all the time, when I was in America. Too many, I guess. I've certainly lost the taste for them since.'

'You have lived in America?'

'I tried to. I didn't make much of a success of it.' He turned his head to look at her. 'You've been there yourself?'

'No. It must be a fascinating country.' Meya turned to the drink tray again. 'Perhaps, then, you would like whisky? I

94

think you are that sort of man.'

There wasn't much sorcery about that, Blair thought, a trifle sourly. There must have been at least one bottle of whisky in his cabin the night this woman had occupied it.

He said, 'Whisky would be fine.'

'A whisky-soda?'

'No. Straight, if you don't mind.'

'With some ice?'

'Good heavens, no!' Blair shuddered at the thought.

Meya poured his drink, and a Campari-soda for herself. She gave Blair his glass, and then raised hers in smiling, mock ceremony.

'To you, Captain Blair.'

'To you, Miss Nordstrom.'

'Meya, please.'

'Bruce,' Blair said.

She sipped her drink. She said, 'Bruce—that is not a common English name?'

Blair tasted his whisky. He said, 'It's not English at all—it's Scottish. British, if you like. The Scots are one of the more primitive British tribes.'

'Primitive? I do not know—'

'It means rough, uncivilised, wild.'

'And you are a very wild man, Captain?'

'No.'

'But you are. You are a wild, lawless, wicked man, Captain Blair.' She drank again, and her eyes mocked him over the rim of her glass.

Blair said, 'You seem to know a good deal about me.'

Meya gestured briefly with her cigarette. She said, 'How should I not know a great deal about you? So does every other idle woman like myself who passes the time by looking at papers and magazines.' She gestured again. 'Everywhere—pictures of the bold *Il Capitano Blair!* Captain Blair with his guests, aboard his launch at Sorrento, and not one of them anything less than a *conte* or a *contessa!* Captain Blair with his skin-diving party at Taormina, and every one of them a film star! Captain Blair, always surrounded by rich and beautiful women!' She shrugged, with sudden distaste, it seemed, and her voice was tart as she added, 'Oh no, it is not difficult to know all about you, Captain Blair.'

'Not quite all,' Blair said, piqued in his turn, and his own voice a trifle curt. The picture this woman had drawn of him was absurdly exaggerated and out of focus, but there was still enough truth in it to annoy him.

'What else?' Meya said. She was smiling again, teasing him gently once more. 'You are a magnificent swimmer—I have seen that for myself this afternoon. And I have read of your exploits with the aqualung.'

Blair said, 'Yes. I really am a terrific fellow.'

The smile left her face. She said, 'Now I have annoyed you.'

'No.'

'I am sure I have.' Her tone became pleading. 'Please, do not be annoyed. I was not serious.'

Blair met her look. He said, 'I know. And I'm sorry. I'm afraid I'm just a bit touchy about my great reputation.'

'You do not really like that world?'

'No.'

She was silent for a while, looking down thoughtfully, sifting sand through her fingers. At last she said, 'I think you are a man in a difficult situation.' She paused. 'You are also a long way from home.'

Somehow those last words seemed to Blair to hold a good deal more than their surface meaning. He said slowly, pondering them, 'I think we both are, aren't we?'

'Yes. We both are.'

'Both exiles, perhaps?'

'Exiles?'

'Outcasts.'

She appeared to be considering the words carefully. 'No—I do not think I am exactly that. I came here of my own free will.'

'From Sweden?'

'Yes. From Stockholm.'

'Why?' Blair asked. The question came out unbidden, spontaneously, and he added quickly, 'Just tell me to go to hell if I'm being too personal. I'm afraid I'm a pretty blunt Johnny.'

Meya looked up and smiled at him. She said, 'I like, what you call blunt Johnnies. It suggests they are honest.'

'Then tell me how you came to end up here.'

She shrugged her shoulders slightly. 'Oh, it is a very common story—for a lot of Swedish girls anyway. I was in drama school in Sweden. I was going to be a wonderful actress. I played a little in the theatre in Stockholm, and then I came to Rome with a film contract. It was only a little contract, but my head was full of dreams. I was going to be another Garbo, another Bergman.' She laughed quietly, without rancour. 'How many silly, empty-headed girls must there be that think like that!'

She broke off and Blair nodded, not so much to her as at the realisation that his guess about this woman had been pretty accurate. This was exactly the history he had invented for her before he'd ever met her.

And no doubt the rest would run true to form—a wealthy lover, who kept her in his bower of bliss on Capri.

That was the first impression he had formed. He'd forgotten it, because she didn't seem that sort of woman at all. But now she'd confirmed it more or less out of her own mouth. Her talents lay in bed, not on the film set or the stage. She was a rich man's mistress, nothing more than that, no better and no worse than a thousand others of her kind.

A sudden anger flared up in him at the thought of it, anger not against her, but against the man who had cheapened her. But there was an element of uncertainty in the feeling too, because he would still have sworn that there was nothing cheap about her. Nothing at all.

He said, 'So it didn't work out?' He put the question reluctantly. He didn't want to hear any more, and yet he felt he must.

She said, 'No. It did not work out at all.'

'I'm sorry.'

'Please—you do not need to be.' She reached out and touched his arm. 'I am not sorry for myself. It has taught me not to be foolish, that is all.'

Blair tried to be cynical about it. What she meant, he told himself, was that she had learned which side her bread was buttered. She had found her own particular way of paying the rent. But somehow it didn't work. He couldn't believe that that was the real truth of it. Somehow she had got herself into an equivocal situation. No one knew better than he how easy that was to do. And, like himself, she might very well not like it.

Meya sipped her drink. She said, 'So—that is the story of my life, and now you must tell me about yourself, in return. You did not come to Italy to be a film star?' Her voice was teasing again.

Blair said, 'Nothing so glamorous.' He

threw his cigarette away and watched it smouldering on the sand. He felt a strange compulsion to talk to her about the thing he'd kept jealously locked away in his heart for the past two years. Why her—rather than any other woman?

He hesitated, then said, 'I ... well, I made a bit of a mess of my life back home, so I just cleared out.'

'A—business mess?' Meya said quietly, without looking at him.

'No,' Blair said. 'I have a—a sort of farm, I suppose you would call it.' His thoughts went back briefly to the old house and the broad acres of the Blair estate high up over the Clyde. 'That goes on, whether I'm there or not—the factor manages it more efficiently than I ever could.' He paused, and then added abruptly, 'If you must know, my wife left me.'

There was a silence. Then Meya said softly, 'I am very sorry.'

Blair looked at her. He said, 'We're very sorry for each other, aren't we?'

He was trying to get the conversation back on to its old light level, but she didn't take him up on it. Instead she said seriously, 'She is a very beautiful woman.'

Blair's eyes narrowed. He gave her a puzzled glance. He said, 'Now I know you've got a broomstick somewhere about.'

She looked puzzled in her turn. 'Broomstick? What is that, please?'

'The thing witches ride on.'

She smiled and shook her head. 'No—I am serious, Bruce. She is very lovely.'

'She is,' Blair said. 'But how the devil do you know?'

Meya was trickling sand through her fingers again. She said, 'Again it is very simple. There was a photograph of someone very beautiful in your cabin. It was your wife?'

'Oh,' Blair said abruptly. 'Yes. That was Ann.'

'And you were very much in love with her? I feel sure that you were.'

'Yes,' Blair said. There was no point in not admitting it. In fact it gave him a great sense of relief to be able to do so, to be able to talk about it at last. He said, 'I was much more in love with her than she was with me.' He shook his head, thinking back. 'Though I don't think it could ever have worked, not permanently, even if she'd felt the same as I did. We were too far apart.'

102

'Apart—in what way?'

'She was American.' Blair's mouth twitched in a rueful little grimace. 'The deepest-eyed kind of American—from the deep south. Scotland—my home—was so foreign to her that it might have been on another planet. She couldn't bear the sort of life I led there—and I couldn't take her country either.' He gestured briefly. 'We had no common ground—it was as simple as that. I can see now that there wasn't a chance in hell of it working.'

Meya said, 'So. You are separated?'

'Divorced. I gave her grounds, enough to satisfy the law anyway. It was the easiest way.'

'This was a long while ago?'

'Two years.'

'And—do you know what has happened to her? She has married again?'

Blair shrugged. 'I don't know. When she went back to America, it was a complete break. I don't know whether she's alive or dead.'

'But you are still in love with her?'

Blair hesitated a long time about answering that. It seemed vitally important that he was completely honest in what he said.

103

He said at last, 'No. I was until just a little while ago, or I thought I was. But I'm not any more.'

'But you still keep her picture.'

'It's time I threw it away.'

He drank some of his whisky. There was no sound except for the faint wash of the small waves on the beach, and the solitary cry of a bird high on the cliff face above them.

Meya said, 'And that is why you do not like mint juleps?'

Blair laughed shortly. 'That's right. Rather a tedious explanation, wasn't it?'

She shivered suddenly, though the air was hot and still. She said, 'I do not know why we have told each other these things.'

Blair hugged his knees, staring out to sea. He said, 'I'm glad we have. It's good to be able to tell someone.'

'I'm sorry, but I do not agree.'

Blair turned his head to look at her. 'Why?'

'Because it is too painful. It brings unhappiness back. It—it makes everything too real.'

'You think it is better to keep things on the surface?'

'Yes, it is better.' She sounded quite vehement. She went on quickly, 'It would have been much better in this case. I did not want to find out these things about you.'

She got suddenly to her feet and stood with her head turned away. She seemed very distressed. Blair got up too, wondering just what it was that had upset her so much.

'Meya—' he began.

'I think you should go now.'

'Meya—look at me.'

She turned. Unwillingly she lifted her eyes to his. He saw in their blue depths, anxiety, apprehension, something that seemed like fear.

'If I have said anything—' he began.

He got no further, because suddenly she was in his arms. She clung to him as he kissed her. She yielded to him, but only for a moment before she tore her mouth away from his and pushed him fiercely off. He let her go and she turned and ran from him, up the beach and into the bathing pavilion.

For a minute or more he stood there helplessly, staring after her and waiting for the hammering of his heart to quieten.

Then he followed her up to the pavilion and went in to dress. There was nothing else he could do. His thoughts were very confused. He was puzzled and worried because she was so strangely distressed and afraid—because he knew now that it was fear that he had seen in her eyes. But at the same time he was conscious of a sense of surging exhilaration. He had never dreamed he would be able to feel like this about a woman a second time. It was like coming alive again.

He got quickly into his clothes, but when he went out on to the sunny beach again, he found that Meya had been even quicker. She was already there, waiting for him.

He went up to her. She was staring out to sea. He put a hand gently on her arm and said, 'Meya—'

She didn't seem to be aware that he had spoken, or even that he was standing there at her side. She didn't turn her head when he touched her.

Then she said, expressionlessly, 'It is what I feared. It is too late now.'

Again he didn't understand. She didn't seem to be speaking to him.

She was still staring seaward. So far all his concerns had been for her, but now he followed her gaze and saw what it was that was holding her attention so mesmerically. A large white motor yacht was heading in to the jetty.

'Visitors?' he asked. He tried to make his voice sound casual.

'Yes.'

'Friends?'

She didn't answer.

Suddenly he thought he knew what the situation was, and why she had been so anxious to get rid of him. A taste like gall seemed to fill his mouth.

'Or is it just the boy friend?' he said, with overwhelming bitterness. 'That's it, is it? You want me to clear out before he gets here.'

Meya shook her head. It was a little, helpless, trapped sort of movement.

She said, 'It is too late. He will have seen us now.'

Blair glanced at her. She was more than afraid. She was in an extremity of terror. He stared at the incoming yacht. She was approaching at high speed. In a matter of minutes she would be alongside.

There had been something familiar about her right from the first moment he'd spotted her. And now, as her lines

107

became clearer, he recognised her.

She belonged to Volpi; Leonardo Volpi, ex-American mobster and racketeer; the man whose name, in a few short months had come to strike terror throughout the underworld of Naples.

Volpi ... The man who, Blair was convinced had been responsible for Sam Everett's brutal murder.

His thoughts, confused before, became a racing whirl. Suddenly he knew that it must have been Volpi who had instigated the trip which Meya had made from La Goulette aboard the launch. Why? To observe him, to sound him out and report on whether he would be worth taking into the Volpi outfit—or whether he would be better rubbed out, like Sam? Or to intrigue him and entice him, with the intention of contriving a later meeting with Volpi, in circumstances where, as now, Volpi would have the upper hand? If so, he thought savagely, she had succeeded better than either of them could possibly have hoped—because he had come running. He hadn't been able to wait to catch his foot in the trap, to stick his head into the noose.

He knew he had been enticed, betrayed, by the woman at his side, the woman he had opened his heart to, whom he had kissed and who had clung to him so desperately only a minute or two before. He thought of the response she had aroused in him there on the beach a few moments ago, and he was full of disgust with himself for being so naïve.

He could see it all. He must have been tailed ever since he got back to Naples. Someone had seen him catch the Capri boat. Someone had reported to Volpi, and Volpi had briefed Meya to meet him when he got to Capri. That so accidental meeting down at the harbour! He recalled how completely he had fallen for it, the fatuous nonsense he had talked about this woman being a witch. She had said it had all been very simple—and by God it had! He had taken the bait, hook, line and sinker.

He pulled himself together. This was no time for futile self-recrimination. One thing was clear, and that was that what he had been half-afraid of all along had happened. It had happened to him the way it had happened to Sam. Suddenly shockingly, he was involved in the Naples smuggling racket much deeper than he had ever intended to get. And, standing there watching the big white yacht come in he knew that his own life wasn't worth much more now than Sam's had been when the Volpi crowd caught up with him.

Unless he played it very carefully indeed.

He watched the yacht reduce speed and slide alongside the jetty. 'Volpi ...' he said, half under his breath. He still could not quite believe it.

'Yes.' Meya turned to him at last. All at once she was fiercely, desperately alive again. 'It is Leonardo Volpi. It is best for you to meet him. Only, be very careful what you say to him, for your own sake.'

Blair scarcely heard her. He had only one thought in his head at that moment—that this was the man who was keeping Meya. That she should be the mistress of a man like that!

He said, 'Meya, for God's sake—'

But she was already walking away along the beach towards the jetty. There was nothing he could do except follow her.

The yacht made fast. Volpi had disembarked and was standing on the jetty waiting for them when they came up.

Blair had never met him, nor in fact so much as seen him before. He saw in front of him now a short, stockily-built man immaculately dressed in a white silk suit. His hair was black and smooth. He was a handsome man, and a cruel one. The hard eyes and the thin line of the mouth betrayed that. He was a head shorter than Blair, but there was a great sense of physical strength about him, a sort of controlled power. It showed in the easy assurance with which he stood there waiting.

Meya said in a low voice, 'Leo—this is Captain Blair.'

Volpi offered his hand. He said, 'Hallo, Captain.' His voice and manner were relaxed and casual, his accent strongly American.

Blair took the proffered hand. The grip was firm and cordial. He didn't say anything.

Volpi said, 'It was you, I believe, who brought Miss Nordstrom across from Tunis.'

Blair nodded. 'I did.'

'It was kind of you to find room for her on that trip. I understand your passenger list was full.'

There was a silence, until Meya said, expressionlessly, 'We met again this afternoon, down at the Marina Grande.'

Blair said, 'Quite by accident, of course. Miss Nordstrom was kind enough to ask me back here to swim.'

'Fine.' Volpi took them each by an arm and gently urged them shoreward. Meya shook him off and moved away from him. Volpi frowned a little, walking between them, still keeping a companionable hand on Blair's arm. He said, 'I am glad for Meya to have other company. She gets a little bored with me now and then—or at any rate with my absences—don't you, honey?'

Meya didn't answer and Blair felt that there was a proud, cold disdain in her silence.

They reached the shoreward end of the jetty. Blair stopped there. He said carefully, 'I ought to be on my way—I've got to get the steamer back.' He looked at Meya. 'Thanks for the swim.'

'Nonsense,' Volpi said. 'You must come up and have a drink with us—dinner, if you feel so inclined ... mustn't he, Meya?'

Meya didn't answer. Instead Blair said quickly, 'I've got to get back to Naples.'

Volpi said, 'Don't worry about that. I am returning to Naples myself to-night. I

112

should be delighted to take you with me.'

Blair knew there was nothing he could do but accept. He was conscious of being very much on his own. There were pretty obviously only two ways off the beach where he now stood. One was by sea from the jetty—and the Volpi yacht lay there, with God alone knew how many of the Volpi thugs aboard. And the other was through the grounds of the villa high above him; Volpi's villa, no doubt staffed with others on the Volpi payroll.

'Well—' he said. '—Okay.'

Volpi said, 'Fine. Why don't we go on up?'

They walked on towards the foot of the cliff. Blair couldn't see any path up it. He wondered just how they were going to get up to the villa.

He found out a minute later. From just beyond the root of the jetty, so well landscaped with small trees and shrubs as to be invisible from a few yards off, a small funicular led steeply upwards.

They boarded the car, and Volpi took the controls. The car was electrically operated, and they rose smoothly and silently through thickets of myrtle and rhododendron. When they stopped and

dismounted, the cliff levelled out and
their way lay through a grove of cool
and fragrant lemon trees. The villa lay
beyond the grove, across a wide, paved
terrace.

They sat out on the terrace. A man-
servant wheeled out a drink trolley, and
withdrew. Volpi officiated at the trolley,
with a smooth, slightly mocking courtesy.

With a whisky in his hand, Blair stared
at the view before him. It was almost
unbelievably beautiful. The whole of the
upper part of the cliff was a garden, with
the blue sea in the distance. It was a
work of art, not of nature, and fleetingly
he wondered what it and the elegant villa
at at his back must have cost. He couldn't
even begin to guess. He wondered too,
cynically and without much interest now,
what sort of woman rated such a love-nest,
and just what she had to do for it.

Volpi made such conversation as there
was. Meya said very little. When Volpi
spoke to her, she scarcely answered
him. And Blair spoke only curtly and
mechanically. He was too occupied with
his own predicament to do anything else.

Volpi did not seem to be aware that
anything was wrong. He offered Blair a

cigar. It was an expensive Havana. When Blair refused it, Volpi lit one for himself. He leaned back in his chair, lazily puffing smoke. He said, 'You have been running this launch of yours for some time?'

Blair nodded briefly. 'Two years.'

'You enjoy this charter work?'

'It's a living.'

'You seem to do pretty well at it. You skim off the cream of the customers.'

Blair said, 'You must have been reading the papers too.'

Volpi examined the ash on his cigar. He said, 'Yes. Captain Blair, the sea-going gigolo. It seems a hell of a way for a man like you to make a living. You're big and tough. Or just big, perhaps?'

His change of tone was so sudden that it took Blair by surprise. He felt a mounting irritation but he fought it down. Volpi was deliberately needling him—but why? Was there some jealousy here, a desire to belittle him in front of Meya?

Volpi waved a hand lazily. 'Forget it,' he said. 'You're tough enough. Tell me about the smuggling. You've done all right at that too, haven't you?' He raised his hand again as Blair was about to speak. 'Don't go all innocent on me, please. I know as much about what you've been running as you do yourself.'

Blair realised that that was probably true. He said expressionlessly, 'I've done all right.'

'You know the honeymoon's over, though?'

'Meaning?'

'The meaning is obvious,' Volpi said coldly. 'There's no room for you small-time amateurs any more.'

'Now the big-time professional has moved in, you mean?'

Volpi smiled. It wasn't a pleasant smile. He said, 'Precisely, Captain Blair.'

'So?'

'So—how do you feel about it?'

Blair shrugged. 'I presume I have been warned. If I don't want to be found one day soon, riddled with bullets on a drifting boat—'

Volpi's eyes narrowed. He said, 'I find you a little too—tactless, my friend.' He waved a hand dismissively. 'But no matter. I am really quite impressed with you. I think I could use you.'

Blair said, 'I'm flattered.'

'You should be.' Volpi smiled again. 'I choose my men carefully.' His tone changed suddenly once more. 'But this must be very dull for Meya. Shall I just suggest that you think about it?'

Blair said, 'I'll do that.'

The talk languished after that. Volpi made a deliberate effort to draw Meya in, but she remained withdrawn and unresponsive; and Blair still had too much on his mind to do more than answer mechanically when he had to.

Dinner was served on the terrace. It was an exquisite meal, but only Volpi had any appetite for it. For Blair it was an ordeal, and so, obviously, it was for Meya too.

After dinner, the evening seemed to Blair to drag interminably. The whole thing was a farce, and they all knew it, but it plainly pleased Volpi to play games. Even he tired of it in the end, though, and at last he made a move. He said, 'Well, I guess it's time we were on our way.' He finished the last of the brandy in the glass at his elbow and got up. He leaned over the back of Meya's chair and kissed her on the cheek. 'Good night, honey. I'll call you.'

Blair was on his feet by then, and Meya got up too. They stood looking at each other. She said, 'Good night ... Bruce.' His name seemed to catch in her throat. She

117

turned and walked quickly away and in through the french windows which opened out of the drawing-room of the villa on to the terrace.

Blair stared after her. It was torture to see her go like that. In spite of the bitterness he felt against her for the way she had delivered him into Volpi's hands, he couldn't forget what had passed between them on the beach. And, from the way she'd used his first name just now, it seemed that neither could she.

Not only that. It seemed clear to him now that Volpi must have some hold over her, to keep her here. How else could the unspoken but obvious conflict between them be explained?

Volpi said, 'If you're all set—'

Blair turned away. The only thought in his head just then was the crazy one that Volpi was leaving too, that this was one night at least that he wouldn't be spending with Meya.

Volpi led the way down through the lemon grove. The path was dappled with moonlight. As he and Blair reached the head of the funicular, two men came out of the shadows. Volpi said, *Ciaou*, Corvo—Cellini.' He turned to Blair. 'Two of my boys. They like to come up to the villa for an evening now and then. The maids are pretty.'

Neither of the men spoke. They stood aside while Blair and Volpi boarded the car, then got in behind them. Volpi operated the controls again and the car slid smoothly down the cliff. The two silent men at his back gave Blair a chill down his spine.

They reached the foot of the funicular and walked out along the jetty, still as a close foursome. Blair felt that he was under escort. They reached the yacht and Volpi led the way aboard. He ushered Blair into the saloon and, crossing to a sideboard, said over his shoulder, 'Another little drink, Captain?'

'No thanks.' Blair was looking round him, at the saloon's cedar panelling, the soft, indirect lighting, the deep, thick carpet, the luxurious settees. He'd been on a good many luxury yachts in his time, but never one of quite this class.

Volpi said, 'In that case perhaps you'd like to go to your cabin.'

Blair's head jerked round. He said, 'Cabin? It's not more than an hour to Naples.'

Volpi said, 'But you're not going back to Naples.'

Blair turned quickly, instinctively towards the door. Corvo and Cellini were lounging there. They looked almost bored but their eyes were watchful and cold.

Volpi said, 'You heard me. You're not going back to Naples, Captain Blair.'

His voice was as smooth and deadly as the gun in his hand.

4

The night passed somehow. Blair spent a good deal of it pacing his small prison, trying to work out just what was likely to happen next. It was an unprofitable exercise, and in the end he gave it up. There was nothing he could do except wait and see what Volpi's next move would be.

After a long while he lay down on the bunk, but he did not sleep. It wasn't until well after dawn that he fell at last into a fitful doze.

He was awakened by the sudden throb of the yacht's engines and the sound of men's movements and voices over his head as she got under way. He got up off the bunk. Anger flared in him again at the way he had been shanghaied, and he all but hammered on the door and demanded to be released. But he knew that would be senseless, and he fought the temptation down.

An inner door led from the cabin into

121

a small bathroom. He had reconnoitred it in his prowlings during the night. He went through into it again. It was provided with towels, a razor, soap, everything he needed to make his toilet. He shaved and took a shower and felt better. He dressed again and sat on the edge of the bunk, watching the cabin door.

After a while there were footsteps outside. A key turned in the lock. The door opened and a man in steward's whites appeared. He said in Italian, impersonally, 'Follow me, please.'

Again Blair was seized by an impulse that almost got the better of him, this time to push past the man, find Volpi, and demand to know what the hell was going on. But he knew that that wouldn't do any good either, and once more he controlled himself. He'd had a long time to think about the spot he was in, and he was very conscious of the fact that he'd got to play the very poor hand he held very close indeed to his chest if he wanted to stay alive.

He followed the steward. The man led the way to the saloon. There was a smell of good coffee and the sound of voices.

There were three men at breakfast in the

saloon. Volpi ... Corvo ... Cellini ....

Volpi turned in his chair as Blair came in. He said, 'Ah, here's our friend.' He waved a hospitable hand. 'Come and sit down, Captain.'

Blair stood his ground in the doorway. He said, 'What's the bright idea?'

Volpi said, 'Don't be like that. Come and sit down, there's a good guy, and have some breakfast. Then we can talk.'

Play it Volpi's way. Blair told himself yet again that for the moment it was the only thing he could do. There was a place laid at the end of the table farthest from the door. He walked to it and sat down.

'That's better,' Volpi said. 'There's no reason why we shouldn't be friendly, is there?' He drank from his coffee cup. 'Let me introduce you, first of all. You met these two boys of mine last night, but it was all kind of informal, wasn't it? Corvo here is my skipper. And Cellini's what you might call my aide-de-camp, my right-hand man.' He smiled. 'I don't know what I should do without Cellini.'

Corvo grunted and shovelled food into his mouth. He was a huge, swarthy brute, a gorilla of a man bursting out of his creased white uniform. Blair wrote him off as just

123

a thug. Cellini was a different proposition altogether. He was wearing a lounge suit and sat smoking impassively, with just a flicker of a look in Blair's directions when Volpi made his 'introduction.' He was narrow-shouldered, with a long, thin, lipless face and formidable quality of stillness about him. Blair made another mental note. Cellini would be a good man with a knife or a gun—preferably a knife. If it came to any rough stuff with these two, Cellini was the boy to watch.

Another steward, younger than the one who had fetched him from his cabin, offered him food from a chafing dish. He waved it away. He let the man pour him a cup of strong black coffee and drank it at a single draught. It scalded his throat but made him feel better. He lit a cigarette and said, 'Right. Now let's have it.'

'Sure.' Volpi lit a cigarette for himself and sat back in his chair. 'But first I want to apologise for kidnapping you like this.'

Blair said shortly. 'You can skip the play-acting.'

'It's not play-acting,' Volpi said. 'I really am sincerely sorry that I had to be so crude about it. I'd intended a much subtler approach.'

Blair's thoughts flew to Meya, and her distress of the previous day. He felt sure that had been genuine. In some way or other she was Volpi's victim just as much as he was. The thought made him furious.

He said savagely, 'So you sent your mistress to feel me out?'

Volpi frowned as though the word offended him. He said, 'I already knew a good deal about you, but only from hearsay. I decided it was time we met—discreetly, of course. I thought Miss Nordstrom might make the first contact.' He smiled blandly. 'I guess she did pretty well.'

Blair was silent.

Volpi drank from his coffee cup. 'As I've said,' he went on, 'I was prepared to play it with a little more finesse, but that was some days ago. The picture had changed a lot since then.'

Blair sat back and drew a deep breath. He said, 'Okay. Suppose we stop talking around it. I'm here. What do you want?'

Volpi said, 'I want you.'

'What for?'

'Because you're only a small-time smuggler at the moment—and, as I told you last night your future at that is strictly limited. But you look to me like a good man, and I thought you might like a chance at the bigger stuff.'

'What makes you think that?'

Volpi shrugged. 'You're not stupid. You could use some real money, couldn't you?'

Blair said, 'I'd rather run my own boat. I like working for myself.'

'So did Sam Everett.'

Blair looked slowly round the table. Volpi was as relaxed and easy as ever. He was smiling as though at some private joke. Corvo was hunched over the table. His face was beaded with sweat, and Blair knew that for some reason he was afraid. Cellini hadn't moved. He met Blair's eyes with a hard, expressionless stare.

Blair looked at Volpi again. He said, 'Meaning I could get the same treatment?'

'You could, if you're foolish.'

'So—you don't leave me much alternative, do you?'

Volpi's smile broadened. He said pleasantly, 'None.'

Blair ground out his cigarette and lit another. 'Okay. What do I do?'

Volpi said, 'Fine. I'm glad you're going

to be reasonable.' He paused. 'I decided in the first place that I might be able to use you in a general sort of way. I needed a few more good men, and you looked like one, that was all. But since then something rather unusual has come up. I am glad we were able to pick you up so quickly, because I think you may be just the man for the job.'

'What job?'

Volpi leaned forward. For the first time there was a trace or urgency, of excitement in his manner. He said, 'I need a diver—a skin diver—and I need him quick ... You're pretty good with an aqualung, I believe?'

Blair said curtly, 'I can use one.'

'I need someone who can use one better than most. You hold some sort of record for deep diving, don't you?'

Blair nodded.

'You can go down to what sort of depth? A hundred feet?'

'Maybe.'

'You could do a job at that depth?'

'It depends on the job.'

Volpi gestured dismissively. 'It shouldn't be very taxing. All I want you to do is to locate a small vessel that was sunk

127

recently and salvage some stuff from her. Nothing very big or heavy—and we'll have a boat there to haul it up. Your job is to locate it and get a rope on it.'

Blair felt for his pipe. He brought it out, and his tobacco pouch. He said as he thumbed tobacco into the bowl, 'Just what small vessel is this?'

'A tunny boat. She went down off Ischia a few nights ago. You remember the big storm?'

That, Blair realised, must have been the night when he and Vic had done their last cigarette run. He tamped the tobacco down in the bowl of the pipe, wondering as he did so what Vic had made of his disappearance.

He put a match to the pipe and looked narrowly at Volpi over the jumping flame. He said, 'What do I bring up—fish?'

Volpi shook his head. He said, 'I may as well be quite honest with you, my friend.' He spread his hands in a little frank and open gesture. 'The tunny boat was meeting a launch to take off her cargo and run it ashore. Unfortunately, while they were making the transfer, the launch rammed the tunny boat and she sank.' He gestured

128

again, curtly this time. 'I still want her cargo.'

As he finished speaking, the note of the yacht's engines changed. She was reducing speed. Corvo got up and went out of the saloon.

Blair said, 'You still haven't told me what I'm going down after.'

Volpi looked at him. He said deliberately, 'What I want are the six canisters she had aboard. They're each about three feet long and a foot or so in diameter. They're metal—aluminium, and, as I've already told you, not very heavy. They were in the hold under the fish.'

Blair said dryly, 'You intrigue me. What's in them?'

Corvo looked in through the door. He said nervously, 'We're coming up to the spot now.'

'Good,' Volpi said. He spoke without looking round, keeping his eyes steadily on Blair. He said, 'What is in them doesn't concern you, Captain. All you need to know is that you get a thousand good American dollars if we recover them safely. A thousand bucks for an hour or so's work. That's the sort of money you'll be getting if you work for me.' He pushed back his chair and got up as though there was nothing more to be said. 'All right—let's go.'

Blair hesitated a moment, then got to his feet. He followed the others to the door. Cellini stood aside to let him through. 'After you, *capitano.*' The Italian's face wore a thin smile.

Blair followed Volpi out on deck. He could feel Cellini at his heels. The three of them moved over to the starboard rail. The yacht was scarcely moving now, and Blair saw that, about a cable ahead and just off her starboard bow, there was a boat at anchor. She was a battered work-boat, with the words *Golfo Salvaggio* painted in large red letters on her dirty side.

He took a quick look round to get his bearings. There was land out beyond the yacht's bows, high land rising steeply to a central peak, and he recognised it as the eastern silhouette of Isola d'Ischia. It was some two or three miles off.

The yacht was edging up to go alongside. There were half a dozen men on the salvage boat's deck, standing at her rail and watching the yacht approach. One stood a little apart from the others, and suddenly Blair reaslised who it was.

It was Vic.

The yacht closed the salvage boat. She ran alongside and got a line across from the bow. Corvo was in command up on the bridge, and at his gruff order she went briefly astern, then cut her engines. A stern line snaked across. Both bow and stern lines were hauled in and made fast. The two vessels lay side by side on the calm blue sea.

Blair didn't wait for orders from Volpi. He jumped down on to the salvage boat's deck. Vic came to meet him, and the boy looked a mess. His jaw was swollen and he had a long gash over his left eye. The eye was almost closed, and the side of his face was crusted with dried blood.

Vic said, 'What goes on?'

'Plenty,' Blair said briefly. 'What happened to you?'

'They were waiting for me when I got back aboard last night.'

'They beat you up?'

'I tried to run for it.' Vic managed a lop-sided grin. 'I didn't make it.'

Volpi and Cellini came aboard the salvage boat. Volpi spoke to one of her crew and then came up to Blair. He said, 'Toschi reckons we'd better use a net.'

Blair said, 'Who the bloody hell's Toschi?'

'Here he is. He runs this boat.'

Blair glanced at the man. He was tall, cadaverous, grey-haired, with the weather-beaten face of a seaman.

Toschi said, 'We have brought your equipment.'

Blair had already seen it, lying beside the salvage boat's tall, narrow wheel-house. His lungs, masks, diving trunks, heavy underwater torch, all his gear seemed to be there.

He looked around him. Besides Vic and himself there were seven men on the salvage boat's deck. Volpi and Cellini had been joined by Corvo, and also there were four of the salvage boat's crew, including Toschi.

A small yellow buoy floated on the surface of the sea ten yards or so from the side of the salvage boat. It was plainly a marker buoy. Blair turned to Toschi. He said, 'That the wreck?'

'*Si.*' He shrugged. 'Somewhere there.'

Blair leaned over the rail. He could see the buoy's mooring line angling down in to the depths. The water was very clear, and he could follow the lead of the line

132

for perhaps fifty feet.

The water was clean. It invited him, offering him escape, if only for a little while, down there, where no one else could follow him.

He stripped off. He pulled on his trunks and Vic came across to help him on with the lung. Neither of them spoke. There was nothing to say. A diver's ladder had been rigged over the side. Blair went down it, mask in hand.

Volpi came to the rail. 'Good luck,' he said. The excitement in his voice was very marked now.

Blair spat in his mask and rinsed it out. He put the mask on. He pushed off from the ladder and swam with a few slow strokes to the buoy. When he reached it, he dived.

He went down through the familiar spectrum; the pale, radiant blue, roofed with the dazzling patina of the sun on the surface. Then darker blue, shading to purple. No fish, no life of any kind—only a great, free emptiness. Then a lightening of the thick, lurid technicolour twilight as he reached a floor of sand.

He was very deep. Volpi's estimate of a hundred feet had been a bit on the low side. He knew he couldn't stay down there long. He could see a smudge on the sea bed which was the grapnel with which the marker buoy was moored. No wreck, but that didn't mean that it was far away. At that depth his field of vision was very limited.

He swam, a few feet above the bottom, in a circle which had the grapnel at its centre. He could see nothing but smooth, empty sand. He surfaced and turned towards the salvage boat. He shook his head when Volpi leaned over the rail and called to him. He swam to the boat and climbed up the ladder on to her deck.

Volpi said, 'You haven't found it?'

Blair shook his head again. 'Did you expect me to—first time down? If Toschi says it's only "somewhere there,"' the odds are it's going to prove a long job.'

He rested, then dived again; rested and dived taking a new bearing on the buoy each time, and each time swimming in an exploratory circle along the bottom. He was anxious now to find out what it was Volpi was after. But the sun blazed up to high noon, and still he had found nothing. Volpi got more and more impatient each

134

time he came up to report failure, but Blair ignored him. He went down again only when he was good and ready. He was beginning to feel the strain.

It was shortly after noon when he found the boat, and he caught only a glimpse of her before he had to surface. He came up immediately above her. He was about two hundred yards from the marker buoy. He trod water, signalling to the boat to move up over the spot. She came up and anchored again, and he climbed wearily aboard.

Volpi clapped him on the shoulder as he heaved himself up over the side. 'Bravo—bravo!' he exclaimed. He was a man transformed, tense with excitement, all his composure gone.

'Don't get too worked up,' Blair said shortly. 'There's something down there, but I don't know what. I didn't have time to see. It may not be her.'

Volpi said, 'Another dive—'

'Later,' Blair told him. 'Much later. I'm going to break off for a couple of hours before I go down again.'

Volpi was almost beside himself at the thought of the delay. But he could see there was nothing he could do about it.

Grudgingly he said, 'Okay. If you want to eat—'

Blair shrugged himself out of the lung. His body was already dry in the sun. He stripped off the trunks and got into his clothes. He went below and ate sparingly of the food that was put in front of him, then found a bunk and slept.

When he woke, someone was sitting on the edge of the bunk. He said quietly, 'Hallo, Vic.'

Vic said, 'Hallo, *capitano*. How do you feel?'

'A bit busted.' Blair hoisted himself up on one elbow. 'Got a cigarette? Not one of those stinking damned things of yours.'

Vic pulled a pack of Luckies out of his trousers pocket. He put a cigarette in Blair's mouth and lit it for him. He said, 'You should not dive again to-day.'

Blair said, 'I don't have much option, with that lot.' He drew on the cigarette. 'You know it's the Volpi crowd?'

Vic nodded. '*Si.*' He frowned. 'But how is it that you are here?'

Blair said, 'I walked right into it.' He laughed bitterly. 'Volpi went fishing and caught me. I'm on the hook. He dangled a pretty little piece of bait in front of me, and

136

I swallowed it right down to the tail.'

Vic looked puzzled. He said, 'I do not understand.'

Blair gestured briefly with his cigarettes. 'It doesn't matter now. I'm doing a job for him because I don't have any alternative, that's all.' He swung his legs off the bunk.

'What sort of job?'

'Just looking for something. Damned if I know what.'

Vic repeated stubbornly, 'You should not dive again to-day.'

Blair shrugged. 'What else can I do? I've got to play along. Volpi tells me he thinks I could be useful to him.' He paused, looking at Vic long and thoughtfully. 'If he wants me, he'll have to take you too. It's a slim chance, but the only one we have. It's the best we can do.' He got up off the bunk. 'Come on—let's get on with it.'

They went up on deck. Volpi was pacing across in front of the wheel-house. He was no longer the suave, immaculate character he had been when Blair met him. He was sweating and dishevelled, and he looked as though he'd been biting his nails. Blair smiled tightly at what the delay had done to him.

137

Volpi stopped pacing when he saw Blair and walked quickly over to him. He said, 'You are rested now?'

'I guess so.'

'You are going down again at once?'

Blair paused deliberately before replying. Then he said, 'I don't know what it is you've lost down there, but you're certainly damned anxious to get it back.'

He turned away to his gear once more. Vic helped him on with the lung. He went over the side and down the ladder.

This time he was able to go straight down to the wreck. He swam round her. She was a fishing boat all right, and he soon saw that she was one of the tunny boats that operated in the Gulf of Naples. She was the boat Volpi had been talking about.

And she had certainly taken a crack from the launch that had hit her. She was lying drunkenly over to port and she had a great, gaping hole in her starboard side, just about amidships.

There was a litter of debris scattered over the sea bed. Among it Blair found two identical and symmetrical shapes lying on the sand, and he knew that these must be two of Volpi's precious canisters.

138

Then, close under her bows, he found a third, and it looked as though this one must have been ruptured by the collision. Its thin metal casing was torn open, and some of its contents had spilled out. It seemed to have contained a number of smaller cylinders, because there were several of these scattered around it.

Blair picked one of them up. It was about nine inches deep and six in diameter ...

He felt a sudden chill—a chill that had nothing to do with the temperature of the water.

The cylinder had a screw top, with a sealing of tape round the joint. He tore off the tape and unscrewed the lid. As the water rushed in, something rose from the cylinder in a ghost-grey cloud ....

Blair knew then that he had found the same thing that Sam Everett had dredged up in his trawl. He remembered Nicolo's description of it.

A little pot ... full of white powder.

He remembered the silence in the Bar Marina after Nicolo had said that. And, staring at the thing he now held in his hand, he felt that he too, like Sam Everett, was a dead man.

5

Blair squatted on the sea bed, the empty container still in his hands, trying to assess the stunning implications of his find. But it wasn't easy to think straight. He was already beginning to feel drunk and dizzy again, although he hadn't been down more than a minute or two. He knew the truth of the matter was that he had had more than enough diving for one day.

His brain was getting more blurred and foggy every moment. He couldn't get any real grip on his thoughts at all. The only thing that got through to him with any impact was a realisation of the fantastic size of the cargo Volpi had been running.

He dropped the container and swam carefully up towards the surface. When he had risen to within a few feet of it, he checked his ascent and hung motionless in the translucent blue, waiting for his head to clear.

After a while his thoughts became more lucid. He remembered now the rumours he had heard, time and time again over the past two years, of a tremendous cache of war surplus drugs that had been built up somewhere in Tunisia. Now he knew that he had found it, or part of it—in transit to Naples. The stuff must be fifteen years old, or more, the gleanings of the great battlefields of the North African campaign; but, hermetically sealed in those containers, there was no reason to think it had lost any of potency.

Somehow Volpi had got his hands on it. He had been running it across to Naples in one tremendous contraband operation. And it was staggering to think what the contents of those six canisters could mean, in terms of sheer human misery to countless human beings, once the stuff got on to the illicit drug market.

He floated up the last few feet, broke surface into air and sunshine, and pushed up his mask. He had no illusions now as to where he stood with Volpi. It was quite plain to him that Volpi wanted him for this one job, and that, as soon as it was completed, he would be strictly expendable. That 'come and work for me' talk had been just a line. It might have been true once, when Volpi was first thinking of adding him to the general strength of his outfit. But, as Volpi himself had said, the picture had changed since then. Again, on Volpi's own admission, there hadn't been time to recruit him carefully. So Volpi couldn't be sure of him. And Volpi wasn't likely to keep anyone he wasn't completely sure of, not after a job like this.

Blair's thoughts were still muddled, but one thing was quite clear. Once he had done what was required of him, he would be ruthlessly rubbed out. His first reaction had been grimly to the point. He'd get the same treatment Sam Everett had got.

Suddenly he remembered Vic. The boy would get the chop too. That must be why he had been picked up and brought out here. Vic had known too much, or so Volpi must have thought. He'd known that Meya Nordstrom was a passenger aboard the launch on that ill-fated-passage from La Goulette; and he could have known about his skipper's visit to Meya on Capri. That was very little to know, but it was enough to sign his death warrant. He could have started an inquiry that would lead to Meya, and perhaps farther. And Volpi wasn't going to leave anyone around who might, even as an outside chance, bring the present affair home to him ....

Blair came back to the present, realising that someone was calling to him from the salvage boat. It was Volpi, wanting to know how the dive had gone. Blair ignored him. He swam slowly back towards the boat.

He could only stall for time. He'd got to put on an act of diving again. But he knew that the stuff down there on the sea bed must never fall into Volpi's hands, more for the sake of the evil it might do in the world than even for his own sake. Once it had been salvaged, his own life—and Vic's too—would be worth less than nothing, but that realisation paled almost to insignificance in the face of the other.

He climbed slowly up the ladder. Volpi himself leaned over the salvage boat's side to help him aboard. Volpi's voice was rough and taut with impatience as he said, 'What's the matter with you? Can't you answer me?'

Blair said, with a weariness he didn't have to pretend, 'Why don't you try a few deep dives? You wouldn't have much breath to talk.'

Volpi gestured curtly. 'Forget it. Tell me how it's going.'

'It isn't.'

'What in hell do you mean—it isn't?'

Blair took his time getting out of his gear. He almost enjoyed keeping Volpi in suspense. He took the cigarette Vic passed to him and lit it very deliberately.

'Look,' he said, 'let's get this straight. You told me yourself, didn't you, that the canisters are in the hold under the catch? Well, that probably means clearing several tons of fish. And before I start on that little chore, there's the hatch cover to be got off. I haven't got inside the damn' boat yet.'

Volpi glowered at Blair. But he was completely in Blair's hands over this operation, and he knew it.

'Okay,' he said at last. 'How long is it going to take?'

Blair shrugged. 'I doubt whether I'll manage it to-day.'

Volpi's face darkened dangerously. But again he managed to control himself.

'I told you I'd give you a thousand bucks for the job,' he said. 'If you finish it to-day, I'll double it.'

Blair smiled tightly. 'That's big of you,' he said. 'I'll see what I can do.'

144

He dived again as soon as he felt equal to it. This time he took a small crowbar down with him, as colour for his mythical attack on the hatch over the fish hold. He had little idea what he was going to do once he had reached the wreck, but as he swam down he was seized with a compulsion to find out whether the remaining canisters were there or not, to make sure that none of them had been transferred before the boat was sunk.

It took him three more dives to do so. Fighting against an ever increasing exhaustion, he struggled in three times through the rent in the tunny boat's side, fighting his way into a nightmare cavern full of dead fish. The huge, flabby bodies made his skin crawl as he groped among them. Now that he was working inside the boat, he had to use his torch, and the scene its light illumined was like a madman's dream.

He found the remaining canisters and, without quite knowing why he did it, dragged them out and laid them on the sea bed with the others. When he surfaced for the last time, he was weak with dizziness. He swam tiredly back to the salvage boat, searching his weary brain for details to give

Volpi as to the progress he had made. As far as Volpi knew, he had not yet cleared away the hatch cover.

Volpi waited this time until he had slipped out of his gear. Then he asked abruptly, 'Well?'

'It's a tough one,' Blair said. 'And the list she's got on her doesn't help. I'll probably shift it next time I go down, but that won't be to-day.' He went on quickly as Volpi was about to interrupt. 'It's hopeless to think of doing any more before to-morrow. It's getting too dark.'

Volpi didn't answer. It was obvious even to him that what Blair had said made sense. The sun had dropped below the rim of the sea some time ago, and daylight was fading fast. It was plain too that Blair couldn't have dived again anyway. His long and exhausting day in the water had brought him to the limits even of his endurance.

'All right,' Volpi said at last. 'To-morrow.' He turned to Cellini, who seemed never, all day, to have been far from his side, standing a pace or two apart, a cold, silent spectator of everything that was happening. He said, 'He can stay aboard here to-night—and

146

the kid with him. You'd better stay too and take care of them.'

'*Si,*' Cellini said. 'I'll take care of them.' His thin-lipped smile didn't make him look any less lethal.

Volpi said, 'We'll start again early. I'll be back at dawn.'

He turned and went back aboard the yacht. A minute or two later she cast off. There was a sudden eruption of white water under her stern as her engines woke to life. Then she moved ahead, steaming in a wide half-circle until she was heading back towards Capri.

Blair stood watching her go. When he turned away, he found himself confronting Cellini. The Italian said, 'There are five men aboard this boat to look after you.'

Blair frowned. 'So?'

'Most of them have guns and know how to use them.'

'So?'

'I'm just telling you in case you get ideas. They wouldn't be very good ideas.'

Blair said, 'If you're thinking I'm going to try anything, you can forget it. We're playing on the same team, aren't we?'

'I don't want you to be foolish, that's all,' Cellini said. 'I'm telling you you

147

would very much regret it.' He jerked his head. 'All right—get going.'

'Get going where?'

'Below.' Cellini looked across at Vic. 'You too. I've fixed up a nice little cabin for you both for the night. I don't want you wandering about the boat. I'll be happier if I know where you are.'

Blair hesitated. Then he walked towards the hatchway that led below. Vic followed him.

A few minutes later they found themselves in a cramped little cabin up in the bows of the boat, with the door shut on them and the key turned in the lock. The cabin was stiflingly hot. It was lit by a single bulb in a wire cage over the door. Over against the outboard bulkhead there were two single bunks, one above the other, with a porthole over the top one. The porthole was shut. Blair walked across and opened it to let some air into the place.

He sat down on the lower bunk, slowly filling his pipe. Vic stayed by the door, lounging with his back against it. His attitude was characteristic and as casual as ever, but it was belied by his face, which was drawn and strained.

Blair looked up. He said briefly, 'Sorry about this.'

Vic gestured dismissively. 'Why? It is not your fault.' He paused. 'We're in big trouble, aren't we?'

'The worst.'

'I think—I don't know what this is all about—but I think you have found something down in that boat. Something which has made it worse.'

Blair said, 'I found what Sam Everett found.'

He went on to fill in for Vic the details of the story so far.

Vic licked his lips. 'They killed Signor Everett. You think they are going to kill us too?'

'I'm pretty certain that's the general idea.' Blair paused. 'We're okay just for the moment—until to-morrow. But I shan't be able to stall much longer then. Volpi's not that dumb.'

There was a silence. It was broken by the scrape of the key in the lock. The door opened.

There were three of the salvage boat's crew outside.

'Supper,' one of them said. He came in with a tray while the other two watched

149

from the doorway. On the tray there was *pasta*, bread, a bottle of rough red wine. The man put the tray down on the small flap-table hinged to the cabin bulkhead near the head of the two bunks. He went out. The door shut again. The key turned.

Vic and Blair looked at each other. Vic looked at the food and shook his head.

'Better eat if you can,' Blair said. 'No sense in not keeping your strength up. You may need it.'

Vic said, almost despairingly, 'Need it for what?'

Blair said, 'I don't intend to let them kill us like rats in a trap. There must be something we can do about it.'

They tried to eat. Somehow they got some of the food into them. Afterwards Vic lay back listlessly on the lower bunk, while Blair prowled about the cabin. He stopped and stood for some time close by the door. An occasional slight sound outside told him that there was someone there.

Cellini had posted a guard. He wasn't taking any chances at all.

Blair turned from the door and surveyed the cabin. There wasn't much to survey. Just the double bunk, with drawers under the bottom one; a steel-framed chair; a grubby wash-basin; the hinged metal flap-table, and a couple of pegs for clothing. That was all.

He turned to the door again. It was a sliding door, a steel panel on runners, designed to save space in the cramped forepeak. He stared at it, frowning.

Somebody coughed outside.

He crossed the cabin and heaved himself up on to the top bunk. He looked out of the porthole. The swift Mediterranean night had fallen, and the stars were bright in the sky. He realised that it was going to be a clear but dark night. There would be no moon until just before dawn. There wasn't a breath of wind, and the sea was flat calm.

He discovered he could get his head out of the porthole, but that was all. Quite definitely the only way out of the cabin was through the door.

He lay back, thinking. If they were going to do anything to save themselves, it had got to be done to-night. To-morrow, in daylight and with the yacht back again, there wouldn't be a hope. To-night they had one ally and that was darkness. If they could escape into it ....

The problem stated itself starkly. Somehow they had got to get the door unlocked. That was the only way out. But how could they do it? They couldn't go to work on it themselves. The guard outside would soon be aware of what was going on. And in any case they had nothing to go to work on it with.

There was only one answer. Somehow they'd got to get the gang outside to open up of their own accord. But again—how? Start some sort of fracas in the cabin? He dismissed that almost immediately. There was no reason why that should bring anyone in. And in any case it was too elementary.

He sat frowning in thought. He tensed, then relaxed again. It was no good. But the idea came back again, and this time it kindled a spark of hope inside him.

He said suddenly, 'How far do you reckon we are off Ischia? Three or four kilometres?'

Vic didn't answer at once. Then Blair heard him stir. '*Si,*' Vic said. 'About that. Why?'

'You could swim that far?'

'*Si.*' There was a catch of hope in Vic's voice. 'You think we can get out of here?'

'We can try.'

'How?'

Blair outlined his plan. It wasn't brilliant. In fact it seemed so unlikely to succeed that he again lost heart. 'It sounds just too damn' silly,' he said. He hesitated, then went on stubbornly, 'But at least they'd have to check. They can't afford to take any sort of chance with us, because they know damn' well Volpi will have their hides if anything goes wrong. They won't believe what seems to be happening, but they'll have to check to make sure. Maybe we'll get a chance.'

'And when they open the door?'

'We get out, fast, or do our damnedest to. I needn't tell you it'll be a long shot, even once the door's open. There'll probably be quite a reception committee outside, and they'll be armed.'

'So what? If we don't try it, we'll get it anyway.'

'Precisely.' Blair slid off his bunk and sat down on the foot of the lower one. 'Right—this is the drill. They open up. We make a break through them. Maybe their guns won't be much use to them in the narrow passage out there. We get out on deck, and go over the side. We're on

153

the port side now, so we'll go over the starboard side, swim under the boat and then off on the port beam. With luck they'll be looking for us the other side.' He laughed shortly. 'There's a fair amount of luck in it, isn't there?'

Vic simply said, 'When?'

'We'll leave it a bit—give some of them a chance to turn in. We'll wake them up again, no doubt, but perhaps they won't be quite so bright if they've been in their bunks for a while.' Blair glanced at his watch. 'We'll make it midnight. We'll need most of the night for the swim.'

He got up and prowled restlessly round the cabin again, then came back to the bunk. He sat there thinking. They were both silent. There was nothing more to be said. Nothing to do except wait.

From time to time Blair glanced at his watch, and finally he got up. 'Right. Let's get to work.'

There were coarse blankets on the bunks. They stripped them off. To Blair it was a relief to be doing something, even something that seemed fantastically silly.

Vic tore one of the blankets into strips, sawing the material against the metal edge of the table to start the tear. Out of the

154

strips he fashioned a crude rope. Blair soaked another blanket in the wash-basin, to give it weight. He rolled the blanket up into a sodden bundle, and tied one end of Vic's rope to it. They were ready to go.

Blair said. 'Okay. Let's try it.'

He threw the bundle and the rope up on to the top bunk. Vic climbed up after it. Blair switched out the cabin light and flattened himself against the wall beside the door, leaving room for it to open fully. He stared across the cabin towards the porthole, which showed as a paler circle against the darkness. The circle was obscured as Vic shoved the bundle out through it.

Everything was quiet aboard the salvage boat. As quiet as the night outside. The splash as the folded, sodden blanket hit the water sounded loud in the stillness. It was followed by Vic's voice, not much more than a hurried whisper at first, then lifting into a rapid, urgent jabber in the Neapolitan argot. The boy was really throwing himself into the part. Like al Neapolitans, he had a vivid sense of the dramatic.

There was a commotion in the water outside followed by another heavy splash as

Vic hauled the bundle up on the rope and then let it fall again. Pressed hard against the cabin bulkhead beside the door, Blair had a mad impulse to laugh. It was crazy to hope that this insane little pantomime was going to get them anywhere at all.

But by God, it was! There was a sound of sudden movement outside the cabin door. A hoarse shout. Feet running along the passageway. Then voices, several voices, hurried questions and answers. Then a listening silence.

Vic went through his routine again. He hauled up the bundle and dropped it. Blair clenched his fists and prayed. He had gambled on the fact that to the bunch outside the door it would seem that one or perhaps both of their prisoners had got out of the cabin through the porthole, even though on the face of it that was impossible. And he was banking that they'd check the fastest way they could. If they had sense enough to go up on deck and take a look over the side before they did anything else, it wasn't going to work.

It *was* going to work! He heard the scrape of the key in the lock. The door handle turned. The door was slid violently open on its runners. A man came half a step into the cabin. He called out roughly, 'What goes on?' He was holding a sub-machine-gun at the ready.

Blair got his shoulder against the edge of the door and charged it shut. It caught the gunman cruelly across the forearms, crushing them against the jamb. The man gave a bellow of surprise and pain. The gun clattered to the floor.

Blair dived for the gun and snatched it up. His finger found the trigger. He kicked back the door and fired a spraying burst into the passage outside. There were four or five men there, and he heard a gasp and a heavy grunt. He fired again at the light in the passage. It shattered. In the sudden darkness he made a break for it. A man went down before him, and he stumbled over another lying huddled and groaning on the floor. He made for the ladder up to the deck at a groping, blundering rush, reached it and dashed up it. As he got to the top, there came a single, barking shot from below.

There was someone close at his heels. He could only hope it was Vic. It was. Vic dashed past him as he stopped and turned at the head of the ladder. Blair fired another burst down into the darkness below. He shouted, 'Come on up, if you want some more.' Then he darted across the deck to the shelter of the deck-house.

He crouched there, breathing heavily. It had all gone far better than he had ever dared to hope. He felt a heady sense of triumph, of mastery. He hesitated. Should he try to take them, and the boat? He had a gun, a damned good gun, in his hands, and the advantage of surprise.

But he knew they weren't all down below. He could deal with the bunch in the passageway, but not the others. He couldn't face two ways at once. It just couldn't be done single-handed, not at night and in the close confines of a boat. The only sane thing to do was to get out while the going was good, to make the most of the advantage they had gained so far.

He still hesitated. It was the sound of a splash that finally decided him. Vic was on his way. Best to get after him as fast as possible. Blair ran to the starboard rail and vaulted it, throwing the gun out ahead of him.

He heard shouting and a rush of footsteps behind him, and then the sea closed over his head.

He let himself sink until he estimated that he was deeper than the boat's keel, then turned towards the vessel and swam under her, keeping as tight a check as he could on his direction. It wasn't easy, and he knew he had little hope of making any immediate contact with Vic. It didn't matter. It would be a good thing if they kept together, but they could make contact later, when they were well away. They couldn't be far apart, and a call or two would bring them to each other. A call would carry a long way over such a calm sea.

He swam as far as he could underwater, until his lungs were bursting. Then he angled gradually up to the surface. Gently he let his head break through into the blessed air. He drew it painfully into his aching chest as he trod water, turning as he did so to face the salvage boat.

The boat was a dark, looming shape. She looked horribly near. A torch flashed from her decks, but it was on the far side of her. They were looking for him and Vic over there.

The play of the torch beam seemed vague and undecided, and after a minute

159

it went out. Blair turned and swam quietly again. He heard voices raised in argument aboard the salvage boat. It was taking them some time to sort themselves out. It was a respite, but it couldn't last long. The boat was equipped with a searchlight. The next tricky stage would be when they got that working.

He sensed rather than heard movement in the water ahead of him. Vic? It must be! His heart lifted at the sheer luck of it. Things had certainly gone all their way so far.

Blair slowly overhauled the boy until they were swimming side by side. He said softly, 'We made it. You okay?'

'*Si.*' Vic's voice was thin and strained.

'Watch out for their searchlight. Better swim on our backs and face the boat, then we'll see what they're doing with it. Go under when it comes our way. Gently. A ripple will give us away in this calm.'

The light snapped on almost at once, shining out on the far side of the salvage boat. It swept carefully up and down the starboard side. It wasn't a big light, but it had brilliance and range enough to be very dangerous.

The light slowly and methodically searched

160

the sea on the far side of the boat, close in at first, then gradually farther out. Then it swung abruptly round to port.

'Here it comes,' Blair said. 'Watch it. Now!'

The light was sliding towards them as they sank and let the water close quietly over their heads. Staring up, Blair saw the surface above him illumined to a pale, ghostly green. Then all was dark again. When he came up cautiously for air, the light was moving on towards the boat's bow ....

It carried out the same methodical search off the port side. It seemed to Blair that it would never leave them alone. Time and time again it swept towards them. Time and time again they had to submerge to avoid it. And the strain was obviously telling on Vic. He was beginning to gasp and splash clumsily. Much more of it, and he would be in no shape for the long swim to shore.

But at last the light snapped out. They waited, but it didn't come on again.

'They've given that up,' Blair said. 'Now they'll get under way to look for us. We'd better get going while we can.'

They turned and swam. A couple of

161

minutes later they heard, plainly cross the calm, dark sea, the throb of the salvage boat's engines starting up. Then the clank of her winch as she weighed anchor.

Blair stopped swimming and turned to look back, staring through the clear darkness. He was too far away now to be able to see anything of the boat, but he heard the engine-note change as she got under way.

Then the beam of the searchlight stabbed the night again, and this time its point of origin was moving.

Vic was close beside him. Blair said, 'Same drill. Face it. Watch it. Go under if it sweeps this way.'

At first the boat headed away from them. Then she turned on to a circular course. She swung until she was coming directly towards them. If she held to the same circle, she would, Blair estimated, pass within a hundred yards of them, and the searchlight was sweeping a broad arc in front of the boat's bows.

The boat drew nearer. The light was sweeping ever nearer. They let themselves drift down again. Under water, the beat of her screw was loud in Blair's ears. She was a lot closer than he had estimated, and he thought grimly that it would be an ironic twist of fate if, after the success of their fantastically improbable escape so far, they were to be almost accidentally run down.

The beat of the screw grew louder still until it seemed deafening. Then there was a thrust of pressure as the hull of the boat ploughed past only a few feet away. The next moment Blair was being thrown about by the disturbed water of her wake. He surfaced, gasping.

Vic? Good boy. He was there, a yard or two away ....

Then it was all over. The boat steamed on, still turning slowly, until she had completed her circular sweep. After that she lay stopped for some minutes. Then she cast about ineffectually for a while before finally moving off on a course which, Blair estimated, would take her to Capri.

He got a harsh pleasure out of thinking of the reception the bunch aboard the boat were going to get when they reported that night's work to Volpi.

And he and Vic had made it! They were free! There was nothing ahead of them now but a straight swim to land.

He laughed aloud in triumph and relief.

He said, 'We're in the clear, Vic. And I certainly don't envy those boys. They're going to have a hell of a time explaining—'

He broke off abruptly. He had turned his head as he spoke, and was just in time to see Vic slide quietly under the surface.

Desperately Blair went down after him. He got him just in time, an inert, slack shape drifting down into the black depths. He got the boy under the armpits and kicked hard for the surface. They broke through into air, but Vic was a dead weight in his arms.

He was unconscious. Had the boat hit him as it passed? Blair slapped his face and shook him hard, but without result. He put a hand over the boy's heart. It was beating. He was alive, but he was out cold.

Blair trod water, supporting the boy. He stared around him at the dark, empty sea. Suddenly the swim to shore had taken on a very different aspect.

6

Time meant nothing any more. Blair had very little idea how long they had been in the water. He had no sense of place or distance. The sea stretched black and empty in every direction, merging imperceptibly with the dark sky. Only the vast, brilliant spread of the stars had any order or definition.

He knew his strength was giving out. His thoughts and sensations were muzzy. He could no longer remember clearly what had happened during the last few hours, and sometimes he forgot that he was swimming in the sea. Instead it seemed to him that he was hanging suspended at the centre of some great, dark void. Sometimes he felt the blackness rushing in upon him from all sides, so that he was tempted to struggle violently to prevent it overwhelming him. He fought back the temptation, knowing that he must at all costs preserve his strength.

He had had to hold Vic up all the time.

All the time he had been waiting for him to recover consciousness, but the boy had done no more than mutter faintly once or twice. Blair wondered over and over again what it could have been that had knocked him out. Was it merely shock and exhaustion, caused by the effort and danger of their escape? He couldn't believe that. Vic was tougher than that.

He must have been hurt. Had he in fact been hit by the boat? Blair's thoughts kept returning to that as the only possible explanation. But though he several times ran his hands carefully over the whole of Vic's body, he could find nothing torn or broken.

Not until the last time, and then he thought that perhaps he had found something. Vic stirred and muttered as Blair gently kneaded his shoulders. Some trouble there? He opened the boy's shirt and passed his hand over the firm flesh. Nothing, except a small area of roughness under the right shoulder blade.

He pressed the spot with his fingers. The boy muttered again and tried to twist weakly away. Was this it? It wasn't the sort of injury he would have got from the boat. It was something that had caused very little surface damage, but might have penetrated deeply.

A bullet? Blair suddenly remembered the single bark of the gun aboard the salvage boat. It could be that that one shot had got Vic in the back as he ran for it.

He took his fingers away from the roughness, and it seemed to him that they were sticky. But it could have been the stickiness of salt. And there was no other way of telling whether it was blood or not. He put his fingers to his mouth, but blood had the taste of salt. And it was far too dark to see.

He decided he couldn't take any chances on it. If it was a bullet wound, Vic could have lost a frightening amount of blood already, particularly with the sea stopping any coagulation of the wound.

He laughed weakly. Why the hell was he thinking in terms of not taking any chances, when there was almost no chance at all of either of them surviving this night? Nevertheless he went to work to see what he could do. Awkwardly, lying on his back with his legs in a scissors grip round Vic's waist to leave his hands free, he first took off the boy's shirt and then tore it into strips. He made a pad of some of the material of the shirt and bound it over the place with strips from the rest. Then he took Vic's head between his hands again, in a life-saving grip, and swam slowly on his back, as he had been doing for hours.

It was useless to think of making land. He had given up that idea a long time ago. He could do no more than keep them both afloat, and he wasn't going to be able to do that much longer.

There was only one hope. A boat. But that was so faint that it was no hope at all. A boat could pass within yards and not see them; and even if he shouted—if he could still shout—he would never be heard above the engine noise.

In daylight they would have more chance. If they could survive until dawn. But there was no hint of dawn, and the boy was becoming a terrible weight in his aching arms.

The water, too, was beginning to feel icily cold, although it was a hot summer night. It was all that Blair could do not to stiffen himself against it. With an effort he stayed relaxed, making only the minimum effort to keep himself and his burden on the surface.

He was drifting rather than swimming. His thoughts were drifting too; thoughts of the evil treasure somewhere beneath him in the dark depths ... of Volpi ... of Meya.

Meya. Strangely, he felt no bitterness towards her now. He knew that he loved her, and that she was as much a victim of circumstances as he was himself.

Sometimes he seemed to be drifting in a dream, on the edge of nightmare. He floated through patches of phosphorescence, when both his body and that of the boy in his arms were limned in cold green fire. It felt to him then as though he was borne along in a lurid, vaporous cloud, as though there was no substance at all to anything any more. He could not feel the water, nor the weight of the young body he was supporting.

An immeasurable period intervened. The sea was black and void ... Then it became grey ... A new day was beginning.

The greyness paled. There was a light mist on the surface. Dawn was coming, but Blair was scarcely aware of it. He was barely conscious.

The sun lifted above the horizon. Quickly it drew up the mist, which vanished like an exhalation ....

It was the sun that roused Blair from his stupor. He lifted his head and looked around him. The sea was like silk, a pale, dawn blue.

The sun brought him new hope. He trod water and turned in a circle, searching the horizon. There was no land in the path of the sun—the great, dazzling ball now climbing over the flat rim of the sea. But he did not expect to find land there, to the eastward. He turned to the north, the west. There was no land there, not even where Ischia had been the day before. But he realised that from sea-level his horizon was very limited. It could be there, not so terribly far distant. Though it might as well have been a million miles away for all the hope he had of reaching it.

That didn't worry him. In daylight the chances of being picked up were immeasurably greater. If only he could keep afloat long enough, a boat must come ....

The sun was warm on his face and wonderfully heartening. He seemed to find a new reserve of strength, and his spirits rose. He told himself they were going to make it after all.

He made another slow turn, searching

the sea. It was empty. No boat. But there would be a boat. They were in the Bocca Grande, the main channel leading in to Naples. There was always a lot of traffic there. Perhaps even now there were boats not far away, heading towards him ....

Vic stirred and whimpered. It was the first time he had shown any sign of life for several hours. Blair had almost forgotten him, except for an occasional check that he was still alive. The boy had become merely an impersonal burden, a thing, precious but inanimate, which he must at all costs salvage from the sea.

Blair held the boy off from him and turned him to face him. It was a shock to him to see that Vic's eyes were open. They stared at him, dully, sightlessly. The boy's face was slack and puffy, a muddy grey colour. The rough bandage round his shoulder was a pale, watery red, with a patch of darker red at the centre.

The sun, climbed higher. Its warmth increased. It brought Vic back to semi-consciousness. A violent fit of shivering seized him, and he began to mumble.

The mumbling went on and on, a never-ending string of incoherent, half-formed words. It got Blair down worse than anything he'd been through all night. It emphasised for him what he'd known all along, that the boy was in a bad way, perhaps dying, and that there was nothing he could do about it. And there was something appallingly incongruous too in the contrast between Vic's grey, stricken face and the blood-soaked bandage, and the serenity of the new day, the peaceful calm of the life-giving sun lifting above the clear blue sea.

Blair turned slowly in a circle once again as he searched the glittering horizon. The optimism he had felt with the coming of daylight was now beginning to ebb away. The slight resurgence of new strength the sun had nurtured in him was deserting him. He was feeling exhausted again, and at the end of hope. There was no boat. There wouldn't be a boat; not, at any rate, until it was too late ....

He had almost completed the full circle of the turn when he checked. Was there something there, a long way away? He stared, painfully. His eyes felt raw with salt.

There *was* something. Something white, a blob of white with a smudge in the sky above it. His eyes misted and he rubbed a hand over them, then stared again. And now he knew what he was looking at. Not a boat. A ship.

Approaching? Passing? She was hull down on the horizon. He was looking at her white upperworks. He could see the smudge of smoke in the sky above her, but no funnel. That suggested that she was approaching.

The white blob grew larger and more clearly defined, and he knew that his guess had been right. She was coming towards him, head on. What he was looking at was the high spread of her bridge. The funnel would be hidden behind it.

She was coming up fast. He could see the needle-thin stick of her foremast, then the flaring V of her bows. She was obviously coming in to Naples. She was steaming at speed, and she was big. She was clearly a passenger vessel, either a liner or a cruise ship.

Soon she was in full view, dazzling white, with a twenty-knot bow wave creaming out from her forefoot. From Blair's viewpoint at zero elevation she looked tremendous. Her bows seemed already to be soaring above him as they knifed mightily through the sea, so that for a moment he feared that she was going to run him down. Then he realised that that was the least of his troubles, a million to one chance. What mattered far more was how near was she going to pass?

Watching her narrowly, he thought he could see a fraction of her starboard side, and her foremast seemed to cut the spread of her bridge a little to the right of centre. That meant she was going to pass to the right of him. She would pass quite near, as distances went at sea, but she might still go by anything from half a mile to a mile away.

It was an effort to take his eyes off her, but he forced himself to do so. He'd got to get nearer. Even a few yards might make all the difference between being seen or not seen; all the difference between life and death, because this was his one hope. He was too near the end of his tether for there to be another.

He turned on his back again, holding Vic under the armpits, and kicked out on an intercepting course. He fought his way through the water, stubbornly refusing to admit how useless and feeble the effort was, shutting his mind to the grim thought that the great ship, twenty thousand tons or more of her rushing inexorably on her way, would never notice his tiny, insect-like struggle for survival on the vast surface of the sea.

He was very nearly finished. His strength was all but gone, and Vic was a leaden weight in his arms. He seemed to be splashing feebly without making any progress at all. And all at once he felt that it was no use. The ship would rush powerfully and aloofly past, and that would be the end.

He stopped swimming and stared round, gasping, to see where she was. A few more strokes. He forced himself to swim again. He stopped once more and turned. Now he could see the whole length of her, from her stem to her stern, the whole of her shining white side, her many decks with their rows of portholes, behind which, lapped in the comfort of their luxurious cabins, most of her passengers would be still asleep, all of them quite unaware of his desperate need.

She was a Cunarder. He could tell that from her funnel. And she was flying the old red duster. She was British. Somehow, absurdly, that fact gave him a last desperate lease of life.

175

He was about a point off her starboard bow, and he knew that it was now or never. If he swam again, he might get a yard or two nearer, but she was drawing abreast all the time. It was only while he was forward of her beam that he would have any chance of being seen at all. If he left it until she was drawing away, it would be hopeless. The watch on her bridge would be interested only in what lay ahead of the ship.

He held Vic up with one hand and began to splash furiously with the other. He tried to shout, but his throat was thick and parched with salt and all he could manage was a hoarse croak. It was useless to shout anyway, since he could never be heard at that distance and above the sounds of the great ship's passage, but he couldn't resist the compulsion to do so.

She was passing, rushing by, without the slightest alteration of course or speed. She was nearer than he had hoped, not more than a quarter of a mile away. He could hear the low, humming throb of her engines, the regular, inexorable beat of her great screws, even the faint rush of the sea along her sides. She looked enormous and very near, but she was sliding away. He splashed and shouted, hopelessly, with a cold dead certainty inside him now that no one would see the tiny commotion he was making. If they did, they would ignore it, putting it down as a flaw on the surface, the leap of a porpoise or a fish.

In the desperation of his efforts he lost his hold on Vic, and they both went under before he could regain his hold. He fought his way up again and dashed the water out of his eyes. The ship was still there, still sliding past.

But—not quite so fast?

He stared at her. Something was happening. Something was different. And then he knew what it was. He could no longer hear the beat of her screws.

Almost as that realisation got home to him, he heard a sudden rumble and saw a great, boiling upthrust of white water under her massive, bulbous counter. Her engines were going astern. She was stopping!

He felt sick and faint. Both ship and sea tilted drunkenly as his sight blurred and misted over. He felt he was going to pass out. Then his sight cleared again. He stared up at the ship. There was a cluster of people at the rail of her boat deck. The boats ... one of them was turning out ... slowly ... slowly ....

It seemed an eternity before the boat hung clear of the ship's side. It dropped slowly, painfully slowly, towards the water. Blair heard the sharp, thin note of its engine starting up.

Then it was afloat. It was clear of the ship's side. He saw it head towards him.

He didn't care any more. He'd done what he'd intended to do. He'd stopped the ship. All he wanted now was to slip away, down into peace and quietness.

He felt himself going under again, and only half-heartedly tried to prevent it. The boat loomed over him. He heard a splash. He could hear the loud, crackling note of the boat's exhaust, smell the stink of it. He was under her stern. Then someone grabbed at him. Someone was in the water with him. Hands tried to take Vic away from him, and he struggled feebly to keep his hold, but he was too weak.

He heard men's voices. They were curt and urgent, and he wondered foolishly why. More hands grabbed at him. There was something under his armpits, cutting agonisingly into his sea-softened flesh. The pain of it brought him partially round and

178

he realised that it was a rope.

His head struck the side of the boat. The rope bit deeper as it dragged him clear of the sea. He fell like a sack over the gunwale and into the bottom of the boat ....

He was lying on the bottom boards. They were hard and vibrating. There was engine noise and a petrol smell. Voices. Something on his mouth. He fought to turn his head away, and wetness spilled over his face. Automatically he licked his lips and tasted the sharpness of liquor. When the flask was put to his lips again, he swallowed. The pungency of the brandy made him choke, but the knot of darkness in his brain dissolved away. He opened his eyes. He saw the gunwales of the boat and the blue sky above.

He sat up and retched violently, his head between his knees. A voice said, 'This one's okay.' He retched again, wearily, and then lifted his head and said, 'Where's Vic?' Another voice said, 'For Christ's sake, he's English!' Then someone bent over him, taking him by the shoulders. A voice said, 'Don't worry, chum. Your pal's going to be all right too.'

The note of the engine changed. The

179

boat was under way. Blair sat where he was until the nausea had cleared a little. Then he lifted his head again. He tried to get up. Hands under his armpits helped him. He slumped down heavily in the sternsheets of the boat, opposite the officer in charge. The officer was fair-haired, young, sun-burned and handsome. His whites were immaculate and he wore the Cunard badge on his cap.

The young officer grinned at Blair. 'Nice bathing weather.' He went on, when Blair made an effort to speak, 'Save it. Wait till you're aboard. Plenty of time to talk about it then.'

The boat sped back to the ship. It was hooked on to the falls and hoisted away. It was turned inboard. Two of the seamen of the boat's crew moved aft to help Blair out of the boat, but he waved them away and got to his feet by himself. He stood there swaying drunkenly. He saw the blurred faces of the crowd of passengers who had gathered to watch the rescue, and he thought, with tired, ironic humour, that this was something extra that they'd got for their money, something special to tell their friends about when they got home again.

There were several ship's officers on the deck. One of them gave a quiet order that was more a polite request than anything else. The watching passengers drew back. There was a considerable crowd watching, most of them men, and most of them in dressing-gowns. Blair realised that it must still be very early in the day.

The officer in the boat motioned to the two seamen to help Blair out, but again he waved them away. He wasn't going to leave Vic behind. A stretcher was handed up into the boat and he watched wearily while Vic was laid on it and the stretcher was lifted and lowered over the gunwale. The young officer in command of the boat superintended the operation, then turned to Blair. He said, 'Think you can make it?' Blair nodded. He climbed over the gunwale and dropped heavily and awkwardly to the deck. He staggered and his legs all but gave way beneath him. He was glad this time of the strong hands that caught him and held him up.

Someone put a blanket round his shoulders. He was grateful for that too. In spite of the warmth of the sun, he was shivering.

An elderly, portly man in a white

towelling bathrobe came and stood in front of him. An officer in uniform stepped forward. He said, 'This is the one that signalled us, sir. He's just about all in, but he doesn't appear to be hurt in any way.'

The older man nodded. 'You say he speaks English?' He frowned at Blair. He said, 'I am the captain of this ship. Who are you, and what is all this about? How did it happen?'

Blair shook his head. With the solidity of the ship's deck beneath him, he felt the last of his resistance melting away. And he was not prepared to answer questions yet anyway. His head was muzzy and confused, but a sharp prick of caution warned him not to say anything. He needed time to work out what his story was going to be. He was lucid enough to realise that telling the truth might not be very healthy.

One of the other white-uniformed officers on the ship's deck spoke, deferentially, but with an authority of his own. 'I think we'd better leave it for a while, sir. We'll get him down to the hospital. Perhaps you could talk to him there.'

The captain nodded. 'Very good, Doctor.

Be kind enough to let me know when he has sufficiently recovered.'

He turned away. One of the members of the ship's crew supporting Blair said, 'Come on, chum.'

Blair allowed himself to be led away. He was taken to the lift and down in it to the white, antiseptic-smelling ship's hospital. An orderly took over there. He said, 'Okay. Let's get these things off you and rub you down. Where the hell did you spring from?'

Blair allowed his sodden clothes to be stripped expertly off him. He said, 'What ship is this?'

'*Highland Queen.*'

'Cunard?'

'That's it. Cruise ship. All the ports of the sunny Mediterranean.' The orderly was a cheerful Cockney.

Blair managed a grin. 'Just as well you included Naples.'

'Just as well for you, boy.' The orderly looked at Blair curiously. 'You haven't told me just how you came to be swimming out there in the middle of the flicking bay.'

Blair said, 'I don't know. I haven't sorted it out myself yet.' The rough towel felt good on his body.

The orderly was brisk and efficient. He snapped the towel. He said, 'All right, get in the bed.'

'Bed?' Blair said. 'I don't want—'

'I said get in the bloody bed. Doc. West will have my guts if he comes in and finds you hanging around like this.'

Blair got into the bed. He said, 'I must find out how my boy is.'

'The other bloke with you in the drink?'

'Yes.'

'They've got him in X-ray. Hurt pretty bad, wasn't he?' The orderly's voice changed a little, became a shade more remote and impersonal. 'Here's Doctor West now.'

The doctor had another ship's officer with him, a captain, by his insignia. The doctor gave Blair a quick check over, and the other officer said, 'How is he, Doctor?'

The doctor grunted. 'All right. Been in the water a long time, but it doesn't seem to have hurt him at all. Tough as blazes, this one.'

'Do you want to give him a shot or anything?'

'I don't think it's necessary. There's nothing wrong with him that a good sleep won't cure.'

The officer came closer to the bed. 'He can sleep later,' he said, 'when we've found out a bit about him.' He said to Blair, 'You've been picked up by a Cunard liner, the *Highland Queen*. I am her staff captain. I want to know who you are.'

Blair had wondered whether he could pass himself off as an Italian fisherman who had suffered some mishap with his boat. He spoke the language well enough. But he had already given his nationality away to the boat's crew that had picked him up. He decided he'd better tell as much of the truth as he could.

He said, 'My name's Blair.'

'English?'

'British.'

'British. Well, Mr Blair—what's your story about all this?'

The staff captain's voice was brusque, almost hostile. Blair guessed that for some reason or other he was already being regarded with suspicion. This wasn't a man to be put off either. He wanted an explanation, and he wanted it now. Blair knew he had got to give some account of himself. And he'd got to watch his step.

He said, 'I run a charter boat out of Naples—or I did. We had a petrol

185

explosion on board. The boat sank and we had to swim for it. Luckily we weren't carrying passengers at the time—there was only my boy and myself on board.'

The staff captain said, 'I see. It was rather an odd sort of explosion, though wasn't it? You know, I suppose, that your boy, as you call him, has a bullet in his back?'

Blair raised himself on one elbow. He said quickly, with no thought now of avoiding the issue, 'How is he?'

The doctor said, 'He's alive.'

'You can—do something for him?'

The doctor said, 'It's a job for a shore hospital—somewhere with more resources than we have.' He seemed a kindly man, in spite of his clipped, impatient way of speaking. He said, to allay Blair's obvious anxiety, 'We've radioed Naples. They'll deal with him there. There'll be an ambulance waiting for him when we get in.'

'There'll be a police car waiting too,' the staff captain said. 'I think we can leave you to them, Mr Blair.'

The doctor and the staff captain went out together. The orderly brought Blair a cup of hot, sweet tea. He drank it and refused the offer of food.

'How long before we get in?' he asked.

'About an hour.' The orderly didn't sound so friendly now.

Blair lay back in the bed and closed his eyes, but he had no thought of sleep. He was in too much of a spot for that. He'd got to work out what he was going to do when the ship docked. What in God's name *could* he do? Walk down the ship's gangway and into a police car?

He didn't know just what the count against him was. But the chances were that he had killed a man, more than one man, in making his getaway. And Volpi might easily see there a heaven-sent chance to get the police to do what he had failed to do himself. Volpi could brief the rest of the salvage boat's crew into trumping up 'evidence' which would brand him as a murderer .... The salvage boat had been at sea on its lawful occasions. They had come into conflict with the man called Blair, a known smuggler .... It was all too simple.

And what sort of story could he offer on his side? Would the police believe, for a moment, a fantastic tale about a sunken fishing boat and a huge cargo of drugs? Even if they did, what evidence would

187

there be? Blair was sure that, once Volpi knew he was still alive and in the hands of the police, he would get rid of that marker buoy in a hurry, if he hadn't done so already. Then, even if the police did bother to go prospecting for the wreck, it was a million to one that they would never find it.

Blair couldn't see any hope in coming clean to the police anyway. He was on the wrong side of the fence where they were concerned. For months they'd been only too anxious to get something on him. And he didn't know what sort of pull Volpi had with them. Plenty, probably, if they were as corrupt as he had reason to believe they were.

In spite of his situation, his exhaustion was too much for him. He knew he must have fallen asleep, for he came to with a start as someone shook him by the shoulder, none too gently.

He groaned and heaved himself up in the bed. A thick-set, dark-haired, tough-looking character in uniform was standing beside the bed.

'Come on—get moving. We'll be in in a few minutes.'

Blair recognised the insignia on the

lapels of the man's uniform. He was the master-at-arms—the ship's policeman. Blair knew that he was as good as under arrest already.

The master-at-arms had a white cotton shirt and a pair of drill trousers over his arm, and a pair of canvas deck shoes in his hand. He said curtly, 'Get these on—they should fit you near enough.'

Blair sat on the edge of the bed and groaned again, with his head in his hands. Now that he had slept for a while, but not long enough, he felt more exhausted than ever. His limbs were leaden. He stood up and got into the shirt and trousers in silence. He had taken off his own shoes while in the water, but those that the master-at-arms had brought were a reasonable fit. He sat down again on the bed to lace them up, then looked up at the man standing over him. He said, 'Okay. What now?'

'Up on deck.'

A seaman was waiting outside the door of the hospital. He and the master-at-arms escorted Blair along the embarkation deck to the forward gangway entrance. There were no passengers about. Blair knew that most of them would be up on the boat or promenade decks, watching the berthing operation.

The gangway port was open. There were two of the ship's officers standing there. And the ship was already alongside. Through the port Blair could see a section of the quayside, hot and dusty in the sun. There was a small crowd of longshoremen and waterfront idlers, and it was easy enough to see what had aroused their curiosity and brought them there. Drawn up on the quay abreast of the gangway port was a white ambulance. And a black police car. Two tough-looking *carabinieri* were leaning against the car, smoking, their guns in their gleaming black holsters very prominently displayed.

A gangway was run up to the port and secured in place. One of the two policemen came up it. Blair saw that he was a lieutenant. The policeman glanced at Blair, then turned to the master-at-arms. 'This is the man?'

The master-at-arms nodded. 'One of them.'

'The other is the one for the ambulance?'

'That's right.'

The lieutenant turned brusquely to Blair. 'Come with me.'

190

'*Momento,*' Blair said.

There was a stir of movement farther along the deck. The lieutenant noticed it too, and turned to look. Four of the ship's crew were carrying a stretcher along to the gangway. As they came up, one of them said, 'Stand aside, please.'

Blair and the lieutenant stood aside. As the stretcher passed him, Blair found himself looking down at Vic. A blanket covered the boy up to his chin. His face was very pale and his eyes were closed.

The bearers manoeuvred the stretcher down the gangway and started across the quay towards the ambulance. The lieutenant put a hand on Blair's arm, but he shook it off. He was watching the bearers lift the stretcher into the waiting vehicle.

For the moment the moment the police lieutenant made no further move. He was watching too. And suddenly Blair knew that this was his chance. It wasn't much of a chance, but it was the best he was likely to get.

There was nothing he could do for Vic. The boy was on his way to hospital, which was the best place for him to be. He'd be cared for there. He'd be safe from Volpi.

191

And he hadn't much to fear from the police. He wasn't seriously involved in all this ....

Blair shoved the police lieutenant violently aside and hurled himself down the gangway towards the quay. There was a startled shout behind him, and ahead the *carabiniere* by the car was reaching for his gun. Blair rushed him. The man staggered backwards and the gun went clattering down on to the cobbles of the quay.

'*Fermatalo!* Stop that man!'

Blair heard a confusion of voices shouting, from the ship and on the quay. He came to an abrupt stop for a split second to get his bearings. He saw the ambulance, ran for it and dodged round it. For the moment he was out of sight from the ship and the startled crowd on the quayside.

Then there were more shouts, and the sound of running feet. Off to his left, two workmen were watching him curiously, unsure as yet just what was going on. He saw a line of railway trucks ahead of him. He raced towards them and ducked between two of them, under the coupling.

After that it was easy. His heart was pumping and his legs felt as weak as water, but there was plenty of cover on the quayside. He was on familiar ground too—he knew the Naples docks and quays a lot better than most of his pursuers. He slid quickly along the side of a warehouse and was out into the street before the gatemen had a chance to suspect what was happening. He slipped quickly across the waterfront road. A minute later he was lost in the labyrinth of alleys on the other side.

He slowed his pace to a fast walk. Where now? He couldn't stay in the streets for long. What sort of a bolt-hole could he find? Instinctively he thought of going to earth for a bit in one of the innumerable dingy bars, but he realised at once that that wouldn't work. He hadn't a lira in his pocket.

He walked quickly on, putting distance between himself and the waterfront. But he knew he was still far from safe, even temporarily. The whole of the Naples police would already have been alerted, and also the news of his escape would spread through these warrens like a forest fire. He knew he was walking among a mob of loafers, down-and-outs, beggars, any one of whom would gladly turn him in for the price of a drink.

He worked his way gradually up to the seething centre of the city. On the broad main streets he felt easier. But he was still in bad trouble. Apart from anything else, he wasn't going to be able to keep walking much longer. He'd got to find somewhere to rest.

After a while he came to the busy intersection where the Capodimonte grotto yawned like a black and stinking mouth. He stopped outside it. The grotto was a cave, a hole in the ground, inhabited by the most hopeless of the Naples poor. It was a place of last resort. And so it now seemed to him. Here was refuge, of a kind at least. And he could go no farther.

He turned blindly, staggering, in through the grotto entrance. After a pace or two the light and warmth of the sun were cut off. There were steps leading into the depths, and he stumbled down them. They were wet and slippery. The place stank of urine. He felt nausea heaving inside him, but he stumbled on.

It seemed to him that he was walking into a nightmare. He had left the sane realities of daylight and fresh air behind. Ahead was

Inferno. The grotto was lined with cell-like dwellings, roughly fashioned out of old packing crates and sheets of cardboard and tin. Each housed a family. The only light was the fitful flicker of devotional candles, set before crude pictures and statues of the Virgin, and the redder, more lurid glow from the charcoal buckets that were used for cooking. The whole place was crowded with men and women, dogs and children. It was a place of the lost and the damned. He knew that tuberculosis was rife in the grottos, and the fever of the disease filled the air. White, ghostly faces stared at him as he passed, and a clamour of febrile voices reverberated under the low, rocky roof.

He groped his way on, deep into the farther recesses of the cave. He was like an animal now, seeking the deepest burrow he could find. He came at last to one of the cells that appeared to be unoccupied. A heap of straw in the corner of it provided a pitiful bed. He dropped down exhausted upon it.

He was at the end of his tether. He had no strength left, no courage, no self-respect. He was no better than a hunted animal. He had gone to earth among the very dregs of the city's poor, and for the moment he felt no better than the worst of them.

His very exhaustion brought him merciful release. Gradually the babel of noise, the screams and the curses, died away. The light-flicker faded, and blissful oblivion came. He slept ....

A new clamour of voices woke him. He sat up dazedly on the straw, and at first he did not know where he was. In the dim light he saw a crowd of pale, white faces staring at him. They were gathered at the entrance to the cell, and they were shouting at him, fiercely, threateningly. Then the shouting stopped and a babble of high-pitched chatter took its place. He could not make out what was being said, but he knew that, whatever it was, it was hostile to him.

A big, cadaverous man in stinking rags lurched forward and tried to pull him up off the straw. The shouting started again.

And then another shrill voice rose above the rest. A small figure fought its way to the front of the crowd.

It was a boy. He was small and thin, and not more than ten years old, but he turned and faced the others, standing between them and Blair as though he would keep them all at bay. And he screamed at them with a shrill fury that forced them to listen to him.

There was enough light for Blair to recognise the boy. He looked wraith-like in the semi-darkness, a hollow-eyed little ghost. And it was hard for Blair to believe that he was not a ghost.

It was Tomaso. Little Tommy, the boy Sam Everett had employed on his boat, and who had disappeared when Sam was killed.

7

Tomaso's voice was an impassioned screech, and the Neapolitan slum argot he spoke made it difficult for Blair to catch much of what the child was saying. He heard the word *polizia* several times, and gathered that he was being explained away as a fugitive from the law.

That seemed to do a good deal to dispel the antagonism of the crowd, none of whom had any cause to regard the police with anything but fear or hatred. And the sheer fury of the boy's attack did the rest. Gradually the hostile little mob dispersed, drifting back to their own unsavoury corners, muttering and grumbling.

When the last of them had gone, Tomaso turned and stood staring down at Blair. His narrow chest was heaving, and his eyes were great, dark, sunken hollows in his pinched, young-old face. He said, 'It is all right. They won't bother you any more now.'

Blair said, 'You certainly turned up in

the nick of time. How did you manage it?'

Tomaso said, 'I saw you come in. I knew you must be in trouble, or you would not have come to a place like this. I came after you to look for you, and you were sleeping. Then the others came and began to shout at you.'

Blair looked at the boy curiously. He said, 'How is it that you're here yourself?'

Tomaso gestured briefly. He said, 'It will be best if you come back with me to my place. Then no one will come to disturb you. The man who lives here may come back soon.'

Blair struggled to his feet. He followed the boy back through the grotto.

Tomaso's 'place' was another pitiful little corner, even smaller than the others. His bed was a piece of ragged, dirty sacking. The child gestured to it with a touching little gesture of hospitality, and Blair sank down upon it.

Tomaso squatted beside him. From a box he unearthed a bottle of water and an old fruit can. He poured water into the can and offered it to Blair. Blair's stomach heaved at the mere thought of drinking from such a container in such a place, but again the gesture touched him, so much that he could not refuse. He took the can and drank. The water was tepid and stale, but after the first mouthful he swallowed it greedily.

'Now tell me,' he said. He reached out and touched the boy's shoulder gently. 'Everyone was wondering what had happened to you.'

The boy sat staring in front of him. He said tonelessly, 'Signor Everett is dead.'

'I know.'

'Alessandro is dead.'

'I know that too. They were both murdered, weren't they?'

'Si.'

'How did it happen?'

'Some men came and killed them.'

The boy's voice was a frightened whisper now. Blair put a hand on his arm. He said, 'It is all right now. You can tell me—you know I was Signor Everett's friend.' He paused. 'Do you know who the men were?'

'No.'

'It happened on Signor Everett's boat?'

'Si.'

'How?'

'Another boat came alongside. The men

came on board. They had guns and they shot Signor Everett and then Alessandro.'

'They didn't bother about you? You were on board the boat too?'

'*Si*. I was on the boat. But they did not see me.'

'Tell me how it was.'

Tomaso hesitated. For a moment he seemed too afraid to say anything more. He gave Blair a quick, nervous look. Then he went on to tell Blair about it, and, once he had started again, the words came out in a rush.

'Alessandro and Signor Everett were on deck,' Tomaso said. 'I was in the cabin. I heard the other boat come alongside, but I did not think anything of it. Then I heard angry voices—Signor Everett's voice, asking what they wanted. I heard some men laughing. They were laughing at Signor Everett, and I knew they were bad men. I heard them tell him to go below. I was frightened and hid in the store cupboard.'

'And then?'

'They came below into the cabin. I heard them talking. And then'—the boy's voice fell to a terrified whisper again—'then I heard the gun firing. I heard Alessandro

201

shout, and then the gun fired again. After that the men went away. I heard their boat leave.'

'What did you do then?'

'I stayed in the cupboard. I was very frightened. I was afraid they would kill me too, if they knew I was there. But then, when the other boat had gone away and there had been silence for a long while, I came out. Alessandro and Signor Everett were lying on the cabin floor. There was blood all over the floor.'

'And after that?'

'I—I do not know. I tried to make them speak to me, but they wouldn't. I tried to make them drink some water, but they wouldn't. I could not do anything. They were both dead. I did not know what to do. The men had stopped the engine and the boat was drifting. I did not know how to make it go.'

Blair's face was grim. He was thinking of this poor, terrified waif alone on a drifting boat with two murdered men; one of them the only man who had ever showed him any real kindness in his unhappy little life.

He said slowly, 'I see. What happened after that?'

Tomaso shook his head. 'Nothing. Nothing for a long time. It grew dark, and then it was light again. I think perhaps I went to sleep. Then another boat came, or perhaps it was the same boat, and so I hid again.'

That, Blair realised, must have been the Partici brothers, when they found Sam's boat ....

'Go on,' Blair said.

'Some men came aboard Signore Everett's boat,' Tomaso said. He was talking more freely, less apprehensively, now. 'They came down into the cabin. I heard them moving about there, and their voices, but I could not tell what they were saying. I did not know who they were. Then they went out of the cabin, and in a little while the boat began to move. The engines were not running, so that I knew it was being towed.'

'You still stayed in hiding?'

'Si.' The boy nodded vigorously. 'I was still afraid. I stayed there until the boat ceased to move again. It was a long time before that happened, though I do not know how long. Then I heard sounds that told me that it was in harbour.'

'Naples?'

'*Si.* Though I did not know that until later. All I knew was that there were suddenly many men and many voices in the cabin. I stayed there until they had gone.

'I still waited, until everything had been quiet a long time, and then I came out. It was dark by then. I looked out of a porthole and saw that the boat was in Naples, and I went up on deck and ran away. There was a policeman standing on the deck, but he did not see me.'

'And then you came here?'

Tomaso shook his head. 'Not at once. I did not know what to do. I was still very afraid.'

'What did you do?'

'I stayed in the streets.' The boy hesitated. 'After a time I came back to the waterfront. I was looking for you.'

'For me?' Blair said, startled.

'*Si.* I wanted to tell you what had happened. I knew you were a good friend of Signor Everett.'

Blair said slowly, 'I was at sea that night.'

'Yes. Your boat was not there. But two nights later she had come back—'

'You mean you were hanging about all

that time waiting for me?'

'*Si,*' Tomaso said simply. 'And when I saw that the boat had come back, I kept watch on it. I knew you would come ashore. I saw you go to the Bar Marina, and I followed you there. I waited outside. Then you came out I wanted to speak to you, but I dared not. I was still afraid someone else would see me. I followed you back again to your boat. I did not know what to do. I saw Vittorio Massena go back aboard. All this time I wanted to speak to you, but I was still afraid.

'So I ran away again, and that was when I came here. I did not feel safe in the streets. I did not think that the men who killed Signore Everett and Alessandro could know about me, but I still had great fear that somehow they would find me and want to kill me too.'

Blair frowned, recognising the unreasoning fear that this child must have felt as he wandered about the teeming, brutal streets of Naples. He had felt the same fear himself.

He put an arm round the boy's thin shoulders. He said, 'Don't worry about it any more, Tommy. It's all over now. I'll see to it that no one hurts you.'

205

It was a stupid, pointless thing to say, when he was a fugitive himself. Blair recognised that. But it seemed to satisfy Tomaso. The boy looked up at Blair and smiled. He said, 'I am not afraid now.' He scrambled to his feet. 'I must go out. You will want to eat—I will go and find food.' He looked down at Blair anxiously, beseechingly. 'You will be here when I come back?'

Blair said quietly, 'Don't worry. I'll be here.'

In a moment Tomaso was gone, scurrying away into the shadows. Blair watched him go and then sat staring round him.

After a while he lay back on the sacking and closed his eyes. But he could not close his ears or his nostrils to the horrors of that vile place.

He was still weak with hunger and exhaustion, and during the next few minutes his spirits sank to their lowest ebb yet. He thought back wearily over the events of the past few days. He had known, for too long, that he was asking for trouble, but had never thought that he could have come to such a pass as this.

His thoughts turned to Vic. If the boy died ... He thought of the bright-eyed, laughing girl who was so in love with Vic ....

And Meya. He felt her in his arms again, felt the hunger of her mouth under his.

Had it all been nothing but an act? Didn't she belong to Volpi? Wasn't it at Volpi's bidding that she had hired him, duped him, betrayed him? And yet she had not done it very cleverly, or willingly. It had distressed her. Of that much he was certain.

He clutched at the one straw of hope he had clutched at before, where Meya was concerned. If she had done what she had done, if she had betrayed him, it was only because she had been forced into it, because she had no alternative.

He tried to hold on to that. It seemed to bring her nearer. He tried to forget everything except that he loved her.

A great surge of longing swept over him to see her again, to hear the sound of her voice, to hold her once more in his arms. He knew that, somehow, though it was madness even to think of it, he had got to be with her again, soon, whatever the risk. He would manage it somehow. He *must* manage it.

With that resolve, torn by his thoughts

207

of her but at the same time inexpressibly warmed and comforted, he felt himself sinking down into oblivion once more ....

When he awoke again, Tomaso was back. A stump of candle burned on the box. The boy was sitting motionless, watching him by its weak and wavering light.

When Tomaso saw that he was awake, his urchin's pinched face came suddenly to life. He said quickly, 'You have slept well, signor.'

Blair grunted. 'Have I? I don't know how long.'

He looked at his watch, but it had stopped. He wound it. It was supposed to be watertight, but he wondered whether it had survived its long immersion in the sea. The sweep of the second hand began. It was all right.

He turned and looked along the grotto towards the entrance. It seemed to him that the faint daylight there had been there earlier had gone.

He said, 'What time is it?'

Tomaso said, 'It is dark outside. It has been dark a short while.'

As he spoke, he picked up a newspaper parcel which lay at his side. He unwrapped it with the eagerness and pride of a child displaying some cherished treasure, glancing up at Blair every now and then as he did so.

In the paper lay a small loaf of bread, some tomatoes, and a stalk of bruised bananas.

Blair said, 'You've done well.' The sight of the food made his stomach feel hollow.

Tomaso said, 'To-day I stole. It was necessary.' He groped for his bottle. He said, 'I will get more water. Then we will eat.'

He picked up the bottle and darted away. He was soon back, and they ate together. As they did so, Blair felt the dragging emptiness within him ease. He felt his strength returning and spirits lifted a little from the depths they'd sunk to earlier.

By the time he had finished the simple meal, an almost uncontrollable restlessness had come upon him. He was no longer the helpless fugitive he had been an hour or so ago. He needed to be doing something, instead of cowering in that sordid burrow. He became conscious again of the foulness of the place. He felt he'd got to get out into the open, with space around him and clean air to breathe, if only for a while.

And there was two things he had got to do. He had got to find out how Vic was faring. He shut his mind against the possibility that the boy might be dead. And secondly, he'd got to talk to Meya. If he could do nothing else, he'd got to hear the sound of her voice. It was still madness, but he didn't think he could go on without some kind of contact with her.

He turned to the boy. He said, 'I'm going out. I've got things to do.'

Tomaso immediately became agitated. He reached out and gripped Blair's arm with a thin hand, as though to restrain him. He said, 'Why must you go? You are safe here.'

'I'll be safe outside now it's dark. I know my way around.'

'But you will come back?'

Blair frowned. He suddenly saw this boy as a responsibility. He realised that he couldn't leave him to fend for himself, not in this place; and particularly not after what had happened to bring him here.

He said slowly, 'Don't worry—I'll come back. And I'll not be gone long. Not more than an hour.'

He got up and made his way along

210

the grotto to the entrance. He paused there for a moment, reluctant at the last moment to leave what was after all a place of comparative safety. Then he slouched out, like a loafer, trying to make himself as inconspicuous as possible, but none the less feeling naked in the lights and the bustle of the crowded street.

There was danger out in the open—but there was air. He drew it deep into his lungs. Even the stale after-dark heat of the city seemed fresh and clean after the foulness he had been breathing.

He walked away along the street. As usual after dark, the city was turgid with light and movement. He was heading instinctively towards the harbour, but after a while he realised that that was a foolish thing to do. They would be on the alert for him there. All he wanted anyway was a telephone kiosk, preferably one in some reasonably quiet spot.

An alley opened ahead and he turned into it. It was poorly lit and there was no one about. He made his way along it, and then through a succession of other narrow ways. He came out into a drab little piazza and saw a phone kiosk on the far side.

He didn't yet know what he was going to

do about Vic. He didn't even know which hospital he had been taken to. There were a dozen at least in the city.

He decided that first he would call Meya ....

He had no money for a phone call, and he did not know the number. He didn't even know the name of the villa, and he doubted very much whether the number would be listed under either Volpi's or Meya's name. But it shouldn't be too difficult to find.

It wasn't. He called the inquiries operator, who was co-operative and got in touch with Capri. The foreign blonde woman who lived in the villa on the cliff was well enough known, and in a few moments he had the number.

He picked up the receiver again, gave the number, and said he wanted to make a personal call to Signorina Nordstrom. He wished her to accept the charge for the call, since it was an emergency call and he had no small money available. The operator was reluctant to make the connection. He told her it was a matter of life and death, but that seemed to make little difference.

Then he had an inspiration. It was, he gave her to understand, a liaison ....

The girl said, 'Very well. It is irregular, signor, but I will see what I can do.'

Blair waited tensely, listening to the chattering of the exchange. Meya might not be there. Or Volpi might be with her. At that thought, his bood began to pound, not with fear but with anger.

A voice spoke at the other end. Meya's voice. She said, 'Yes—who is it?' Her voice was taut with strain.

Blair said, 'Meya—'

'Bruce!'

Blair said harshly, 'You're alone?'

'Yes ... Bruce—is it really you?'

Blair said, 'Where's Volpi?'

There was a pause. Then she said, 'I—I do not know. Not here.'

She had hesitated. Why? Uncertainty and mistrust surged up in Blair again. Was she lying? Was Volpi there? Was he standing at her elbow, listening to her replies, watching her as she talked? Or, if he weren't there, wouldn't she get in touch with him as soon as she could, as soon as this call was over? Volpi obviously had a powerful hold over her. Dare she deceive him?

He thrust such thoughts fiercely away from him. If he loved her, he'd got to trust her. It was the only way.

He said, 'You're surprised to hear from me. Did you think I was dead?' The tension made him laugh shortly.

Meya said, 'I prayed that you were alive, but I feared that you were dead. And then it was on the radio that you had been picked up. There is much about it also in the newspapers to-night.'

She must have known of his escape from the salvage boat before she heard it on the radio or read about it in the papers, or she could not have feared that he was dead. Blair thought quickly back. The salvage boat had returned to Capri to report the escape to Volpi, and he must have told Meya. How had he told her? In anger, thrusting it upon her? Or had he told her as he would an accomplice? Was she still that, even if an unwilling one?

Meya broke in on his thoughts. She said quickly, as though afraid that they hadn't much time to talk, 'Bruce—please, where are you now?'

'In Naples.' That told her nothing. She knew already that the call was from Naples.

'I must see you.'

Blair's heart leaped at the words. He

said, 'God knows, I want to see you too.'

'Where can we meet?'

'Can you come to Naples?'

'Of course. When?'

'To-morrow?'

'Yes. Tell me where to meet you.'

'No one will question your leaving the island?'

'Of course not. I am often in Naples—to see my dressmaker, or for a hair appointment ....'

My dressmaker. A hair appointment. It was another and completely different world, and for a moment the difference between them destroyed Blair's faith in her. How could he possibly mean anything to her? Standing there in the stiflingly hot phone kiosk, he passed a hand over his eyes. Dare he trust her? And if so, where could they meet that would be tolerably private and at the same time accessible to him? He couldn't go to a hotel or a restaurant, or even a respectable bar in the condition he was in. It would have to be somewhere in the open air.

He thought of a place that might serve. He said, 'There's a little public garden down by the harbour, just behind the San

215

Antonio church. You think you could find your way there?'

'Of course. I will come by taxi.'

'Don't go straight there. You may be followed. Try to make sure you aren't.'

'I will make sure.'

'Tell the driver to take you to the church. Go in there for a few minutes. When you come out, walk through the garden. I will be waiting for you there.'

'Tell me at what time to come.'

'At noon?'

'At noon. I will be there.'

Blair felt weak and giddy again. He said thickly, 'Don't fail me, Meya. I need you. I need you badly.'

He hung up and leaned against the wall of the box. It was done. He would be there at noon to-morrow, because he'd got to see her. And if she was faithless, if he had set a trap for himself ....

He couldn't help it. He was in her hands.

He tried to think about other things. There was still Vic. How was he going to find out about the boy? He realised, guiltily, that he had been so obsessed with thoughts of Meya that he had made no real effort to think that one out.

216

There was one way of finding out. It would mean waiting till to-morrow, but he couldn't think of any alternative. After he had seen Meya, he would go out to Porto Sannazzaro and seek out the Pieroni family. They would be sure to know, because of Gina.

They might refuse to tell him. They would blame him for what had happened to Vic. That seemed only too probable. They might even try to turn him over to the police. But that was simply another risk that had to be taken.

He pushed the door of the kiosk open. The little piazza outside was deserted. He crossed it quickly, and plunged into the alley on the farther side. He made his way back to the grotto by the way he had come.

Tomaso was asleep, lying sprawled in innocent, childlike abandon on his bit of sacking. Blair sat down beside him and leaned back wearily against the suppurating wall.

His last thoughts that night were of Meya. He saw her coming towards him, down the dark tunnel of the grotto, fair and lithe-limbed and golden, in a pure white dress.

217

8

It was a blue dress, pale, powder blue. From where he stood, just inside the garden behind the San Antonio church, Blair saw her get out of the taxi at the church door. She looked as cool and lovely as ever. He longed to run out of the garden and rush across the street to her, but with an effort of will he stayed where he was.

He saw the taxi move off, saw her go into the church.

The garden was a shabby, neglected place. It was unlikely that many people were ever attracted there, and just now, at the hot noon hour, it was completely deserted. In the middle of it there was an ornate but crumbling stone fountain, long since dry. Its mass would cover their meeting. Blair walked over to it and waited for her there.

Long minutes passed. Then he heard footsteps. He could feel that they were her footsteps. She did not see him until she was almost upon him. She checked suddenly when she did, and said, 'Bruce!' Her face was strained and pale.

He went to her and gripped her arm. 'Meya!'

'Bruce—you are all right? You look ill—'

'Along here,' Blair said. 'Then we can talk.'

He led her to the garden's most secluded spot. There was a stone bench there, sheltered by a gnarled and ancient fig tree. They sat down on the bench. Blair glanced about him. There was no one in sight.

'Bruce—' Meya turned impulsively to him, taking one of his hands in both of hers. Her voice was taut and trembling.

She looked anxiously, searchingly into his face. Their gaze met and held, and Blair thought that her eyes were bluer than ever—and that the shadows under them were darker than they had been before. Her lips were quivering, and he could see that she was near tears.

She had never looked more beautiful to him, and beside her fresh and immaculate grooming he felt dirty and demoralised in his stained and crumpled clothes and with a stubble of beard on his face. He said, as lightly as he could, partly in apology

219

and partly to try to keep things calm and level between them, 'I'm afraid I must look pretty rough.'

She didn't seem to hear. Her grip on his hand tightened. She said, 'You are sure you are not hurt?'

Blair said, 'No. I'm not hurt. Sound in wind and limb. Just dirty.'

'But you are in great danger.'

He nodded. 'I know.' He put his other hand over hers. 'I had to see you, Meya.'

'Thank God you wanted to.' She closed her eyes, shuddering. 'I was so terribly afraid, until you telephoned.'

Blair said, 'Don't worry. I'm not done for yet.'

'But—he would have killed you. He will still kill you, if he can. And he is so powerful. So terrible—'

She seemed on the verge of breaking down completely, and that wouldn't do either of them any good. He said, as composedly as he could, 'Meya, darling, don't distress yourself so. We haven't very much time together.'

She turned her head away from him, her body rigid with the effort she was making to keep herself under control. Then at last she relaxed, with a slow exhalation of breath that was almost a sigh. She turned to him again. 'I'm sorry.' She smiled at him tremulously. 'It is wrong for me to worry you.'

Blair pressed her hand. He looked round the garden again. He said, 'I'm all right for the moment. I'm probably being melodramatic anyway, seeing bogy men everywhere I look.'

Meya looked up at him. She said simply, 'I love you.'

'And I love you.' Blair shook his head. 'I never thought that this could ever happen to me again—no, it isn't "again" either, because the first time was never like this.' He laughed wryly. 'A fine time I've chosen for it too, haven't I? I wonder why I always have to do things the hard way?'

He was still trying hard to keep things light, but Meya could not respond. She could not match his mood. She said, 'What are we going to do? Oh Bruce—what are we going to do?'

Blair said, 'First I'd like to get a few things straight between us.' He hesitated. 'That first time we met, on the trip from La Goulette. You made that trip on Volpi's orders?'

She bit her lip. 'You know I did.'

221

'Why?'

She gestured helplessly. 'I did not understand what I was doing.' She looked up at him. 'I have not known Leonardo Volpi long. I have—lived with him only a little while. I knew from the first that he was not a good man, but he was strong, and could protect me, and in the condition I was in at the time that was all that mattered to me.' She shivered. 'And then suddenly I was afraid of him. I had to do what he asked ....'

She bowed her head. The sunlight was golden on her hair. Blair felt a sudden tearing compassion for her. He said, 'It doesn't matter—about the trip, I mean. It's all old history now.' He hesitated again. He hated doing this, but he had to do it. He said, 'Did you know then what he wanted me for?'

She gestured quickly, defensively. 'No. I—'

'Did you know that it was something shady?' He saw from the quick, nervously inquiring glance she gave him that she did not know the word. He tried again. 'You knew it was something against the law?'

'I—I am not sure what I thought,' she said. 'And I did not know about you, what

222

sort of man you were.'

'Did you know that he was a drug-peddler and a murderer?'

'No.' Her voice was a whisper.

'Do you believe me when I tell you now?'

She said expressionlessly, 'I do not need you to tell me. He told me himself ... When the men on the boat came to tell him that you had escaped ...' She put a hand up before her eyes as though to shout out something horrible.

Blair said gently, 'Tell me about it.'

She looked at him and away again. For a moment she didn't seem to be able to go on. Then she said, 'After he had left you on the boat, he came back to the villa. He was there when the men from the boat came. It was during the night. The men came and talked to him. I do not know what they said, because it was late and I had gone to bed. But I heard him screaming at them.'

She didn't seem to be able to speak Volpi's name. 'It went on for a long time. Then they went away, and he came up to my room. I had locked my door—you know why.' Her eyes met Blair's briefly, and the colour heightened in her cheeks.

223

'But he beat upon it and shouted that he would break it down if I did not open it. I opened it, and he came in.' She put a hand up to her face as though she had been struck. 'It was terrible. He was like a maniac. He raged about the room, shouting at me. He told me about the American—'

Blair said quickly, 'Volpi killed Sam?'

Meya closed her eyes and gave a shudder of revulsion. 'He ordered the American to be killed—and you were to have been killed too, once you had done what he wanted. He raved about drugs at the bottom of the sea ....'

Blair put an arm along the back of the bench and drew her to him. He said gently, 'It must have been frightful.'

He didn't want her to have to relive any more of that nightmare time. But there was something else he badly needed to know. Something he *had* to know.

He said, 'Tell me just one thing more, if you can. I had to use a gun to get off that boat. Did I kill anyone?'

'All this talk of killing!' Meya's mouth quivered and she clenched her fists to hold on to herself. With a tremendous effort she managed to answer in a level voice. She said, 'I do not know that. He did not speak of it.'

'He wouldn't,' Blair said grimly. 'If any of his stooges got rubbed out, it wouldn't mean a thing to him.' He drew a deep breath. 'But it could mean plenty to me.'

They looked at each other in a strained and desperate silence. Then Meya's eyes filled with tears. She said, 'Oh, Bruce, Bruce—what are you going to do?'

Blair gestured. 'I don't know. I've got to work on it.'

Meya put a hand on his arm in sudden, urgent appeal. 'Can you not go to the police? Isn't that the best—the only thing to do?'

It was a simple, direct question. And to Blair it was more than that. It awoke in him a sudden upsurge of comfort and happiness. Because it meant that, from the way she obviously thought of the police as protectors, she herself could not be seriously involved with Volpi.

She was just another of his victims. Somehow she had come into his clutches— had perhaps been attracted to him before she knew what he was; perhaps hadn't even cared very much what he was, because at the time she hadn't cared very much about herself or what happened to her ....

Blair realised suddenly that she was watching him anxiously; that she was waiting for his answer. Her eyes were searching his face, pleadingly.

But what answer could he give?

It was a long time before he spoke. He knew how important it was that he make her understand what his position was. He knew that, as in her case just now, what he said would indicate his own degree of involvement with the whole rotten business. An innocent man, or even one not guilty of any great crime, would surely go to the police in the desperate situation he was now in. It was a simple issue. And that was how it must seem to her.

He answered her at last. He said slowly, 'The police? I don't know.' He met her gaze levelly. 'I'm quite sure they'd be very glad to see me—they've been gunning for me a long time. They've never had anything on me—but they might be able to hang something on me now, over the little matter of last night aboard the salvage boat, particularly if Volpi co-operates with them. If I killed anybody then—and the odds certainly are that I did—then it could be murder. And I'm sure Volpi will have seen the possibilities of the situation already. He could frame me for that one very easily—and it might give him quite a kick to fix it that way.'

He laughed shortly. 'I can see how it would work. To all intents and purposes, that salvage boat was a respectable outfit. I got aboard it, for some shady purpose or other. I tangled with the crew, and killed one or two of them in the process.

'There's the rest of the crew as witnesses. They could tell some trumped-up story as to what it was all about—it couldn't sound wilder than the story I'd have to tell. Volpi could brief them on it, and never come into the thing himself. He could fix it so that the police did his dirty work for him. All he would have to do would be to sit back and watch.'

Meya was looking sick with horror when he finished. She said desperately, 'Then you are in terrible danger on both sides. There is only one thing you can do.'

'Which is?'

'You must leave Italy.'

'That's easier said than done.'

'It must be done. It is the only way.' She spoke rapidly, urgently. 'Bruce—I have money. It is all yours. Anything I have is yours—'

'I know.' Blair reached up and touched her hair, smoothing it back from her face. 'And don't think I don't appreciate it, my darling.' His expression hardened. 'But it wouldn't be easy—and it wouldn't be the real answer anyway. They could still bring me back. Or try to. At the best I'd be on the run for the rest of my life.'

'Then—what *can* you do?'

Blair rubbed a hand wearily over his eyes. 'I don't know. I've got to work on it some more.'

He glanced towards the gates of the garden and tensed. Two men had just come in and were walking towards where he and Meya were sitting. They passed, talking volubly together, without turning their heads towards the bench. But they left him on edge. He said, 'We'd better break it up. I'm dangerous company.'

Meya said, 'You mean I must leave you and—go back?' Her voice was dead, expressionless.

Blair got to his feet and stood looking down at her. 'It's the only thing you can do, isn't it?' He couldn't keep the bitterness and jealousy he felt out of his tone. But then a wave of love and pity for her came over him. He said, 'You must go back, my darling, for your own sake as well as mine. You must not let Volpi see you behaving in anything except a normal way. It would alert him at once. It could lead him to me—and it would be very dangerous for you.'

She got up too and faced him. 'I don't care about myself—'

'You must, for my sake. Because I love you.' Blair took her by the shoulders and looked at her gravely. 'We'll come out of this somehow, and we'll come out of it together. But right now you've got to go back to Capri. It'll not only be the safest thing for both of us, but the best for me. I shall know where you are. I shall be able to contact you.' He paused. 'Tell me a name I can use on the phone.'

Meya hesitated. 'Vivaldi,' she said at last. 'He is my hairdresser. A call from him would not excite interest.'

'Vivaldi,' Blair said. 'Good.' He hesitated in his turn. 'Meya, I hate to have you go back, you know that, don't you? But you know you must?'

There were tears on her cheeks, but she nodded. 'If it is what you wish—'

Blair said almost roughly. 'It's not what I wish—it's what you've got to do.' He dropped his hands and turned away from her. 'I'd better go first. You'll need to make up your face—'

'Don't go yet.' She opened her handbag, fumbling with the clasp in her haste. 'I have brought you money.' She pressed a roll of notes into his hand. She closed her eyes, and seemed to sway. 'Parting like this—I do not think I can bear it. Not to know where you are, or what you are doing, what is happening to you.'

'Don't worry—I can take care of myself,' Blair said. The words seemed weak and fatuous to his own ears, but there was no other comfort he could give her. He bent and kissed her quickly on the lips. 'I'll phone you and keep you posted—but don't worry if you don't hear from me for a while. I'll only contact you when I've got something to tell you. It will be risky, however careful we are, so I'll only phone when there's something to justify the risk.'

He lifted his hand and touched her cheek gently. Then he walked away. He did not look back ....

The city was somnolent in the early

afternoon heat. He made his way back through the torrid streets to the black hole of the Capodimonte grotto.

Tomaso was waiting there in his wretched little den. He got quickly to his feet when he saw Blair. He said, 'It is good that you have come back. You have been away a long time. I was afraid that something had happened.' He turned and, dropping to his knees, began to search behind him. 'You want food ... drink? There is still a little—'

'No,' Blair said. 'I'm not hungry—or thirsty right now.'

He squatted down beside the boy, staring at him. For a moment he felt impatient, almost angry. He had no time to play wet nurse to a kid. And yet he knew he could not abandon the child. He could not go away and leave him alone again in that hopeless, terrible place.

He made a sudden decision. He said, 'Tommy—how would you like a bus ride?'

'Come?' The boy didn't understand.

'I'll be taking a trip out of Naples to-night—on a bus out along the coast a little way. Do you want to come with me?'

'Si!' Tomaso was all eagerness now. He hesitated, and then said, simply and

231

seriously, 'I will go anywhere with you, Signor Blair.'

'Good.' Blair felt very touched. 'I don't know that I'm the right sort of company for you to keep—but never mind that.' He lay back. 'We'll leave as soon as it gets dark. Until then I'd like to get a bit more rest.'

He lay with his hands clasped behind his head. He shut his eyes. He didn't expect to sleep—he had too much to think about. But he did fall asleep. When he woke, he got up and walked towards the entrance to the grotto. Night had fallen. He had slept until dark, as he had done the day before. The street outside was garish with light.

He went back to where Tomaso lay and, bending down, shook him gently by the shoulder. The thin little figure tensed at once, shrinking away from Blair's hand. In the unprotected life of the waterfront and the alleys of the city, he had learned to sleep lightly, always prepared to scurry away to a new hiding-place.

Then he saw who it was that had awakened him. He sat up and said quickly, 'It is time to go now?'

Blair said, 'Soon. Maybe we ought to eat something now, before we go.'

They ate again from Tomaso's sad little store of stale bread and bad fruit, and drank the last of the tepid water. As soon as they had finished the scanty meal, Blair got to his feet. Tomaso scrambled up too and stood looking up at Blair anxiously, as though afraid that at the last moment this big man whom he obviously now regarded as a friend and protector would change his mind and leave him behind.

Blair looked down at the child. He saw what Tomaso was thinking, and he put out a hand and ruffled the tousled, dirty hair. He said, 'Okay? You'd better take with you anything you've got here that you particularly want. I don't suppose you will be coming back again.'

'Not come back?' Tomaso stared up at Blair doubtfully now. That place, wretched as it was, was the only shelter, the only home he had.

'Oh, for God's sake, let's get out of it,' Blair said curtly. 'You won't be leaving anything behind that you'll not be well rid of.'

He walked off towards the grotto entrance. The boy stood his ground where he was for a moment, looking

233

uncertainly round him. Then he ran quickly after Blair.

They came out into the harsh, revealing brightness of the street. Blair turned and walked quickly away down towards the docks, towards the little piazza from which Vic had caught the bus out to Porto Sannazzaro. A clock told him that it was nearly nine. He seemed to remember, from the times Vic had left the launch to go out to Porto Sannazzaro, that the buses left more or less on the hour.

He reached the piazza with Tomaso close at his side. They were lucky. There was a bus waiting. It was almost full. The passengers were typical of the people of the outskirts of Naples and the small coastal towns of the bay. He and Tomaso found seats together at the back. Tomaso was now no more than just an excited small boy, wriggling with impatience for the ride to begin. Blair realised that the child had almost certainly never been on a bus before.

The bus started. The driver handled it in true Neapolitan style. It roared and swerved its devious way out of the city and through the suburbs, and then went bustling along the winding coast road.

It was an hour's ride to Porto San-nazzaro. Very few of the passengers were going that far. They dropped off in one's and two's at nearly every stop. By the time the bus arrived at its destination, it was all but empty.

Blair and Tomaso got out in the quiet square of the little town. The few other passengers left had got out in front of them and were already drifting away.

Blair knew that the Pieroni hotel was called the Albergo Italia. He asked the bus driver if he knew where the place was, and the man pointed up the hill to the north of the harbour.

'Straight up. You will see it on your left.'

Blair and Tomaso started up the steep street. Tomaso stared about him as they walked. He said after a while, in a voice that was only a little above a whisper, 'This is a very silent place.'

Blair glanced down at the boy. He was walking even closer to him, and there had been a marked note of apprehension in his voice. Blair realised, with another twinge of compassion for the child, that he could not understand a silence that wasn't ominous, an absence of people that meant merely peace. In Naples, at that time of night, the alleys were only quiet and deserted when some danger threatened.

He said, 'It's all right, Tommy. No one's going to hurt you here.'

He held out his hand. Tomaso took it and held it tightly and trustingly. They went on together like that up the hill.

They had no trouble in finding the Albergo Italia. It was a tall, narrow white house fronting directly on the street about half-way up the hill. There were lights in most of the rooms. The door of the small entrance hall stood open, and there were sounds of activity inside.

Blair paused for a moment before entering, wondering what sort of reception he was going to get. He reminded himself again that the Pieronis, and Giannina in particular, had no reason to love him, after what had happened to Vic. But then he shrugged and told himself it didn't matter much. The only reason he had come was to find out how Vic was. At least they'd tell him that.

He walked in, still holding Tomaso's hand. As he did so, Giannina herself came into the hall through an inner door.

She stopped dead in her tracks. 'Signor!'

'Hallo, Giannina.' Blair tried to be as easy as he could. He saw that she had gone very pale.

The girl stared at him, her hand at her throat. Then she said, in a voice only a little above a whisper, 'Why—why do you come here, signor?'

'To see you,' Blair said. He grinned at her and nerved himself to ask the vital question. 'To find out about Vic—how he is.'

Giannina said, 'He is—' Her hand was still up to her throat, over her small, heaving bosom. 'He is—'

She broke off again. There were footsteps on the stairs. Two women were coming down, obviously two of the guests at the hotel. They looked English to Blair. Elderly—schoolmistresses, perhaps? They glanced at him and Tomaso with genteelly veiled curiosity, and Blair was suddenly conscious that he must look a pretty rough customer.

Giannina recovered herself enough to smile at the two women as they passed. Then, when they had gone out through the street door, she turned to Blair again. 'Please—' she said.

She turned back to the door she had

237

come through. Blair followed her. The door led along a short passageway into the kitchen. There was a sudden wave of heat and a strong smell of garlic as Giannina opened the kitchen door.

Momma Pieroni was at the stove. Papa sat at a big, plain wooden table, wiping cutlery with a cloth.

Giannina said, in a ghost of a voice, 'See who has come.'

Momma Pieroni turned from the stove, an outsize spoon in her hand. Papa looked up, stared, and then got hurriedly to his feet. There was a shower of spoons and forks on to the floor. It went unregarded.

Blair said, 'I'm sorry to intrude. I was worried about Vittorio. I wanted to know how he is.'

There was a silence. Both Giannina and her mother were looking towards Papa Pieroni. He was the head of the house. This was a situation that he must handle.

Papa said slowly, 'He is—alive.'

Blair said, 'Thank God.'

'Si,' Momma said. 'Grazie a Dio.'

Blair said, 'He was badly hurt?'

Papa Pieroni nodded. 'Si. It was very bad. There had to be a big operation. But it was successful. Now he is going to get well, but it will be a long time.'

Giannina was sobbing quietly, her face in her hands. Blair turned to her. He said, 'Giannina—what can I say to you? It was because of me—'

Papa said fiercely, unexpectedly, 'You saved his life, signor.'

Blair said, 'But if he hadn't been working for me—'

They wouldn't let him speak. It was Momma who broke in this time. She said, 'You saved him for our daughter, signor. You saved him for us—for he is one of us now. He is the only man for our daughter. We did not think so once, but we know it now, now that we have seen her love and her grief.'

Papa said, 'So we can only thank you, signor, for saving him from the sea.'

'And you are in trouble, signor,' Momma said. 'We know that, and it is easy to see.' Her glance fell suddenly upon Tomaso, who had been standing timidly in the background throughout all this. 'And the poor bambino—who is he?'

Blair tried to explain. He was bewildered. He had never expected a reception such as this. He had been prepared to meet with suspicion, hostility, a flat refusal to have anything to do with him, to tell him anything; but certainly not this unqualified and impulsive gratitude.

And soon he was more bewildered still, as the Pieronis' overwhelming hospitality engulfed him. He and Tomaso were all but driven to seats at the big kitchen table. Momma set great bowls of steaming *pasta* before them, and Papa fetched wine, the best he had.

The family crowded round, all talking together now, interrupting each other, asking a hundred questions.

Vic had told them as much as he could remember of the long swim, which was very little. They had heard of the cruise ship's part in the affair on the radio, and read of it in the newspapers. They knew that Blair was wanted by the police, but they appeared to have no idea what lay behind it all. Blair didn't enlighten them on that score. He told them a little more about the night he and Vic had spent in the water, and countered the barrage of questions they fired at him as well as he could.

At last there was a moment of pause. He was grateful for it. He was sleepy with good food, and for the first time in days he felt really relaxed. He didn't know how he was going to get up and leave, but he knew that he must. He couldn't endanger these good, simple people with his presence under their roof any longer.

He got heavily to his feet. He said, 'Well—we must be on our way—'

Giannina said, 'But where will you go?'

Blair shrugged, 'I don't know. It doesn't matter—'

'Pouf!' Momma Pieroni faced him, her hands on her hips. 'You will go nowhere at all to-night, signor, not while we have good beds where you can rest.' She moved her great bulk round the table and put a plump hand on Tomaso's shoulder. 'And this poor infant—where do you think you are going to drag him to at this hour of the night? He should be already long asleep.'

Blair said, 'But you could find yourselves in trouble—'

'Trouble?' Papa took over from Momma. 'And aren't you in much more trouble than we are ever likely to be?' He blew out his cheeks, almost angrily. 'Momma is right. You are not going anywhere to-night.'

The thought of a good bed and a quiet, safe night's sleep weakened Blair's resolution to vanishing point.

'It is—good of you,' he said.

'Good—*Santa Maria!*' Momma exclaimed. She seemed angry too. 'Do you think we are the kind of people to turn anyone in need away from our door?' She patted Tomaso's thin shoulder. 'Come, little one. We will go upstairs.'

Tomaso turned and looked doubtfully at Blair. The child, full of food, probably for the first time in years, was scarcely able to keep his eyes open. But he was still uneasy, baffled by the Pieroni family's kindness, and suspicious of it. A house, also, was strange territory to him. His eyes pleaded with Blair for reassurance.

Blair said, 'Put him in with me, if that's possible. He wouldn't be happy in a room on his own. He's never been used to that sort of thing.'

Momma said, 'I will do that. The hotel is full, praise God, but it can be arranged.'

She led the boy away and after a little while came back.

'He's asleep already,' she said. 'He looks like an angel, now that he is clean.'

Blair stayed on in the kitchen a little longer, answering more questions from the family. Then Papa took him upstairs. Papa found him a razor and toilet things, a nightshirt and a light dressing-gown, then said good night and left him.

Blair stood for a moment looking round the room he had been given. There were two beds in it, and in one of them Tomaso lay fast asleep between the sheets, looking very small, and, if not exactly angelic, at least unnaturally tidy and clean.

It reminded him of his own filthy state. He found the bathroom and indulged in the luxury of his first civilised wash for days. He shaved too, for the sheer joy of it. He went back to his room and, a few minutes later, somewhat grotesquely attired in the nightshirt—it was one of Papa's and made up in girth for what it lack in length—got thankfully into the other bed.

The bed was soft and fresh-smelling. It was a delight to lie there. Still dog-tired though he was, however, he did not sleep for a long while. He lay relaxed but wakeful, watching the thin white curtain at the window blowing gently, hearing the soft, distant murmur of the sea.

He did not want to sleep. There was something about that moment that he was reluctant to let go. He felt wonderfully heartened and restored, not only in body but in spirit too, not only by the good food and the comfort of the bed, but also by the honesty and the goodness he had met with that day. He had almost forgotten that such people still existed. People like Meya, with her love and concern for him; and like this simple, kindly, warm-hearted family who had so generously taken him in.

His brain was clear. He thought back calmly, without remorse or self-reproach, over the headlong, catastrophic chain of events of the last few days. For the first time he was able to view the whole miserable business with lucidity and detachment.

He came slowly to a decision. There was only one thing he could do. He could not go on running away. If he was going to regain any self-respect at all ... if he was to be worthy of Meya's love ... if he was to justify his presence in this house to-night ... he had got to stop and face the music, take what was coming to him, at any rate as far as decent society was concerned.

There was only one thing he could do and to-morrow he would do it.

In the morning he would go to the police.

9

In the morning his resolution was still strong. He got up determined to get back into Naples as soon as possible and go to police headquarters.

When he came downstairs, he found Tomaso in the hall, looking lost and obviously waiting nervously for him to appear. The sight of the boy reminded Blair that he still had a problem there. When he had brought Tomaso to Porto Sannazzaro the night before, he had done so on the spur of the moment, simply because he could not possibly have left the child behind in his dreadful slum. He had not thought beyond that.

It turned out, however, to be no problem at all. Momma solved it easily, for the time being at least. Blair and Tomaso breakfasted with the Pieroni family in the kitchen and, when Blair announced that he had to return to the city, Momma seemed to know instinctively what was troubling him.

'You wish to go alone?' she asked.

Blair hesitated. 'It would be easier,' he said. 'At any rate for what I have to do next.'

'You are thinking of the bambino?'

Blair hesitated again. 'Yes.'

'Do not worry. He can stay here.'

'I may be gone quite a while. I can't be sure when I'll get back.' It occurred to him, suddenly and uncomfortably, that he might never get back at all.

Momma lifted a plump hand that smoothed away all difficulties. 'No matter,' she said. 'He will be safe—and he can be useful. There are many things in a hotel that a boy can do.'

Blair silently blessed this big, good-hearted woman. He said, 'It's wonderfully kind of you.' He looked at the boy. 'Is that all right with you, Tommy? You'll stay here with Signor and Signora Pieroni until I come back?'

The boy stared at him and then at Momma. He looked nervous and apprehensive again. Then Momma leaned across the table and pinched his cheek, and quite suddenly he looked up at her and smiled. It was plain that the boy had taken a great liking to her. Perhaps, it

246

struck Blair, it was because he saw in her the mother he had never known, or could not remember.

Papa said, 'He will be doing us a good turn if he stays. *Santa Maria,* but we will make him work! He can clean the shoes, help here in the kitchen. Eh, Tomaso?'

Tomaso looked from one to the other of them. It was pathetic to see how hard it was for him to realise that at last someone wanted him. But then he grinned, with shy pleasure.

'*Si,*' he said.

So it was fixed. Blair tried to leave some money for the boy's keep. The Pieronis were insulted and outraged. They would not hear of it.

'But he needs some decent clothes,' Blair protested.

'So?' Papa said fiercely. 'Do you think we are so poor, that our business is so unsuccessful, that we cannot buy him the few things he needs?'

Blair gave in. But he needed something decent to wear himself. He said so to Papa, who took him to an outfitters in the town where he was able to buy a fairly respectable two-piece suit of a thin, light-grey material. He added to this a shirt, a tie, and a pair of shoes. He went back to the Albergo Italia and changed.

'You look fine now—*bello, bello.*' Momma nodded her head approvingly when she saw him. 'Very smart.'

Blair didn't feel fine, nor in the least smart. He was in a tense, short-tempered mood. His brief respite was over. Now he'd got to get on with what he'd made up his mind to do, and he was beginning to get keyed up at the prospect of what lay ahead of him. He didn't kid himself that it was going to be at all pleasant.

Tomaso was hanging around, still wistful, still a little lost. He said, 'You will be gone long, signor?'

'No—not long.' Blair squeezed the boy's shoulder. 'I'll be back as soon as I can.'

Papa was looking at his watch. 'If you wish to go, the Naples bus leaves almost at once.'

'I'd better get cracking then.' The whole family seemed to have gathered to see him off, and he turned and waved a hand as he started out into the street. '*A la rivederci.* I'll be back soon.'

'Good luck, signor,' Papa called after him.

And he was going to need it, Blair told

248

himself as he hurried down the steep street to the bus stop.

The bus came almost at once and he boarded it. It rattled away towards Naples.

Blair spent the first part of the short journey trying to work out what sort of tactics he was going to employ with the police, but after a while he gave up the attempt. It was past the time for tactics. All he could do was to tell them his side of the affair as directly and straightforwardly as he could. It was too late in the day for anything else.

Maybe he could 'help them with their inquiries'? He smiled ruefully as he recalled that old euphemism of the police back in Britain. He had no illusions about the spot he would be putting himself in; but somehow, now that he had steeled himself to it, he felt that he could take whatever was coming to him. It would even be a relief to pass the burden of it all to somebody else.

He left the bus at its terminating point in Naples and made his way on foot to police headquarters. The Naples *questura* was a gaunt, shabby building. He walked in through the big doors, wondering just when and how he would come out again.

Just inside the main doors there was an inquiries desk with a thick-set, tough-looking *sergente* sitting behind it. He went over and said he wanted to see somebody in connection with the British cruise ship affair. The *sergente* seemed bored until Blair gave his name, but then he looked up sharply. He picked up a phone on the desk and spoke into it. When he replaced it, he pressed a bell. A *carabiniere* came out from an inner door. The *sergente* said, 'Take this man up to Lieutenant Forla.'

Blair followed the *carabiniere* along a corridor, up a flight of stone stairs, then along another long, shabby corridor on the floor above. The *carabiniere* stopped before a door, knocked, then opened the door and stood aside, jerking his head for Blair to enter.

A tall, thin, almost cadaverous man with a sallow complexion, his smooth dark hair flecked with grey, sat behind a big desk under the window. He had a file of papers open in front of him. He closed it and looked past Blair at the *carabiniere,* who was waiting in the doorway. 'You needn't stay,' he said. The door closed, and the man behind the desk waved a hand at

Blair. 'Forla, investigation,' he said. 'Sit down.'

Blair sat down on the hard chair in front of the desk. He looked at Forla. The Italian detective was wearing a light-brown lounge suit with a green and brown polka dot tie. He was a lean, narrow-shouldered man with a thin-lipped, ascetically handsome face. His eyes were dark and piercing.

There was a silence. Blair guessed that it was mean to disconcert him, and it did. This Lieutenant Forla was pretty obviously a formidable character.

Blair said, at last, 'I rather imagine you have been looking for me.'

Forla had been studying his fingernails, which were immaculately clean and well manicured. He flicked a glance at Blair. He said coldly, almost contemptuously, 'That's a brilliant deduction.'

'Well, I'm here now.'

'Why?'

Blair drew a deep breath. 'Because I've been thinking things over. I've realised I'm in a mess.'

Forla took a pack of cigarettes from his pocket and lit one. He didn't hurry over it, and he didn't offer one to Blair. He sat back in his chair, his fingertips just

251

touching the edge of the desk. Blair noticed how long and thin they were, and that they were heavily stained with nicotine.

'So?' he said.

'So I decided my best bet was to go to the police and tell them about it.'

Forla took the cigarette out of his mouth and blew a thin jet of smoke across the desk. He said, 'I shall be most interested to hear what you have to say, Signor Blair. Particularly if it is the truth.'

There was another silence, and once more Blair felt at a disadvantage. He said, uncertainly, 'It's a long story.'

The Italian said dryly, 'I can believe that. So maybe you'd better start talking, signor. I'm a busy man.'

Blair's hand moved towards his own pocket, 'May I smoke?'

'No.' The fingers of Forla's right hand tapped impatiently on the desk top. 'Just start talking.' He reached out and flicked a switch. 'I hope you have this long story of yours well prepared, my friend, or that you have a good memory. This is going down on tape, and you'd better remember what you're saying, because we may want to hear it from you all over again, just to check.'

Blair shrugged. 'You don't need a good memory if you're telling the truth.' He paused a moment. 'I'd better take it right from the beginning.'

'That seems to me to be a good idea.'

Blair hesitated just a moment longer, to collect himself. Then he started in. He kept nothing back. He began by describing the set-up in the local contraband racket as it had appeared to him at the outset of all this trouble; how, during the last six months or so, it had come increasingly under the dominance of the organised and ruthless gang which he now knew to be directed by the man called Leonardo Volpi; how this monopoly had constituted an ever-growing threat to the one-boat operators, including himself.

He told Forla frankly about his own smuggling operations, and then about that last trip to La Goulette, which had been the beginning of his own brush with Volpi. He hated like hell having to reveal Meya's part in the affair, and for a moment he toyed with the idea of covering up for her. But he put the temptation behind him. He knew that, if he was going to do any good at all, he'd got to tell the whole truth, and Meya was essential to the picture. He tried to console himself with the thought that she wasn't really seriously implicated.

He couldn't see it or hear it, but he knew that somewhere a tape was whirring, perhaps in another room. Forla, his thin, dark face impassive, was also making a note or two, chiefly, it seemed, of names.

Blair paused. Forla looked at him. He said, 'You may smoke now.'

Gratefully Blair lit a cigarette. He needed it. He drew on it and relaxed a little.

He said, 'I put Miss Nordstrom off on Capri that afternoon, and was back in harbour here an hour or so later. In the evening I went along to a bar I used to go to—a little waterfront dump called the Bar Marina, which was one of Sam Everett's drinking holes too. They told me there that Sam had been found dead—and that was when I really saw the red light at last. I decided I'd better get out, and fast, before the same thing happened to me.'

Forla said, 'That was very wise of you. So?'

Blair told Forla of the trip he had made to Capri.

'Why did you do that?'

Blair shrugged. 'I wanted to get away from Naples, to give myself a chance to think about what I was going to do.' He paused, wondering whether to leave it at that. But then he thought: *The whole truth.* He added, 'I also wanted to see Miss Nordstrom again.'

'Why?'

'I was—attracted by her.'

Forla smiled sardonically. 'You certainly stick your neck out, don't you, my friend?' He waved a hand, dismissing the matter as of no importance. 'So. And then?'

Blair went on to tell him the rest. About Volpi's nicely arranged arrival at the villa and his imprisonment on the yacht; the diving for the canisters—he had to go back a bit there, to tell about the 'little pot' Sam had had with him in the Bar Marina; then his imprisonment again on the salvage boat, with Vic this time; their escape and the long swim; their rescue by the cruise ship; the second escape from the ship; the Capodimonte grotto; Tomaso ....

It was done at last, and Blair sat heavily back in his chair. He felt exhausted. The ash-tray Forla had pushed across the desk towards him was littered with butts, though he couldn't remember lighting or smoking any cigarette except the first.

'There's only one thing that worries me,'

he added, 'and that's whether I killed anybody on that boat. I realise what it could mean for me if I did.'

Forla didn't at first appear to hear. Then he said, 'We've heard nothing about the boat as yet. Maybe we shall, when they know you've come to us.'

The matter scarcely seemed to interest him. He had something else on his mind. There was a tension, a certain excitement in his manner—though he was plainly not an easily excited man—which dated from the moment Blair had mentioned drugs.

Suddenly the lieutenant rose. He walked quickly round the desk and then came to a stop, looking down at Blair. He said, 'The wreck with the canisters—you could locate it again?'

Blair met his gaze. 'That's a tall order. They won't have been fools enough to leave that marker buoy there.'

'You don't think they can have recovered the stuff already?'

Blair shook his head. 'They haven't had time. They'd have had to get hold of another skin diver—a good one—or else suit divers, with all the equipment that means. Not only that. Once they knew I was still alive, they wouldn't dare

256

do anything. They wouldn't know that I hadn't given the game away.'

Forla beat a fist into the palm of his other hand. 'I hope you are right, signor.' He took a pace away from Blair, then swung back upon him. 'Why in the name of God didn't you come here before?' He took a deep, harsh breath. 'I promise you, my friend—if we are too late to stop this, you will wish you had never been born.'

Blair said, 'I tell you they can't have got the stuff up.'

Again Forla didn't seem to hear. He said, '*Santa Maria*—don't you realise that we've got to be sure of that?' Savagely he lit a cigarette, 'And the only way to be sure, to make certain that the stuff never gets into wrong hands, is to recover it ourselves.'

Blair said, 'I'm willing to help. I'll do anything I can.'

Forla gave a jerky nod of approval. He flicked a switch on the intercom on his desk and spoke rapidly into it. Within a few minutes he had laid on a boat, and two police cars were waiting outside the *questura* to take a salvage party down to it.

A police lieutenant called Bonelli came

into Forla's room. Bonelli was taking charge of the operation. Forla briefed him on the situation. When he had finished, he gave a curt nod of dismissal.

Lieutenant Bonelli got up from his chair. Blair got up too. He followed Bonelli towards the door, but before he reached it he stopped and turned.

'Just one thing,' he said.

Forla said impatiently, 'What is it?'

'Miss Nordstrom. I want you to understand she hasn't really been involved in any of this.'

'No?' Forla said. He smiled unpleasantly. 'She's an accomplice of Volpi's, isn't she? That's what you've told me, even if you didn't put it quite so plainly.'

Blair said helplessly, 'She—'

'Forget it,' Forla said. 'We'll worry about her later. I'm after something a lot bigger than that right now.'

Blair had to be content with that. He went out of the room. Bonelli was waiting for him outside.

The two big black police cars sped powerfully down to the docks. Blair and Lieutenant Bonelli rode together in the leading car. They rolled in through the dock gates and stopped outside the waterfront offices of the Bay Salvage Company. A salvage tug lay alongside the dock wall in front of the offices.

The tug was already manned and ready to go. Bonelli led the way aboard her. Blair and the rest of the police party followed. There were seven other men in uniform, *a sergente* and six *carabinieri*.

A big, burly man with grizzled hair was waiting at the inboard end of the tug's gangplank. Lieutenant Bonelli said, 'Captain Renato?'

Renato grunted. '*Si.*' He jerked his head at Blair. 'This is the diver?'

'*Si.*'

Renato turned to Blair. 'You'd better look at the gear.'

The diving equipment was lying on deck close by. A glance at it was enough for Blair to see that it was standard stuff. He nodded. 'That's okay.'

Captain Renato grunted again, turned on his heel and stamped away up to his bridge. The tug cast off almost at once and steamed for the harbour entrance.

Blair stood at the rail. He was impressed with the speed and efficiency with which the operation had been got under way. And there was, he realised, one man responsible for that. Forla. He was, he had to admit, very impressed with Forla.

The tug steamed out into the bay. Naples slowly fell astern. Capri lay off the port beam, Ischia ahead.

Bonelli came down from the bridge and joined Blair at the rail. 'They tell me we'll be some time yet before we get there,' he said. 'You want to eat before you dive? There's food in the saloon.'

'Thanks.' Blair went below. The police were eating there. He wasn't interested in food, but he was glad of a cup of coffee. He drank it and smoked a cigarette, then sat back and relaxed. He knew he'd got another tough time ahead of him.

Half an hour later one of the tug's hands came down to tell him that Captain Renato wanted him on the bridge.

He went up. There were three men on the bridge—a seaman, at the wheel, with Renato standing beside him; and Bonelli. The tug was in touch with police headquarters by radio telephone, and Bonelli was talking to someone. Blair guessed it was Forla.

Bonelli finished speaking and hung up the receiver. Blair said to Renato, 'You wanted me?'

Renato gave a brusque nod at where Ischia was growing slowly in detail ahead. 'Can you give me a course that will take us roughly to the right spot?'

Blair took a long look at the profile of the island. 'I don't think you're far out now.' He moved up behind the helmsman and glanced at the compass. 'You might alter five degrees to port.'

Renato gave the order. The man on the wheel twirled the spokes, and the tug altered course slightly.

'We have underwater detection gear,' Renato said.

'That should help.'

Renato shrugged. 'It will detect wrecks. But there are many wrecks in the bay.'

As the tug steamed on, they worked out a plan of operation. Blair was to estimate as nearly as possible the spot at which the wreck of the fishing boat lay. The tug would drop a marker buoy there, and would work out from that centre. Both Blair and Renato knew that it was likely to be a long job. It was too much to expect that the first estimated position would be anything like accurate.

The wreck lay two or three miles off the island. At least that had been Blair's earlier estimate, and he didn't think it was far wrong. When the tug came to within something approaching that distance, he spoke to the captain. Renato rang down for half ahead and ordered the detection gear to be switched on.

There was a feeling of expectancy, almost of excitement, in the air now.

Blair was looking anxiously at the sky. It was another hot, still day, but there were signs that the settled weather was going to break, at least temporarily. There was a clammy oppressiveness in the air, and a thickening over the horizon to the southward.

Renato caught Blair's eye. He said, *Scirocco?*'

Blair nodded. 'Looks like it.'

'It won't make things any easier.'

'It may not come to anything much.'

Blair was watching the island ahead narrowly as he spoke, trying to recall just what sort of outline it had presented that day when he had dived for the canisters. He frowned, and then shook his head. They weren't right yet. They needed to get a bit more to the westward.

He said as much to Renato. Renato moved away from the helmsman's side.

'You'd better take over,' he said.

Blair ordered a slight alteration to port. As far as he could recall, the twin sharp peaks of Monte di San Nicola, which formed the precipitous summit of the island, had been almost in line, appearing as one.

He ordered another fractional alteration and checked the depth on the echo-sounder. The wreck lay at about a hundred feet ....

He took Renato's place at the helmsman's side, carefully conning the boat. He edged her towards the land until she had about the right depth beneath her keel. Then he turned her parallel with the island's shoreline, staring at Isola d'Ischia and watching the two peaks of the mountain slowly draw together.

Now that the real search was beginning, the sea suddenly seemed a very big place, and the fishing boat a very small thing to find. In the end it was more a matter of instinct than anything else.

'Here,' Blair said suddenly.

'Stop engines,' Renato ordered. 'Full astern ....'

The tug lost way rapidly as her screws threshed in reverse.

'Stop both.'

The boat lay motionless. Two of her hands were busy with the marker buoy. A minute or so later it went over the side.

The detection gear had already picked up several wrecks. As Renato had said, there were many of them in the Bay of Naples, most of them grim reminders of World War Two and the Allies' great seaborne invasion of southern Italy. But all of those that had come up on the fluorescent screen so far had been a great deal too large to be what the salvage boat was looking for.

At an order from Renato, the tug's engines woke to life again. She began to steam in a circle round the marker buoy. Blair got ready to dive ....

He dived five times that day, each time after the detection gear had picked up something on the sea bed that seemed worth investigating. Each time he found a wreck, but not the right one.

By the time he surfaced from the fifth dive, he was exhausted. The day was far advanced too. The light was going, earlier than usual, because of the weather. The whole sky was overcast, and the sea was grey, with the beginnings of an uneasy swell.

Renato looked at Blair. 'Leave it until to-morrow?'

Blair nodded. 'We'll have to.'

'We will carry on again at dawn.'

Blair glanced at the sky. 'If the weather lets us.'

Renato shrugged, and then, suddenly and surprisingly, his face cracked into a friendly grin.

'To hell with the weather,' he said. 'Come down to my cabin. You could do with something warm in your stomach, my friend ...'

The tug spent the night at anchor at the spot where Blair had made his last dive. Blair slept heavily and awoke feeling still weary but at the same time anxious to get on with the job. But the deterioration in the weather was now very marked. The barometer was still falling. The damp wind was much stronger, and the sea was grey and lumpy. The tug was beginning to roll quite heavily.

Conditions for diving were difficult but not impossible. Blair and Renato conferred, and agreed to carry on for as long as they could. It was Blair that really made the

265

decision. He hated the thought of giving up the search, even temporarily. He badly wanted to get the whole unpleasant business over and done with.

'I have a feeling we need to try still a bit farther west,' he said.

The marker buoy was hauled up and dropped again. A new concentric search was begun. Both Blair and Renato knew that it was going to be a much tougher business than the search of the day before. The usually sunny, blue and placid waters of the gulf were now a waste of heaving grey. There was no sign of any of the pleasure craft normally to be seen in the area. As Blair got ready for his first dive, the only vessel in sight was a fair-sized launch which passed close to the tug, heading for Ischia, and then dropped anchor off the island, as though uncertain whether to stay at sea or not.

To-day Blair put on a sweater and slacks over his swimming trunks while he waited to dive, for the weather was much colder now. The tug steamed in a gradually increasing spiral round the new mark, wallowing and pitching so heavily that it was a tricky business operating the detection apparatus.

Blair dived twice, to investigate doubtful contacts, and found nothing. Getting back on board the tug was a dangerous and exhausting business, even with the ladder they put over the side for him.

Renato was looking worried. He said, when Blair had got back on board after the second dive, 'We had better give it up.'

Blair shook his head. 'I can manage one or two more.'

It was on his next dive that he found the wreck.

He dived to investigate another object picked up by the detection apparatus, but by then the day was so overcast and visibility so bad on the sea bed that he went down with very little hope of seeing anything at all. Even the powerful underwater torch which he took with him was little use, but it did serve to show him the vague outline of a sunken boat. He swam round it. From the size of the wreck, the angle at which it lay, and the cargo that had spilled out of it, he knew that his search was at an end ....

He squatted on the sand for a moment, staring at the spectral hulk and the sinister long pods of the canisters, his thoughts inevitably going back to the time when he had first found the canisters and discovered what was in them. He felt a strong resurgence of the fear and tension he had felt then, mixed with almost overwhelming revulsion for the whole evil, murderous business.

But then, quickly overriding both, came a surge of triumph at his success.

He surfaced as fast as he could, shoved up his mask and shouted the news. There came an answering shout from Renato on the bridge of the tug. The tug's engines began to turn again and Blair trod water, trying to keep, as nearly as he could judge, immediately over the wreck, while Renato slowly edged his vessel up to him. It was a perilous manoeuvre, for the tug's bows were surging and crashing in the swell. But Renato was a good salvage man, which meant that he was something more than just a good seaman.

Renato had a man up in the bows of the tug, signalling yard-by-yard directions. Renato brought the tug up until she was abreast of Blair and only a yard or two from him. The tug's engines went briefly astern and she lay rolling on the swell. A moment later a small marker buoy with a sinker and a light line attached were thrown over the side.

Renato shouted to Blair again, asking him if he wanted to come aboard to rest. But Blair was too tense and too excited to break off the operation, now that the end seemed so near. He dived again as soon as the buoy was riding steadily to its line, following the thin thread of it down into the gloom.

The sinker was lying on the sea bed only a short distance from the wreck. He picked it up and dragged it with him over to the wreck, repositioning it near the canisters. He surfaced then, and was hauled aboard the tug.

Captain Renato and Lieutenant Bonelli were waiting for him at the rail. Their faces and voices betrayed the same tension that Blair was feeling himself.

'You have found it—you are sure?' Renato said.

'Sure,' Blair said. 'The stuff we want's all there, right down at the bottom of the buoy rope.'

Bonelli said, 'I will make a report to headquarters.'

He went up to the bridge to talk to Forla on the radio-telephone. Renato followed him to position the tug ready for the actual salvage operation. During the previous searches he had held the tug in position on her engines, but now that they had found what they were looking for at last, it was necessary to anchor her. He edged her up again and dropped the hook so that she rode to her cable, as precisely as he could judge, over the exact spot where the canisters lay, allowing for the drift of the marker buoy on the wind and what small tidal set there was.

When the tug was at last in position, the buoy was riding just off her starboard quarter. A weighted net was swung out over the starboard side on a davit. It remained only to lower the net, and for Blair to go down again and load the canisters into it.

He had to dive twice more before all the canisters were safely in the net. When he surfaced for the last time, he had had more than enough. The crew of the tug helped him back aboard, and on deck he stripped off the lung. He was panting for breath and shivering, with reaction rather than cold.

The tug's crew were already hoisting the net. The police, who had been increasingly bored spectators of the long-drawn-out operations up till now, caught the sudden feeling of excitement in the air. Those who had been below had come up when the wreck was located. No one except Renato and Lieutenant Bonelli, and Blair himself, knew what the search had been for, but now there was a small crowd of men gathered round the davit, eager and intrigued to see what was coming up.

Blair left them to it. His part was done, and he had no further interest in the operation. He went below to get into his clothes.

He had left his things on a spare bunk in the cramped crew's quarters up in the bows of the tug. He made his way down there, glad to get out of the weather. He stripped off, rubbed himself down, got into shirt and trousers, and sat down on the edge of the bunk to smoke a much-needed cigarette.

The boat was silent save for the surge of the sea against her plates, the occasional crunch of her bows, and the muted blustering of the wind overhead. He heard no sound of the operation aft—it was too far away. He knew, though, that it would take some time to complete. With the big sea now running and the way the tug was rolling, the recovery of the net would have to be a slow and careful business.

Suddenly exhaustion came flooding over him in a wave, overwhelming, irresistible. He lay back on the bunk, and closed his eyes ....

He was jerked out of a half-doze by a sudden shouting. A moment later a heavy bump shook the tug from stem to stern. He sat up, his immediate thought being that the tug was in collision with some other vessel.

He was off the bunk and making for the fo'c'sle doorway when the shots came; two of them. Followed by a high-pitched, choking scream.

10

The shots brought Blair to a sudden dead stop at the foot of the ladder. He stood there tensely poised, listening. For a few moments he heard nothing except the familiar sounds of the wind and sea. Then a voice came from somewhere aft, distant but incisive, giving orders. Then silence again. No other sound. No more firing.

He went cautiously up the ladder. Whatever the trouble was, it was taking place well aft. He raised his head cautiously above the level of the hatch coaming and the first thing he saw was a big motor launch surging against the tug's port side.

At first sight it looked like a collision. But the shots still rang in his ears. If it had been a collision it had been a deliberate one. A boarding.

The launch was pretty obviously the vessel which had been lying at anchor some distance off. Probably everyone else, like Blair himself, had been aware that it

273

was there. But no one had taken much notice of it, in the excitement of recovering the canisters.

Blair frowned, trying to plan what to do. He knew that, before he could make any move at all, he'd got to get a better idea of what was going on.

The tug's bridge and deck-house hid his view aft. Similarly, they hid him from anyone on the tug's stern. He climbed quickly out of the hatch and made for the port rail at a crouching run. He could have been seen from the launch, but he was gambling that anyone left aboard her would be too interested in the snatch—for that was obviously what it was—to be looking forward.

On the tug's port side, under her bridge, there was a life raft on a quick-release chute. The raft faced outwards. He ducked through the rail and climbed into it. He could not be seen from the launch now, for he was close—dangerously close—under the surging flare of her bows. He was completely hidden from the tug's deck too—but he'd got there only just in time, for he had scarcely gained the cover of the raft when a man with a machine pistol came running forward along the port side of the tug's deck. Blair thought he looked like one of the Volpi mob, but he couldn't be sure. The man passed within a couple of feet of him, heading for the fo'c'sle hatch. Blair waited for him to disappear down it, but instead he slammed the heavy steel hatch cover shut, hammered the clips home with the stock of his gun, and then mounted guard over it.

Blair pressed himself closer into the protection of the life raft. Frozen there, he again tried to assess the situation. He didn't doubt that it was the Volpi gang that had made the raid. And, quite obviously, they were already in possession of the tug. Speed and surprise, and the sheer daring of the attack, had given them complete command.

Or almost complete. It looked as though he were the one free agent they didn't know about. No doubt they thought he was still below in the fo'c'sle ....

What was going on aft now? He'd got to know.

He inched his way across to the after gunwale of the raft, and cautiously raised his head until he could see over it. From that position he had a diagonal view of the broad stern of the tug. He could see two

275

men standing there, one of them with a pistol in his hand.

The man with the gun was Volpi himself.

The net with the canisters in it lay on the stern deck. The boarding must have been timed to a split second, the launch coming alongside at the moment the tug had hoisted the net aboard.

The man with Volpi was now attaching a new rope to the net, a rope which led up to a davit on the launch's stern deck. Volpi was watching the operation. He waved the gun impatiently, trying to hurry things up.

There were two bodies sprawled on the tug's deck. Blair could not identify them. There was no sign of the rest of the police and the tug's crew, and he guessed that they had been herded below. The guess became a certainty when he saw half a dozen armed men come up on deck from the companionway aft. Among them he recognised Cellini, and two others of the Volpi mob.

He could only watch, helplessly.

Suddenly the man busy over the net stood up and moved away from it. Volpi's head jerked up as he called to the launch.

The rope attached to the net tightened. The net drew up around the canisters until they slithered across the tug's heaving deck towards the launch's side. It lifted and drew up the launch's side until it swung inboard and disappeared from Blair's sight ....

The sudden opening of the launch's throttles roused him from a state of semi-stupor. The raid had come so unexpectedly, and he had been so powerless to do anything about it, that he was still crouching and watching from the life raft, bereft of the power to take any kind of initiative. He saw the man who had been standing guard over the fo'c'sle hatch run back along the port side and leap aboard the launch. Volpi and the others aft were already back aboard. And at the last moment another man came dashing up from below decks on the tug and jumped across to the other vessel.

The launch was on her way. Blair heard the sudden upthrust of water under her stern as her screws turned. She began to slide slowly past him.

Her bows surged and dropped close above him as she got under way. They were so close that a sea on her starboard bow, swinging her a little, would have

277

smashed her high flare into the life raft where Blair was hidden, crushing him to a pulp. That could in fact have happened at any time while he had been hiding there, but he hadn't thought about it. He didn't think about it now. All that registered with him was that the launch was making a clean getaway with the canisters on board.

She reared and rolled heavily as she began to forge ahead. Then, on a roll to port, her midships section slammed against the tug's side. The point of impact was some distance aft of the life raft, but the shock of it almost tore Blair from his hold. He turned his head and stared up at her, still unafraid, still unconscious of his own danger, possessed only by a bitter feeling of frustration that was now flaming into a furious anger.

Volpi was at the centre of his thoughts. It was Volpi who was responsible for all that he had been through in the last few terrible days; Volpi who had enmeshed him deeper in the way of life he had been determined to get away from; Volpi who had tried to kill him. And it was Volpi who now, in spite of all the effort that had been made to prevent him, was getting away with his cargo of human misery and servitude after all.

The swine wasn't going to get away with it! Not yet, anyway. Blair was suddenly determined that, if the deadly canisters were being snatched away at the very moment when they'd seemed safe, he was going to go with them.

He thought briefly of the men shut up below aboard the tug. They were in a nasty spot—the the canisters were even more important ....

He waited until the launch rolled towards the tug again. Then he jumped for her. He sprawled through her guard rail on to her deck.

He was abreast of her bridge and below the line of sight from the bridge windows. He got up quickly, looking for some place of concealment. The long deck-house gave him cover from the deck aft, but it only needed someone to come along the port side, or to look out from one of her saloon windows, and it would be all over.

Almost opposite him there was a small door in the deck-house. It was forward of the saloon, almost under the bridge, and it looked as though it might lead into a locker or store of some kind. He moved across to it quickly, hoping to God that it did, and that it wasn't fastened.

He turned the handle and the door opened. He was in luck. The door gave access to a minute compartment that was obviously used to stow cleaning gear. It contained buckets and brooms and various other odds and ends. He slid inside and pulled the door shut after him. For the moment he was safe.

Almost at once the launch's engines opened up to full power. That meant she was clear of the tug. Blair could feel the deck plates vibrating under his feet, and the dizzy lift and swoop and shuddering crash of her forefoot as she plunged at speed into the now big, steep seas. Every time her bows came down, there was a drenching of water a few moments later against the outside of the locker door, which meant that she was taking it green over the bows. And he took comfort from that. No one would be likely to come forward along the open deck in that weather.

He was in complete darkness, which exaggerated the launch's motion and destroyed his sense of balance, so that he could hardly keep his feet. He clung to the door frame, feeling round it until he found a light switch. He clicked it on, and at once things seemed to steady down. He looked round the locker. What he wanted now was something that would serve as a weapon.

He soon saw that there was nothing substantial or handy enough to be effective. He was better off with his fists. He deliberated whether or not to leave the light on, and decided that he had better not. It would be getting dark outside, and any chink of light showing through the door would be more and more noticeable as time passed. There would be little risk of anyone seeing it, since, as he had already decided, no one was likely to be out on deck at any rate until the launch got into more sheltered water, but it was still a risk not worth taking. He turned the switch off again and took up a position with his back braced against the inner bulkhead of the locker. But again the motion of the launch seemed so exaggeratedly violent and unpredictable in the dark, and it was so difficult for him to keep his balance, that after a minute or two he slid down until he was squatting on his haunches.

There was nothing to do but wait. And

think. He didn't have to think very hard to realise that he had again got himself into a very tough spot. It wasn't just a case of staying hidden and making a getaway when he could. He knew that, if there was to be any point at all in his going along with the canisters, he must at some stage or other intervene in Volpi's plans for their disposal; and when he did that, he wasn't going to have much chance of survival. But he was still determined to do what he could to stop Volpi getting away with his loot. It was something he had got to do, at any price.

Meanwhile, where was the launch heading? How long would she stay at sea? He glanced at the luminous dial of his watch and set himself to keep in his head a running dead reckoning of her position from his estimate of her speed and alterations of course, which were the only two things he had to go on.

It proved easier than he anticipated. The launch did not keep on her initial course for long. For another five minutes or so she continued to lift and crash down again, rolling more or less evenly, and a lot of water was still coming aboard. That meant she was still heading directly into the weather. Then she heeled to port and, when she levelled out again, the crashing had stopped. Her rolling became more pronounced, but now she was going over a lot farther to port than to starboard. The sounds of the wind and sea were fainter, and she was no longer taking water over her port side. That meant she had turned to port, bringing the weather on the starboard side, so that the locker where Blair was crouching was in the lee.

Then she turned to port again. Blair looked at his watch and saw that ten minutes had passed since her last alteration. And again there was a marked change in her behaviour. Her motion became a seemingly uncontrolled surging and slithering. Now, each time her bows dropped, her stern was thrown round by the humping of the seas up under it. And the noises of the wind and sea had died away still further to a point where they were almost inaudible. That told him that she was now running more or less dead before the weather. Which meant that she must be running back pretty well on the reciprocal of the course she had taken when she first headed away from the tug.

She ran on like that for half an hour. Then, gradually she steadied, until she was on an even keel in comparatively calm water. That could only mean one thing, that she was in the lee of land. And there was only one lee available in a southerly blow in that part of the gulf. Blair realised that she must be somewhere to the north of Isola d'Ischia.

Another forty minutes passed before there was any further change. Then her engines were cut, to half-speed, Blair guessed; then, ten minutes later, to slow ahead. She was either closing the coast, or another vessel, or making harbour.

Suddenly there were movements on deck. Someone tramped forrard past the locker door. The launch's engines stopped, went astern, then stopped again. There was a slight bump and a creaking, which sounded like timber. She was alongside something built of wood. A pier? She was too steady to be lying against another vessel.

She was lying starboard side to, for the men engaged in securing her were busy on the opposite side of her from Blair's hiding place. He heard them moving about and calling to each other for a minute or two, and then there was silence.

Complete silence. The launch might have been deserted for all the indications of life there were aboard her. Blair knew well enough that she wasn't, and sat where he was for a little longer. But now that the launch had obviously reached her destination, and the transfer of the canisters from her might begin at any moment—if it hadn't begun already—continued inaction was intolerable. He'd got to know where he was, if possible. And, if he could, get some idea of what the next stage of the game was likely to be.

He got very carefully to his feet in the pitchy darkness. He couldn't risk any sort of noise, now that the launch was so deathly still. One clattering bucket could spell the end of everything for him.

He moved a step forward until his outstretched hand touched the door. He groped for the door handle, turned it cautiously and eased the door open an inch.

There were lights on in the launch's saloon, but the windows were heavily curtained. There was no sound from inside. A narrow, pencil beam shining out from the second window along, about

285

ten feet from the locker door, showed that a soft, misty rain was falling. The last of the daylight was going, in a thick twilight fading quickly into night.

Blair pushed the door gently farther open and slipped out of the locker. The freshness of the air was welcome after the stuffiness of his cramped little hiding place. He flattened himself against the deck-house beside the door and looked about him.

Because of the rain and the gathering darkness, he couldn't hope to see much. But his eyesight was preternaturally sharp after his long stay in the pitch-black locker, and he could make out some details of his surroundings. The launch was lying alongside the shank of an L- or T-shaped pier. She was bows on to the land, which showed vaugely as a denser blackness against the sky, low-lying beyond the foot of the pier, but rising to a moderate height on either hand. In the depression between the two stretches of higher ground, a sparse scattering of shore lights winked through the gloom.

After two years in the Gulf, Blair knew pretty well every harbour along its shores. And there was only one place he could think of that had a wooden pier of this particular shape, only one inlet where the general configuration of the land agreed with the silhouette he could now discern. He was certain, or almost certain, that the launch had run into Porto di Miseno, on the northern side of Capo di Miseno, the promontory which reaching out towards Isola di Procida and Isola d'Ischia beyond, marked the north-easterly boundary of the great Golfo di Napoli.

Such a destination added up too with his earlier guesses at the launch's course, and with the time she had taken to make harbour. He recalled that she had run for a long while in comparatively sheltered water, which must be because she had been moving in the lee first of Ischia, then Procida, and then of the Miseno promontory itself ....

The launch was still quiet. He knew that it would be easy for him to slip ashore, and for a moment he was tempted to do so. The time he had spent in forced inactivity in the cramped and oppressive little locker, and the lonely desolation of the scene around him now, combined to drain away his spirits and destroy his confidence that he could do anything effective about the canisters. But he could not give up now, and he realised that that was what he would be doing if he left the boat before anything further developed. If he wanted to find out what was going to happen next, he had got to stick around. There was no place of concealment on the bare length of the pier, and if he went ashore he would lose all contact with the launch.

He thought of making for the little community ashore and alerting the authorities. But Porto di Miseno was very small, little more than a fishing village, and there would be no one of any calibre to alert. By the time he had routed out the local *sergente*—if the place ran to one—and got him to understand what was going on, it might easily be too late. And in any case, even if he got through to the Porto di Miseno police and they decided to take some action, what could they do? The total police strength in a place like that wouldn't amount to more than a *sergente* and a *carabiniere*, at the most—and what could they do against the mob on the launch? Nothing, or worse than nothing, and the result would be two dead policemen. Blair had no doubts about that. He had no illusions left about the ruthlessness of the Volpi outfit.

He debated the possibility of getting to a phone and raising the alarm in Naples, getting on to Forla himself, if he could. But he dismissed that idea too after only a very little thought. It was thirty or forty miles from Naples to Porto di Miseno, along a narrow, tortuous road, and the night was a bad one for speed. By the time Forla's boys arrived in Porto di Miseno, it could easily be too late. The canisters would in all probability be on their way again. It didn't seem likely that the bunch on the launch would lose a lot of time landing the stuff ....

Blair clenched his fists, suddenly angry with himself for so much as entertaining these possibilities. He saw them now only as excuses for him to withdraw from the business himself. His resolution hardened again. He told himself that, having stayed with this thing so far, he was going to see it through, at least until he got some further idea of where the canisters were going, or had a better opportunity of doing something about them.

That meant that for the time being he'd got to go on playing a waiting game.

That was the hardest thing of all to endure, and he urgently and impatiently craved the release of some sort of action; but obviously there was nothing further he could do until the opposition made some further move themselves. He did not know when that would be; though, the way he had rationalised things, it couldn't be long.

The rain was falling more heavily now. He was getting wet and chilled. He moved back into the locker and pulled the door to until it was almost shut. He had a better chance of hearing what was happening if he left it ajar. He flattened himself against the door and stood looking out. The chink commanded a view of the port side deck aft as far as the end of the deck-house. If anyone came out on that side, they would do so from aft, and he would be warned in time to close the door completely.

Time ticked slowly by, and still nothing happened, and he began thinking about the set-up generally. He wondered whether Porto di Miseno was the place where the stuff was to have been landed under the original plan. It seemed feasible. The sunken tunny boat might very well have come out from here—it was an unobtrusive run from Porto di Miseno to the spot where she had foundered. And Porto di Miseno itself, small, sleepy and remote, would be as good a place as any to land the canisters.

They could have been put ashore with her catch of fish. In the normal way, the catch would most likely be transferred straight from the boat to a truck, which would take it to Naples ....

Blair tensed suddenly and listened. Something had broken his train of thought. A sound. Not a sound on the boat, but one far off in the distance. It was a faint humming, and it died away before he could identify it exactly. Then it came again, and this time grew gradually in strength and definition. It faded, and came back again, and now he knew that it was the engine of a car or some light vehicle travelling along the coast road. It grew steadily louder. Whatever it was, it was coming in to Porto di Miseno from the direction of Naples, and coming fast.

It came on, and on. Then the engine note dropped, and Blair guessed that it had reached the village. A minute or so later headlights flashed and swung in the darkness at the head of the inlet.

There was no reason to think that the oncoming vehicle had any connection with the launch, and yet somehow Blair was almost sure that it had. And he didn't have long to wait before he was quite certain of it. Suddenly there were voices and movements aft. It was clear that the others aboard the launch had heard the engine too. It seemed in fact as though they must have been waiting for it.

Blair waited, motionless, staring out through the almost shut door of the locker. Suddenly the deck-house of the launch stood out blackly, in sharp relief against the glare of headlights. The wooden planks of the pier drummed hollowly as the approaching vehicle rumbled out along it. It ran out past the launch. He could not see it now, but he heard it stop and reverse, and knew that it was turning at the head of the pier. He heard it return and stop opposite the launch. Its engine and lights were quickly switched off. A voice called cautiously. There was a curt reply from the launch. Then someone jumped aboard from the pier.

Blair heard more voices, questions and answers. The voices were still subdued so that he couldn't make out what was being said, but it sounded to him as though the tone of the questioner was recriminating, as though the man who had just arrived was being bawled out for being late. No doubt he should have been there when the launch came in. Then another voice cut the argument short. There was a brief silence, and, then heavy movements aft, and on the pier.

It was plain enough what was going on. The canisters were being transferred.

Blair drew a deep breath. This was it. The stuff was on the move again, which meant that it was time he made his next move too. He still had no idea what he could do, but it was obvious that he wouldn't achieve anything by staying where he was any longer. He'd got to do something, and do it pretty smartly, or it would be too late. The canisters would be on their way. Once the van left with them, he would be sunk.

The first thing was to reconnoitre the position a little more closely.

He slipped out of the locker once more, closing the door quietly and carefully behind him. Silently, in the softly blowing, rainy darkness, he moved forward along the port side of the launch, keeping close to her super-structure. He slid round the forward end of the deck-house, under the wheel-house windows, until he reached the starboard, forward corner of the wheel-house. Very cautiously, he peered round.

He could just make out the vehicle on the pier well enough to identify it as some sort of light van. Its rear doors were open and someone was moving there. There were movements too on the launch's stern deck abreast of the van. Something was being passed across from the launch to the pier.

It was obviously one of the canisters. And, watching, Blair knew a moment of panic. Transferring the canisters was an operation that would take almost no time at all. Perhaps it had been completed already—perhaps the canister he had just seen being passed across was the last of the batch. At any moment now the van doors might be shut, the engine would start up, and the van would move off—and he would be left stranded and helpless.

It looked as though he was helpless anyway. There were five or six men there aft, at the least, and he couldn't have hoped to deal with them all, in the darkness, even if he'd had a gun. And as it was, with no weapon at all, any sort of attempt at intervention on his part would be sheer suicide.

There was nothing he could do. Unless, somehow, he could contrive to go with the van ....

He still stood watching, motionless, pressed close against the corner of the wheel-house. He saw another object—another of the canisters—being passed across from the launch to the van. It must have been the last, for a moment or two later he heard the doors of the van being shut.

A feeling of frustration as bitter as gall surged up inside him as he realised that he had left his own move too late. He stood there helplessly, waiting for the van's engine to start.

It didn't. Instead there came a man's ill-tempered voice from the pier. Blair could hear the words this time. The man was obviously the van driver, and he was grumbling about having to drive back again without so much as a drop of wine to warm him on so wet and cheerless a night. There was an argument that seemed to go on interminably, then someone on the launch's deck called out a grudging invitation to the driver to come aboard.

Hope surged up in Blair again. This could be the break he needed. He found himself trembling with anticipation. He watched as a shadowy figure moved across from the van and stepped across on to the launch's deck. The man disappeared behind the after end of the deck-house.

There was no one in sight now, and no sound. Then Blair heard voices in the saloon again. He drew a deep breath. This was his chance, and it was a far better one than he had ever hoped to get. It was an incredible stoke of luck that the van should have been left unattended.

Quickly he slipped aft along the starboard side deck of the launch. As he ducked under the first of the saloon windows, he heard voices again, a short harsh laugh, and then the chink of bottles. No doubt the mob in there felt there was no real harm in taking a few minutes time out for a drink. It must have seemed to them that they were safe enough, on such a night and in such a desolate place.

Blair passed, crouching, under the second window on the starboard side. He reached the stern deck of the launch at a quick, light run. He was now abreast of the van. The launch's stern rail had been taken down to facilitate the passing of the canisters across to the pier. He stepped across on to the pier. A couple of long strides brought him to the van. He dodged round it and his hand closed over the handle of the driver's door. He felt a last-moment, irrational flutter of panic at the thought that the door might be locked.

It wasn't. The handle squeaked a little as it turned. He opened the door and slid in behind the wheel. He pulled the door to and shut it carefully.

It was pitch dark in the front of the van. He located the hand brake and gear shift and felt for the pedals with his feet. He eased the brake off, depressed the clutch and put the van into bottom gear. He ran his right hand over the invisible dashboard controls. The lay-out seemed vaugely familiar. He had an idea that the van was a Fiat, but he couldn't be sure.

Thank God the ignition key was there! With his fingers on it, he turned to glance quickly across at the launch. Everything seemed to be quiet there.

He turned the ignition key and jabbed his thumb at what he guessed to be the starter button. The starter motor whined, terrifyingly loud in the still night. The engine turned but did not fire.

Almost instantly there were shouts aboard the launch. Out of the corner of his eye, Blair saw light stream out from the suddenly-flung-open door of the saloon. There was an eruption of men on to the after deck. He kept his thumb down hard on the starter button, and the motor ground agonisingly round and round. But the van's engine stayed stubbornly dead.

A gun flamed and roared from the launch's deck. The bullet snicked diagonally through the van's thin steel side and went out ahead, shattering the windscreen.

Above the hopeless rasp of the starter there came the sound of falling glass.

11

The engine caught at last. It roared as Blair put his foot down hard on the accelerator. He released the clutch pedal. The van's back wheels screeched on the wet planks of the pier in a standing skid before they took hold. Then the tyres gripped and the van rocketed away, throwing him back against the driving seat.

A volley of shots ripped through the body of the van at his back. Instinctively he ducked away. He scrabbled at several switches until he found the headlights, then wrenched at the wheel as he saw that the van was hurtling towards the edge of the pier. The van skidded bodily sideways until its nearside wheels struck the raised baulk of timber that edged the pier. It tilted up on two wheels and for a long, desperate moment seemed to hang over the dark water. Then the offside wheels came down again, and he had control once more.

More shots blasted from the launch, but only one struck, ricocheting off the rear doors. By this time Blair had changed up into third, his foot still hard down on the accelerator pedal, and the van was travelling fast. He answered the shot that struck with a yell of derisive triumph, knowing that he was rapidly getting out of range.

The men on the launch must have realised that too, for there was no more firing.

Half a minute later the van reached the shoreward end of the pier and bumped off it on to the rough harbour road. Blair headed it up into the silent little town of Porto di Miseno. The one main street was dark and deserted. He drove through it at top speed. Almost at once he was out on the open road to Naples.

He had made it! He laughed aloud and slapped the wheel, in violent, exuberant reaction from the long tension.

Then he forced himself to sober down. He knew what he was going to do. He was going to take the stuff in the van straight to Forla, in Naples. But he didn't kid himself that he was out of the wood yet by any means. The van was light and soggy on its springs, and slithered alarmingly on the sharper bends and the rain was driving in through the shattered windscreen. He had to screw up his eyes against it, and at times he was driving almost blind. He knew that, one way and another, he couldn't hope to make very good time.

He'd got to expect pursuit. The Volpi mob wouldn't waste any time getting after him. If they could find a fast car ....

He tried to work it out. They would guess he was heading towards Naples. In fact they didn't even need to guess, because they would see his headlights on the road. And if they found a car, they could over take him fast.

He'd got something of a start, but he didn't know how much. First they'd got to get off the pier—which, thank God, was a long one, and the launch was lying near the outer end of it. And then finding a car that was any use to them might not be so easy in a place like Porto di Miseno.

He reckoned that he'd got, at the very worst, about fifteen minutes' start along the road. That was something, but not much.

He was pushing the van along as fast as he dared, his shoulders hunched and his eyes narrowed as he peered out into the rain-filled glare of the headlights. The

301

stretch of coast he was driving along was lonely and deserted. The road was a single thread stringing together the coastal towns and villages of the northern arm of the bay. He'd driven along it before, and he couldn't remember that there were any turnings off it, at least for some considerable way. There was nothing he could do to avoid pursuit, no chance of branching off and letting the chase go by.

At last he saw a fork ahead, where a narrow road led off up into the mountains. His foot moved instinctively to the brake, wondering whether to take it or not. If he did, he would have a chance of losing himself. But then he trod on the accelerator again and drove straight on. He wasn't going to go wandering around the mountains, possibly on a road that led nowhere at all. Not with the sort of freight he'd got. The dominating thought in his head was still to get the deadly canisters into the safe hands of authority as soon as possible.

He drove at top speed through another deserted village. As he left it, he glanced in the rear-view mirror. The road was still dark behind. He was keeping a close watch in the mirror. Once he had thought he could see the faint loom of headlights a long way back, but it hadn't come again.

He thought ahead, to Naples. How far now? Twenty miles? The city still seemed a long way away.

Something glinted in the mirror. He peered into it. This time he could see headlights quite clearly. There was definitely something on the road behind him. Something much nearer than it had been. Something overtaking him rapidly. It could be some other quite innocent car, but somehow he was sure it wasn't. No casual car would be coming up at that speed.

He set his jaw and put his foot down harder. He was still thinking in terms of driving right through to Naples. But then, suddenly, he knew that that would be trying to push his luck too far. He would be overtaken long before he got there—and he would be within gun range even before that.

He tried to think what else he could do. He tried to visualise the whole length of the coast road, and his present position on it. He knew that Pozzuoli couldn't be far ahead—and Pozzuoli was a fair-sized town. He made a snap decision to stop at the *questura* there.

He was nearer the town that he had hoped. Two or three minutes later he was driving into the outskirts. He'd made it, but only just in time. A turn of the road hid the lights behind him, but he reckoned that, when he'd last seen them, they'd closed the gap to a mile at the most.

He drove on until he was somewhere near the centre of the town. Then he braked, killed the headlights, and swung abruptly into a dark and narrow alley leading off the road. The alley curved almost at once to the right. He drove round the curve until he was out of sight of the road. Then he doused the sidelights too and sat waiting.

He didn't have to wait long. Not more than a minute later the car went by on the road, headlights blazing and travelling fast.

So far, all right. But he wasn't in the clear yet by any means. As soon as they got out on the open road again, the mob in the car would discover that the van wasn't ahead of them any more. And then they would be coming back.

He jabbed the starter, switched on the lights, and backed fast out of the alley.

The van slewed out across the road. He stared along the street ahead. There was a meagre scattering of dimly lit windows here and there. No one about in the open. One ground-floor window was a yellow smear. It looked like a bar. He drove up to it, hurled himself out of the driving seat and pushed the door roughly open.

Four or five men were drinking in the bar. They looked up at him in surprise, and then with suspicion. But when he asked for the *questura,* his urgency had its effect. One of them came to the door and pointed. The *questura* was just along the road on the left-hand side.

Blair was back in the driving seat of the van before the man had finished pointing. He drove on to the *questura.* An arched gateway led into a yard behind. He swung the van in. There were two police cars there. He parked the van behind them so that it was hidden from the gateway.

A minute later he was inside the building, talking to the *sergente* on duty. The *sergente* seemed to be half-asleep, but Forla's name woke him up, very thoroughly, and he at once put in a call to Naples.

Forla was there, in his office. Blair had been praying that he would be. And now, as he listened to the *sergente's* end of the conversation, he realised that he had been quite sure all along that Forla would be there. He was the sort of man who seemed to have a knack of being always on the job just where and when he was wanted. The dedicated sort of man who never seemed to need to eat or sleep.

Blair thanked God that Forla was that sort of man. He'd felt, ever since he'd snatched the canisters, that he wouldn't be able to breathe easily again until he'd handed them over to the formidable Italian policeman.

The *sergente* held out the phone to him. He took it and said, 'Blair.'

There was silence for a moment at the other end of the line. Then Forla's voice, thin, bitter, very strained. 'Well?'

Blair told him quickly and briefly what had happened.

'Where are the canisters now?'

'In the yard behind the station here. In the van.'

'What the hell are they doing there?'

Blair said, 'For God's sake. I've only just—'

'Get off the line.' Forla's voice was savage. 'Put the *sergente* on again.'

Blair frowned. He hadn't wanted or expected thanks for what he had done, but he didn't see why Forla needed to take that tone. He handed the phone back to the *sergente*. The *sergente* listened, tried to interpose something, and winced. Then he nodded anxiously. '*Si ... si, tenente.* At once.' He put the receiver down in a hurry as though it had suddenly become red hot. He turned to Blair. 'The lieutenant is coming out. He is already on his way. He will be here in half an hour.' He stood up behind the desk. 'And now we must get these things in the van to a place of safety—and we must hurry.' He pulled out a handkerchief and mopped his face with it. He was getting flustered. 'You have the ignition key of the van?'

'Here,' Blair said.

The *sergente* took the key and shouted to three of his men. They left the room at a run. After a moment's hesitation, Blair followed them. The side door they had gone out through led into the yard. The *sergente* had opened the rear doors of the van and was pulling out the canisters. The others helped him. As soon as all the canisters had been unloaded, one of the *carabinieri* jumped into the driving seat of the van. He revved the engine and it shot away through a rear exit from the yard. Blair heard it change up, the screech of its tyres on a corner and then another gear change into top. The engine note began to die away in the distance. He smiled slightly and said to the *sergente*, 'A false trail, eh?'

The *sergente* said worriedly, 'It is the *tenente's* orders. Now we must lock these things away.'

Blair helped the *sergente* and the others carry the canisters into the *questura*. There they were locked in an empty cell, as being the most secure place in the building. Then the *sergente* ordered everyone into the big front office. The *carabinieri* gathered there expectantly, all of them armed. The Pozzuoli *questura* was in a state of siege. Forla obviously reckoned that the Volpi mob wouldn't balk at attacking the *questura*, if they thought the canisters were there.

He wondered what had happened to the pursuit. Had the Volpi crowd realised yet that he wasn't still ahead of them? And if they turned back, would the ruse of the empty van work? They would be bound to spot its headlights on so dark a night.

And, if they stopped to listen, they would hear that it was being driven hard.

Even as these thoughts were passing through his mind, a car passed at speed along the road outside, travelling back from the direction of Naples. He heard the engine roar as the driver changed down, then a squeal of brakes and a scream of tyres.

It could only be the Volpi mob, chasing the van.

Blair turned to the *sergente* again. He said, 'Where's the van going?'

The *sergente* said, reluctantly, 'Just up into the mountains, signor.'

'Then the driver will abandon it?'

The *sergente* didn't answer. He was plainly anxious only to carry out his orders. He didn't know how much he ought to tell this man who had burst upon him so alarmingly out of the night.

Time passed. The tension didn't slacken. It was a nervous business, waiting for Forla to arrive. The *sergente* did so with ill-concealed apprehension—he seemed to be more afraid of the lieutenant than of any attack that might have come. He sat down at his desk and then got up again to prowl round the big, shabby room.

Blair sat on a hard chair beside the *sergente's* desk, smoking one cigarette after another. He felt keyed up, too. And he could sympathise with the *sergente*. Forla on the warpath was likely to be a pretty tough proposition.

The *sergente* sat down again. There was silence in the room, except for a desultory low murmur of talk among the *carabinieri*.

The waiting came to an end at last when a car screeched to a stop outside. It was Forla's car. Forla himself came striding in, with two plain-clothes men behind him. The lieutenant's face was livid with fury. He glared at Blair and snapped at the *sergente*. He demanded to be shown the canisters, to see for himself that they were safe. When he came back into the room, he flung himself down in the chair behind the *sergente's* desk. For a while he sat there glowering, and there was a heavy silence in the bare, ugly room. Then his head jerked round towards Blair. He said, with a trembling, only just controlled passion of anger, 'I suppose you think you're a big hero, eh? I suppose you'll want a medal or something for this?'

Blair stared uncomprehendingly at the

dark, narrow face. He said, 'What the hell are you talking about? What's the matter with you?'

Forla leaned forward. His eyes were venomous. He said, 'You were pretty smart getting off the tug, weren't you? Do you know what happened to her?'

'The tug?' Blair was completely bewildered now.

'Yes—the tug,' Forla snapped. He gestured furiously. 'We knew of her boarding almost as soon as you did. Her radio operator got a message away. An alarm, and a rough position. Then the transmission broke off. We sent a launch out to investigate. We heard from her a little while ago—just before you came through from here. She reported that there was no sign of the tug in the area. But they had found flotsam ...'

Blair felt suddenly sick with horror. In his mind's eye he saw again the last of the raiders coming up from below decks on the tug. What had he been doing down there? Opening the sea-cocks? Setting scuttling charges?

And both the tug's crew, and the police aboard, had been imprisoned down below ...

Forla said, 'They must be mad. Eight of our men ...' Now he was on the verge of tears. With an effort he got a grip on himself again. 'It is obvious what they do. They seek a reign of terror, so that no one, not even the police, will dare to move against them.' He drew a deep, harsh breath and began beating with his clenched fist into the palm of his other hand, the gesture Blair remembered from his interview with Forla in Naples and which so vividly expressed a passion of frustration. 'And it is this man Volpi who is behind it all. Volpi ... Volpi ... Volpi ....'

Blair said frowning. 'Can't you get him now? Can't you pull him in?'

Forla stopped, his fist raised. 'For what? He is too clever. We have nothing against him that we can be sure will stick. There is not a witness that would speak. And he would have the best defence that money could buy.'

'But you can't let him go on like this.'

Forla's hand dropped to the desk top. He said, in a dry, hard voice, 'He will not go on, not for more than a few days longer now. He must not, and I pledge myself that he will not. Only, when we get him, we must be certain of him. When he stands before the judge of the court and the jury, it must be that there can be only one verdict.' He gestured again. He was in possession of himself once more. 'Thank you for what you have done to-day. It was courageous. And a great service to our people.'

Blair shrugged. 'Anything I can do. I told you that. I hate his guts as much as you do. I've plenty of reason to, haven't I? So if you can still use me—'

There was a silence. Forla had lit a cigarette and was sitting slumped in the chair. He was plainly making a big effort to relax. But the hand he raised to take the cigarette from his mouth still shook violently.

'Maybe I can,' he said. 'At the moment what I want you to do is wait.'

'For what?'

The Italian's narrow shoulders lifted. 'I don't know. I only know I may find a use for you. Until I do, I want you to wait. I want you to keep out of the way. I don't want you at police headquarters, because—' He frowned. 'You could go to the hotel at Porto Sannazzaro, where you left the boy?'

'I guess I could.'

'You could stay there for a few days?'

'I don't see why not.'

'*Bene.*' Forla sat up. He was a man of decision again, well in command of the situation. 'The *sergente* will provide a car to take you there now. You will stay there until you hear from me. If anything important should happen, you will contact me. *Capito?*'

Blair nodded. '*Capito.*' He grinned. 'Don't leave me right out of it, though, my friend. I've got shares in this affair.'

Forla's mouth twisted in a bitter smile. 'Somehow I think you will be there for the last act, signor. I think you may even be playing a leading role.'

Five minutes later Blair was on his way. It was not more than fifteen kilometres to Porto Sannazzaro, and the police car soon covered the distance. It dropped him unobtrusively on the outskirts of the little port. He walked on into the town and climbed the hill to the Albergo Italia.

It was Tomaso who came to the door, a very clean and neat Tomaso. The boy stared at Blair for a moment in incredulous delight. 'You have come back, signor!' He seized Blair by the hand and dragged him over the threshold.

As usual in the evening, the family was in the kitchen; Momma, Papa, Giannina. Their welcome was almost as warm as Tomaso's. They greeted Blair as though they hadn't seen him for years.

Tomaso was still close at Blair's side. Blair ruffled the small, dark head. He said to Momma, 'He has behaved himself?'

'*Si,*' Momma said. 'He is a good boy. Except that he will not go to bed.' She shook her head. 'He has been working so hard. He thinks that, if he does not, we will throw him out. Foolish child!'

Papa said, 'What are your plans now, signor? You stay with us, perhaps, for a while?'

Blair hesitated. His presence was still dangerous to this family—more dangerous, in fact, than it had been before. He should have thought of that before he agreed to come here. But it was too late now. He had his orders.

'Thank you,' he said. 'For a day or two, if I may.' He hesitated again. 'And it would be best if no one knows I am here.'

Momma fluttered her hands. 'But of course. For as many days as you wish.' She smiled at him. 'And we will be discreet.'

They were good people. They knew his presence there was again a threat to their own safety, but that didn't diminish the warmth of their hospitality. They told him that he looked exhausted, and pressed food and drink upon him with the same overwhelming hospitality as before.

Blair blacked out, rather than slept, that night. He was bone weary. He got up late the following morning and ate, then went back to his room and slept again.

It was mid afternoon when he surfaced next. He felt relaxed, his nerves no longer jumping, but he was still deathly tired. For the rest of the day he was well content to obey Forla's orders and stay in the hotel.

That night, though, he was restless. He wondered what Forla was doing, and when the Italian would call him in again. He had a strong conviction that somehow his own part in the affair was not yet by any means played out. He had no idea what sort of part he would be playing, but he remembered Forla's last words to him at Pozzuoli. *A leading part.* Forla wasn't the kind of man to say things idly.

Meya, too, was sharply back in his thoughts. He was racked by anxiety for her. It was almost unbearable to think that she should still be living in the villa on Capri; still, ostensibly at any rate, Volpi's mistress. He was beset by a strong temptation to go there and fetch her away. But he knew that that would be madness.

He hardly slept at all that night. By morning his enforced inactivity was chafing him badly. He scanned the newspapers that came into the hotel and listened to the radio newscasts for some account of the events of the previous day. There was nothing. Forla had obviously clamped security down hard.

That day passed without news, without Forla contacting him, without anything happening at all. So did the next. He found it harder, with every hour that passed, just to hang around. He was bedevilled, too, by the desire to find out what was happening to Meya. Several times he went to the telephone, and once he lifted the instrument before he thought better of it. If he rang her, he could at least hear her voice, and reassure himself that she was still all right, tell her that he loved her, that things looked as though they might be going to work out better than he had dared to hope when he'd seen her last. But every time, somehow, he stopped himself making the call. It would be too risky. Too risky for her. He'd only done it before because he was even more desperate than he was now. He must not do it again.

And Forla's hard, incisive voice still rang in his ears. *Do nothing until you hear from me.* So he did nothing. He had promised Forla his full co-operation, as long as the Italian needed it, and he was still resolved to keep that promise.

It was on the morning of his fourth interminable day at the Albergo Italia, when he was lying listlessly on his bed, that Papa Pieroni came up and knocked on his door.

'Telephone for you, signor.'

Blair leaped from the bed and hurried down the stairs after Papa to take the call. He felt relief flooding through him, mixed with a tense, excited feeling of anticipation. Forla would have some news for him, if nothing else.

He picked up the receiver and said, 'Forla?'

But it was not Forla.

12

It was Meya. Her voice was little more than a trembling whisper as she said, 'Bruce—it is you?'

The mere sound of her voice was a physical shock to Blair. For a moment he could not answer. Then he said, 'My God ... Meya ....'

'I was so afraid you would not be there.' She sounded as though she were desperately afraid of being overheard, and Blair had a sudden appalling feeling that she was in some great danger. He said sharply, 'What's gone wrong? You're in trouble?'

Meya said urgently, breaking in on him, 'Yes. Oh, Bruce ...' Her voice broke on his name. 'Bruce ... *carissimo* ... I need you. You must come to me.'

'You mean to Capri? To the villa?' A dozen questions were clamouring for answer in Blair's head, but there was no time to ask any of them.

'Yes. You must come here. At once. You

319

must help me. I am so afraid.'

'But what ...?'

She broke in on him again. 'There is no time to explain. It is difficult for me to say even as much as this. But you must come.'

'But—'

'You must come to-night. I have arranged it. Please listen to me carefully, because I shall not be able to repeat it .... A fisherman called Giorgio Ruffino will bring you across from Porto Sannazzaro. And it will be safe. You can rely on him.'

Blair frowned. There were things about this that he didn't like at all. He had a sudden, overwhelming feeling that he was the one that was in danger. But he thrust it away from him. Meya needed him. And if she needed him, he must go to her.

She was still waiting for his answer. Every moment that he kept her on the telephone could be an added risk for her. He said quickly, 'This man Ruffino—how do I contact him?'

'He will be in Porto Sannazzaro as soon as it is dark to-night. At nine o'clock he will be waiting at the harbour steps opposite the Bar Napoli.'

Blair drew a deep breath. 'Okay.'

'You *will* come?'

'Of course.'

There was a moment of silence, as though she was too overcome to speak. Then she said, 'I—'

That was all, except for the click of the phone. Blair was left listening to a dead line.

He went back up to his room, his thoughts in a turmoil. Papa Pieroni spoke to him as he passed on his way up the stairs, but Blair never heard what the little man said, never saw him.

He stood at the window, staring out, but still seeing nothing. How had Meya known that he was at the Pieroni hotel? What was this trouble she was in?

It smelt like a trap. It smelt of treachery and death. Not a trap on Meya's part; he could not believe that of her any more. But it was possible that once again Volpi had made her his decoy, this time an entirely innocent and unsuspecting one.

He shook his head. It was pointless thinking like that, since, if it was a trap, he was going to walk into it anyway. It might be madness, but he knew he couldn't help himself.

He thought forward to the night. *The*

harbour steps opposite the Bar Napoli, at nine. He scanned the waterfront. The whole curve of the little harbour lay in full view below him. He could see the name board over the Bar Napoli; yellow lettering on a background of faded blue. He noted the break in the harbour wall opposite, which marked the steps where the man called Ruffino would be waiting for him.

He turned from the window and began pacing the room. It still could only be a trap. And yet—why? Why the elaborate set-up? Wasn't it enough for Volpi to know where he was? Blair had no doubt at all about what would normally happen in such a case. There would be two men, perhaps three, calling at the Albergo Italia. The Pieronis might deny that he was there, but it would be useless. They would be pushed helplessly aside. The hotel would be searched. Sooner or later the killers would find the right room and then the guns would blaze. That was the usual Volpi method. Why should he bother this time with anything else?

Why? ... Why? ... Why? ... A hundred questions clamoured in Blair's head, and there were no answers to any of them.

He couldn't even come to any sensible appraisal of the situation. Always, however hard he tried to be sane and logical about it all, there came the thought that Meya was in distress. Every time, that one overriding thought reduced his carefully built up little edifice of reasoning to nothing.

He knew only one thing for sure, and that was that he had got to go. He had got to go down to the waterfront at nine o'clock that night and step aboard that boat, whatever might happen to him then. He had got to go, in spite of his promise to Forla. Meya meant more to him than a thousand Forlas.

He debated whether there was anything he could do to safeguard himself, any manoeuvre that would prevent him walking quite so blindly into any trap that might have been set for him. He wondered whether to ignore Meya's instructions about the boat and make his way to Capri independently, and ahead of the set time. He could go across on the island boat, as he had done before?

He tried for a long time to argue himself into doing that, but in the end he had to turn away from it. It wouldn't do. He didn't know what kind of set-up he would be getting into at the other end. He didn't know just how or where or when he would be able to contact Meya. And he could not afford to do anything at all that might add to the hazard she was in. It came back always, however he argued it, to the same basic thing. If he was going to be any use to her at all, he'd got to do precisely what she had asked him to do. She must know just what her predicament was, and he knew nothing definite about it at all.

He wondered whether to tell Forla, but quickly realised that that was impossible. Forla would take the thing out of his hands. Blair had no illusions about Forla. He knew how ruthless the man was; and, after the sinking of the tug, the Italian's resolve to get Volpi at all costs had plainly become a savage, all-consuming obsession. Forla would only be interested in somehow using this appeal of Meya's to get Volpi, and he wouldn't give a damn whether she got hurt in the process ....

He came back to the window and stopped there, staring out again. He stared at the steps opposite the Bar Napoli. A small fishing boat was lying alongside there now. In another few hours there would be another boat lying there—or it might even be this same one. Perhaps that was Ruffino down there now, waiting—and laughing.

Blair drew a deep breath and squared his shoulders. He knew he was about to do what might easily be the silliest damned thing he'd ever done in his life.

He left the bedroom and went downstairs. He found Papa Pieroni sitting in the sun on a chair on the steps of the hotel. He said, 'Papa, I need a gun.'

Papa started. 'A gun, signor?'

'A revolver. A Beretta, something like that.'

'But I have no guns, signor!'

'Perhaps you know someone who has?' Blair added, seeing the look of alarm and dismay on Papa's face. 'Don't worry. Nothing is going to happen to you here in your hotel.'

'I am worried about what is going to happen to you.'

Blair shrugged. 'I can take care of myself.'

Papa hesitated. Then he said, 'I will see what I can do. Although I do not know how to do it. My friend, the people I know in Porto Sannazzaro do not have guns.'

Blair patted the troubled little man's

shoulder. 'I know. But if you'd ask around. Quietly, of course—'

'*Si.*' Papa got up. 'I will do that.'

The rest of the day passed slowly. There was nothing Blair could do now except wait for nightfall. His thoughts went round and round the same endless treadmill as before, getting him nowhere. He kept hearing Meya's voice on the phone, so strained and frightened.

He was almost beside himself with restlessness. Some of it was apprehension, but there was a strong element of eagerness and anticipation in it too. His heart lifted and his pulse beat faster when, from time to time, he was able to put the rest of the affair behind him and concentrate on the thought that soon, in a few hours, he might be with Meya again.

At last it was evening. The sun went down over the sea. Dusk thickened the hot air. He went down and ate sketchily, and then returned to his room and lay on his bed for a while.

He had no gun. Papa's inquiries hadn't yielded any result. But it didn't matter. A gun wouldn't have reduced the odds against him very much. If there was trouble ahead, it would be lying in ambush, on the fishing boat, perhaps, or on Capri. There wouldn't be much chance for him to use a gun.

He made a move about eight-thirty. He got up and again stood at his window for a while. It was almost fully dark now, a soft, velvet night. Porto Sannazzaro was sparsely lit, and he could not see much from the window. He stared at a faint glow of light round the curve of the harbour, which might be the Bar Napoli. The steps opposite it were invisible, and there was no way of telling whether there was a boat lying there or not.

He went downstairs. Papa was doing some book-keeping behind the little reception desk.

'I'm going out now,' Blair told him. 'I don't know when I'll be back.' He managed a grin. 'Don't worry about me.' He walked towards the door, then checked and turned. 'If a Lieutenant Forla telephones, tell him I'll get in touch with him as soon as I can.'

'*Si*,' Papa said. His eyes followed Blair anxiously to the door.

As Blair reached the door, Tomaso came running out from the kitchen.

'You are going away again, signor?' he

327

asked breathlessly.

'Just for another little while,' Blair said. He found a grin for Tomaso too. 'Be a good boy.'

Papa called suddenly from the desk, 'Good luck, my friend. Please be very careful.'

'Thanks. I will.'

Blair left the little hotel and walked down the hill towards the harbour. The town was virtually deserted. He turned and made his way carefully along the waterfront until he was within fifty yards or so of the steps opposite the Bar Napoli. He could see the steps and a dark craft lying alongside there.

He stopped and watched the boat for a while from the shelter of a pile of fish boxes on the harbour wall. A pin-prick of light, a small red spark, glowed intermittently from her deck aft. Someone was waiting there, smoking. There was only one cigarette, and presumably the smoker was Ruffino.

There was no other sign of life aboard. Blair waited and watched for quarter of an hour, then looked at his watch. It was a minute to nine. He shrugged. He'd made his reconnaissance, for what it was worth, which was nothing at all. There might be half a dozen men hidden aboard the boat. There was no way of telling. Or only one way ....

He strolled slowly along to the steps where the boat lay. The man on her deck was still smoking, still waiting. Blair stopped and called down softly, 'Ruffino?'

'*Si.*' The cigarette arced over the side. 'You are the *inglese?*'

'I guess so.'

'Please come aboard.'

Blair walked down the dark stone steps and jumped aboard. This was it. He was committed now. His eyes searched the deck, but there was no sign of anyone else. Not that there would be.

He said, 'You are alone?'

'*Si.*'

Blair thought it sounded like the truth. It was said simply, without emphasis. But all the same he felt a coldness down his spine as he stared at the black mouth of the open hatch which led down into the fishing boat's cabin.

Ruffino said, 'You wish to go below for the trip?'

The Italian put the question naturally, almost negligently. It was enough to convince Blair that, if trouble was coming to him, it wasn't due yet.

He said, 'No. I'll stay on deck.' He felt he would much rather be out in the open, where he could at least see what was going on.

Ruffino grunted. He started the engine and went forward to cast off. It was only a small boat, with the engine in an open well aft. Blair sat down on the seat at the back of the well. He lit a cigarette. Ruffino came back and stooped over the engine. He was a squat, broad-shouldered, obviously very powerful man. He opened the throttle and put the engine in gear. The boat moved ahead, slowly gathering speed and swinging out from the sea wall in a close, powerful turn. The Italian steadied her on the harbour entrance.

The boat headed out through the narrow entrance. She carried no navigation lights. The night was very dark indeed. Later there would be a moon, but it would be hours yet before it rose.

The sea was dark and empty. Ruffino lit another cigarette. His face was lit up luridly by the flare of the match cupped in his hands. It was a heavy, swarthy face which told Blair nothing.

Blair smoked and stared into the

darkness. He was trying to estimate how long the trip would take—presuming that he was going to be permitted to complete it. He reckoned it would be all of four hours to Capri at the speed they were making.

The boat thrust on. After a while Blair relaxed a little. He didn't attempt to talk to Ruffino. He was scarcely in the mood for light conversation. And Ruffino didn't seem to be a communicative type either. He stood four-square at the wheel, and neither spoke nor so much as turned his head. There was silence, save for the throb of the boat's engine and the hiss of the sea along her sides.

Blair kept a check on his watch. The hands crept round until they had been under way an hour. He got up then from the stern bench and said, 'I think I'll go below for a while—okay?' And, when Ruffino grunted an assent he felt his way down into the blackness of the cabin, found a settee-bunk and lay down on it.

He lay in the dark, resting while he could, once more trying to size up the situation. What was going to happen next? Had Ruffino a rendezvous to keep with another vessel—perhaps the Volpi yacht?

As time passed and the boat still chugged uneventfully on, the likelihood of any development of that sort diminished. And what at last Blair came out on deck again and saw Capri darkly silhouetted ahead, he felt sure that he was at least going to get ashore without incident. He began thinking of Meya again, of how close he was to her now. And he got angry with himself again for not having trusted her. It could well be that this wasn't a trap after all.

His estimate of four hours for the trip wasn't far wrong. It was a few minutes short of that when the boat entered the Marina Grande.

Ruffino throttled down, once the boat was inside the harbour. It glided in towards the jetty. There was only a sprinkling of lights around the water's edge, but there was a bright and lively glow over the little town up on the cliff, and the sound of music came wafting down to the water. Blair had a sudden and vivid mental picture of the gay night scene up there in the cafés and bars. He recalled the times he himself had spent half the night there drinking with the holiday-makers and the tourists. It all seemed a million miles, a million years away now. It seemed to him that, for an immeasurable time, he had been living in some outer darkness.

The fishing boat nudged alongside the harbour wall. Ruffino cut the engine and jumped ashore to tie up. When he had done so, he growled at Blair to follow him, and turned towards the shore.

Blair said, 'Where are we going? The villa?'

Ruffino grunted. '*Si.*'

They went up by the road, with Ruffino leading the way, shambling stolidly a pace or so ahead. They skirted the town, avoiding the square and threading their way through a maze of narrow back alleys until they came out on a steep and narrow road which bore round in a continuous curve towards the right, cutting over the shoulder of the cliff and obviously leading towards the villa.

The air was heavy with the night perfume of a myriad flowers. The road was closely shut in by steep banks topped with dense vegetation. Walking along it was like walking along a trench. It was a death-trap of a road, an ambush all along its length. A score of men, a hundred, could be lying in wait there, ahead, abreast, behind. Blair felt his skin prickling as he tramped along. But then he told himself not to be a damned fool. If anything was going to happen, it wouldn't happen here—not when he was walking so docilely right into the stronghold of the enemy itself. And in any case there was no ambush either here or at the villa. Meya had said that he would be brought safely to her, and he had got to believe that that was precisely what was taking place.

They came eventually to a break in the right-hand bank of the lane. Something showed palely in the light of the stars overhead. It was a gate, a white gate.

Ruffino turned and went in through the gate. Blair followed him. They were in a driveway. The villa lay ahead. Blair could see the ghostly blur of its white walls. There were lights in one or two of the windows.

Ruffino led the way towards the villa, treading silently, keeping to the edge of the drive. He turned off just before he reached the villa, and took a narrow path which wound round to the rear through a thicket of shrubs. A minute or so later he stopped at what seemed to be a servants' entrance. He turned to Blair and whispered gruffly, 'Wait here.'

Blair stopped where he was. He saw

Ruffino open the door. There was a bare, dimly lit passage inside. The door closed, and Blair was alone in the soft, dark night. He waited. His mouth was dry and he was trembling now, not with apprehension, but because of the nearness of the woman he loved. She was there, somewhere, in the long, low white house. In a matter of moments she would be in his arms.

He heard light footsteps on the other side of the door. It opened. There was a drift of perfume which took him whirling back to La Goulette and the night trip on the launch. There was the pale blur of a dress.

He stepped forward and his arms went round her. 'Meya!' he breathed. Desperately, hungrily, his lips sought hers. He kissed her and held her to him. He was dizzy with her nearness.

Meya clung to him. She was trembling. She murmured his name. 'Bruce—oh, Bruce!'

For a long moment they stood there, held helpless, in spite of the place and the circumstances of their meeting, by the torrent of feeling sweeping over them both. Then Meya pushed him gently away from her. 'We must go inside,' she said. 'There is not much time.'

He would have caught her to him and kissed her again, but something in her voice stopped him. There was a sudden, dead hopelessness in the way she spoke. It seemed to him that she was on the verge of collapse. His heart went out to her at the thought of all the strain she had had to endure.

She reached out and took his hand. 'Come,' she said, almost harshly.

She went ahead of him through the servants' quarters. They were deserted. Her hand was clenched hard on his, and it was trembling almost uncontrollably. Once she half-stumbled and Blair had a feeling that she could hardly walk.

They passed through another door, and came out into the large, elegant, opulent room which Blair remembered from his previous visit. Meya turned and faced him there, and he was shocked by the look of her. Her face had a sick pallor that was only emphasised by the hectic patches of rouge on her cheeks. She looked almost grotesque, a caricature of the woman he knew.

He said, 'For God's sake, Meya, what's

336

the trouble? What's happened?'

She shook her head. She couldn't speak at all now. And, when Blair took an urgent step towards her, she closed her eyes. A low, moaning cry broke from her and she swayed.

He caught her to him. As he did so, a voice spoke from the doorway.

'There is no trouble, my friend. Except for you.'

Blair turned slowly, with Meya in his arms. Volpi was lounging in the doorway, watching him with cold amusement.

'Except for you,' Volpi repeated. He moved a pace forward into the room and stopped again. His gun was in his hand. He stared at Blair, and then suddenly he laughed. It was a harsh, derisive sound. He said, 'You fool—to let yourself be deceived twice by the same woman!'

Meya moaned again. She stiffened in Blair's arms and tried to break away from him. Helplessly, he let her go. She turned and stumbled to a chair. He watched her drop down there and bury her face in her hands.

It all seemed unreal. He couldn't believe that it was actually happening. He could not bring himself to believe that she really had betrayed him a second time. He tried to find excuses for her. He could guess at the terrible pressure that might have been brought to bear upon her. Perhaps even a threat against her life. And yet his own life was at stake too. She must have known she was delivering him over to his executioner. Whatever the pressure, she could never have done that; not if she loved him.

Volpi said, 'We may as well sit down too, and make ourselves comfortable. We are going to have a little chat. It may take quite a while.'

He motioned with the gun towards a chair. Blair moved numbly towards it. There was no thought of resistance in him now. His world had suddenly fallen to pieces, finally and irretrievably. Nothing mattered any more, not even his own life. That was all he knew.

An ornate, upholstered and gilded chaise-longue faced the chairs where Blair and Meya were sitting. It was an elegant piece of furniture, covered in a pale-blue silken material. Volpi sat down there. He was immaculately dressed, as usual, in a white linen suit. His dark hair had a glossy sheen. Lounging there, he might have been an elegant gentleman taking his ease, except for the gun on his knee. He seemed to be holding the gun casually, but his finger was on the trigger, and the muzzle was pointing directly at Blair.

Meya was sobbing. Apart from that there was no sound in the room. Blair did not look at her, and yet he was acutely conscious of her presence. She still filled his thoughts almost to the exclusion of everything else, even Volpi. The desperately suppressed, choking sound of her grief took him whirling back to that other time on the yacht, and then his first encounter with Volpi on the beach below the villa. She had been distressed then—that first time she had betrayed him.

The memory of it aroused in him a sudden savage scorn. It was too bad that it should upset her so much to decoy a man to his death. A man she had professed to love.

With an effort he shut her out of his thoughts. She wasn't worth thinking about. He stared across the room at Volpi. Whatever was coming, he wanted to get it over. He felt quite calm about it. He didn't give a damn for the gun in Volpi's hand. In a way, a quick bullet would be a relief.

He said, 'Well, you've been at considerable pains to get me here. Now what do you want?'

Volpi smiled thinly. 'A little talk, first of all, my friend. A little information.'

'What sort of information?'

Volpi hefted the gun he was holding, feeling the weight of it. He said, 'It was you, of course, who stole the van at Porto Miseno.'

'It was.' Blair grinned painfully. This was the one worthwhile thing that had come out of the whole affair; that he had saved the canisters.

Volpi leaned forward. He said, 'I should be interested to know what you did with the contents.'

Blair stared at him blankly for a moment. Then a faint spark of hope was suddenly born inside him. Volpi, he realised, didn't know that the canisters were safe in the hands of the police.

He remembered the ruse with the empty van. Volpi must have thought that he had abandoned it and hidden its deadly load. If Volpi thought he still had the canisters, or knew where they were, there was just a chance that he could bluff something through.

Volpi said, 'We found the van where you left it. Of course it was empty. I don't know what you have done with the canisters—but I assure you I shall do before I'm through with you.' He paused, and then went on in a more reasonable, almost conciliatory tone. 'Come now, that stuff is no use to you. You haven't the means of disposing of it.' He paused again. 'Maybe we could still do a deal.'

Blair turned his head and looked at Meya. She had lifted her head and was staring sightlessly in front of her. She had stopped weeping, but he could see the tears still on her pale cheeks.

He looked at Volpi again. He said, 'What sort of a deal? I hand over the stuff and you rub me out—something like that, eh?'

Volpi said, 'There could be safeguards.'

Blair's lip curled in spite of himself. This was nonsense. It was hardly worth wasting breath on.

'There is more to it than the one deal anyway,' Volpi said. 'Or there could be.' He weighed the gun in his hand again. 'It could be I could still use a man like you.'

Blair looked at Volpi narrowly. He saw

him suddenly as a man who was very much alone. Maybe his power had weakened a little during the last few days? A big-time gangster's hold on his mob depended almost entirely on his being able to feed them one successful coup after another—and this latest affair certainly hadn't gone too well for him. It could be that Cellini and the others were getting nervous or restive, that they were beginning to feel that Volpi was losing his grip. That could mean one or more of several things. Splinter groups within the gang; or, more likely, a bid by anyone strong enough to take over the outfit himself.

Blair remembered that Volpi had personally taken over the boarding of the salvage boat. That didn't seem quite as it should have been. If all had been going well, he would have remained in the background, the big boss, powerful enough to direct operations by remote control. Why had he led the raid? To encourage the others by his personal example? Whatever it was, it now seemed to Blair to have been the act of a desperate man.

It was just possible that Volpi really did need to do a bit of new recruiting.

Blair frowned. He hoped he looked as

though he were seriously considering the offer. He said at last, 'It certainly looks as though you could do with someone. You haven't been making out too well recently, have you?'

Volpi met his gaze. He said expressionlessly, 'I need a new lieutenant.'

'Meaning me?'

'Yes.'

'Taking me in at the top, eh?' Blair managed a grin. 'You think I could hold down the job?' He was talking gibberish he knew. He was still trying to work out what chance he had of getting out of that room with his life.

Volpi said, 'You wouldn't regret it.' He smiled. 'Look—for a start, I'll make a straight fifty-fifty split with you on what we make out of that parcel of dope. That in itself would be a fortune for you.'

Blair frowned again. Something deep inside him rebelled against having any kind of truck at all with anyone like Volpi, of even maintaining a pretence of interest in what the man was saying. He felt nauseated. He didn't know how he could keep the bluff going much longer, even if his life depended on it ....

He didn't have to, for just then there

came an interruption so unexpected and so violent that it took both him and Volpi by surprise. It came from Meya. She jumped up out of her chair and flung herself down on the floor in front of Blair. She looked wildly up at him, beseechingly, her hands gripping convulsively at his knees.

'You must!' she cried. 'You must do what he says! If you don't, he will shoot you down, in cold blood—the way he shot Lieutenant Bonelli and the captain of the tug!'

Her hands slid away. She buried her face in them. Blair stared at Volpi. In his memory there reverberated the two shots he had heard on the tug. They echoed in his brain, one following the other, coldly deliberate. Bonelli ... Renato ....

'Bonelli ... Renato ...' He repeated the names aloud. 'You shot them?'

Volpi nodded. 'With this little gun.' He waved it gently. 'It was necessary. It was necessary to give my men a little example and encouragement.'

Blair drew a deep breath. He knew that this was the crisis. He knew that he couldn't endure for another moment this man who admitted so easily, even complacently, to cold-blooded murder. He

344

understood now something of the rage that had possessed Forla. He felt it himself.

He measured his chances. They weren't good. In fact they didn't even exist. Volpi was a good ten feet away. He had a gun, and he wouldn't hesitate to use it. He would enjoy using it.

He'd be dead before he'd covered half the distance. He knew that as certainly as he'd ever known anything in his life. But just the same his hands tightened on the arms of his chair. He tensed his leg muscles, ready to hurl himself forward.

Volpi came to this feet in a smooth, easy motion. The gun came up in his hand. He said, 'I wouldn't try it—'

Blair flung himself forward. At the same instant a gun roared ....

It was not the gun in Volpi's hand. The shot came from the doorway through which Blair had come into the room. Volpi's gun flew out of his hand and clattered to the floor. Volpi doubled up, screaming like an animal, clutching his shattered wrist. He turned, crouching, snarling now, towards the door.

It was, incredibly, Forla that was standing there, a still smoking revolver in his hand.

345

Volpi crouched, staring at the lieutenant, for a long moment. Then he whirled again, like a vicious beast at bay, his mouth twisted with pain and fury. His eyes sought the french windows that led out on to the terrace.

Two men came in through the french windows. They both had guns in their hands.

The beast was cornered. There was no escape.

13

Blair was back at the Albergo Italia. He was still under orders from Forla, waiting on call, should the police want him for questioning.

It was two days now since Volpi had been arrested. Blair had spent most of yesterday at police headquarters in Naples, where he had made a long statement, and attested the tape-recording Forla had made of the final act of the drama.

Meya was in Naples. She had not wanted to stay on at the villa a moment longer than was necessary. She had crossed with Blair on the boat on the morning after Volpi's arrest. She was staying at the Hotel Cavour. On a special dispensation from Forla, Blair had dined with her there last night.

It had been a long, intimate evening. There was so much they had to say to each other. And even then there remained so much that was still unsaid. The nightmare they had both been living through had ended so abruptly that it had left them stunned. It was strange, but, when the time came for Blair to return to Porto Sannazzaro, they had parted almost willingly. They both needed rest, and some degree of solitude in which to come to their own personal terms with what had happened. And the parting would not be for long. They both knew now, beyond a shadow of a doubt, that they loved each other; and that, for the moment, was enough.

After breakfast Blair took a stroll along the Porto Sannazzaro waterfront. He was due to go to Naples again that afternoon, first for another interview with Forla, and then to see Vic, for the first time since the boy had been in hospital. After that he hoped to see Meya.

He walked slowly in the sun, thinking about her, still unable to realise that their love didn't have to stand the test of death and danger any more. He knew that it might be some time yet before they could be together for good. That rested in Forla's hands. But there was no real or enduring obstacle to their happiness any more.

He paused at the steps where the man called Ruffino had been waiting with his boat to take him across to Capri on that last nerve-racking night. It had been dark then, with death in every shadow. But now the sun shone, and the sea stretched blue and calm before him.

It seemed to him that the same could be said of the turn his own life had taken. A little while ago he had been living in darkness, but now the prospect ahead was bright.

He leaned on the stone parapet of the waterfront wall. He was thinking about Forla now, knowing without a doubt that he had never met and never would meet a man who impressed him more. There had been times when Forla's handling of the affair had seemed nothing short of superhuman.

It had really been a battle between giants all along; between Volpi on the one hand and Forla on the other. There had never really been anybody else in it at all.

He realised that it was a battle that must have been going on for a long while before he had got into it himself. And it was of course the struggle over the drug canisters that had finally brought it to a head. Though even then it might not have come to quite such a lightning-swift end if Volpi hadn't made the fatal mistake of over-reaching himself.

Volpi had got desperate. And his big mistake had been the sinking of the tug, with the cold-blooded murder of her crew and the police aboard her. As Forla had said, it had been a bid to spread terror in the Naples area, among police and civilians alike. And it hadn't worked. Thanks to Forla, it hadn't had time to work. Before its effects could be felt, the Italian lieutenant had struck savagely and decisively back, a formidable man made even more formidable by his burning passion for revenge.

Leaning there now on the harbour wall, smoking and looking out over the calm sea, Blair found himself thinking back to the moment when he and Forla had met at the *questura* at Pozzuoli. It seemed to him that from then on Forla had handled things not only with breath-taking speed, but also with sheer brilliance.

Blair had not understood at the time just how subtle Forla was. He had been puzzled, for instance, as to why Forla should have resorted to the ruse with the van. Why not a show-down with the Volpi outfit there and then in Pozzuoli? Forla, with the local men added to the others he had brought with him, had had a strong force of police at his disposal.

Blair had said as much to Forla, and the lieutenant had smiled, grimly. That would have been too crude, too obvious. That way he couldn't have been sure of getting Volpi. And he had to be sure, absolutely sure.

So it had had to be something more subtle. But what? Forla had shrugged when he said that. For all his ruthlessness, he was a modest man. He had admitted to Blair that in the first instance he had ordered the van to be driven away and abandoned merely to lay a false trail. Or perhaps he had had a hunch that it was a move that might somehow prove useful.

And it had. As soon as Forla looked at the thing from Volpi's angle, he could see how it might. Volpi had found the van, but not the canisters. Therefore they must have been cached somewhere. They must have been cached by the man who had snatched the van from the pier at Porto di Miseno. Forla realised that Volpi almost certainly didn't know who that man was. It occurred to him that it might be a good idea to let him find out. Volpi might think that if he could find that man, he might

351

still be able to recover the canisters.

It was Blair that had stolen the van. Volpi must be allowed to discover that it was Blair. But how?

There was one obvious link between Blair and Volpi: the Nordstrom woman.

Forla had got quickly and secretly in touch with her. He talked to her and was quite prepared to bully her into co-operation with him, but quickly became aware of two things which made that unnecessary. One was that she was desperately in love with Blair. And the other was that, whatever her feelings for Volpi might once have been, she now felt nothing for him except loathing.

There was a third thing too. She was an actress.

So he set his trap. It was really a trap within a trap. She was to return to Capri and, pretending to succumb to one of Volpi's almost insane, threatening rages—it wouldn't need much pretending—was to confess that Blair had been in touch with her, that he had told her about his escape with the van, that she knew where Blair was, and thought she could entice him to the villa. And then she was to get in touch with Blair and beg him to come to her ...

Blair smiled grimly. There must have been quite a scene between Meya and Forla at that point. She had refused, almost hysterically, to betray the man she loved into so much danger. Forla had tried to make her see that Blair would be in no danger, at any rate of his life, as long as Volpi thought he knew where the canisters were. But she had refused to listen. At that point Forla had got tough. He had told her that the police had enough on Blair anyway to send him to prison for a very long time. If she co-operated she might be saving him that. And at that she had yielded.

All that had remained then was to fix the servants at the villa. A tricky business, but it had been managed. Luckily none of them were Volpi's men. He had never used the villa as a headquarters.

Then there had been the placing of the microphone, with one of Forla's beloved tape-recorders in the next room, and the stationing of the police for the final scene. Forla had been pretty sure that, in an interview with Blair, Volpi could not help but incriminate himself. And Meya was present too, to steer the talk, if necessary, the way Forla wanted it—as she had done so effectively ....

Blair flicked his cigarette butt into the harbour and turned away. The Bar Napoli across the road caught his eye, with the yellow lettering on the faded blue board. He crossed the road and went in.

He ordered a Scotch, and made a wry face when he tasted it. It reminded him of the stuff he had drunk at the Hotel Oasis in La Goulette—how many years ago? It seemed like a different life.

It *was* a different life. He was through with all that now. Even the drink. He realised, with what was almost a shock of surprise, that his craving for liquor had completely gone. He knew that, from now on, drink was a thing he would be able to take or leave alone.

He put his glass down and looked round the bar. It was as sleazy a place as it had seemed to him to be when he'd first spotted it from the window of his room up at the Pieronis' hotel. It was like all those little waterfront dumps, hot and airless, pungent with the sour smell of wine slops. The one or two drinkers looked seedy and down-at-heel, and the obese, elderly proprietor was wearing a shirt that had only very long ago been clean.

The place reminded him of the Bar Marina, and all at once he knew why he had gone in there. He was thinking of Sam Everett. He raised his glass half-ceremoniously and drank to Sam. Poor devil—he was best out of it all. And, in his way, Sam had done his bit to bring Volpi and the Volpi gang to book.

He looked at his watch. It was nearly ten o'clock. He left his drink half-finished on the counter and went out and back to the Albergo Italia.

He was due to drive in to Naples with the Pieroni family. Papa had business there, and later they were all to meet at the hospital. Blair found the whole family waiting outside the hotel in Papa's large and ancient car. Papa was behind the wheel, in a wing collar that made his moustache look fiercer than ever. Momma was beside him in the front, a vast, shining, panting mass of black silk and pale, perspiring flesh. Tomaso was sitting almost obliterated between them, an eager, excited look on his face. This would be his first ride ever in a car!

Giannina, fresh and pretty in a new mauve dress, was alone in the back seat. She was the first to see Blair coming, and she called out to him, 'Hurry, hurry! We must not be late!'

'*She* says we must not be late!' Papa shouted. 'Who is it that has made us late so far? It is always the same with these girls, with all their prinking and preening.'

Blair got in the back with Giannina.

'We are not late at all,' Momma said. She turned to the two part-time woman servants standing on the Albergo Italia's steps watching the departure and screamed last-minute instructions for looking after the hotel while she was away. Then she turned back to Papa. 'Well, get on with it! Signor Blair does not want to sit here all day!'

Papa engaged the gears with a flourish, and the ancient vehicle rocketted away.

An hour later, thanks in large manner to the dexterity of other drivers and the agility of the pedestrians along their route, the Pieroni juggernaut arrived in the centre of the city without mishap.

Blair dropped off at a convenient traffic hold-up and walked to police headquarters. Papa had wanted to drive him to the door, but he needed a few moments to collect himself. He knew that to-day Forla was going to pronounce sentence, unofficially at any rate, on his own part in the Volpi affair.

The desk *sergente* phoned Forla's office. He hung up and said, 'The lieutenant asks you to wait. For the moment he is busy.'

Blair sat down on a bench against the wall. He wondered again if there was ever a time when Forla wasn't busy. He grinned to himself. Maybe at that very moment the lieutenant was putting a new reel on his tape-recorder, to take a note of the coming interview.

Five minutes later a young *carabiniere* came for him. He said, 'Follow me, signore, if you please.' He led the way up to Forla's office.

Forla was at work at his desk. He ignored Blair for a long minute. Then he looked up, as unsmilingly as ever. He sat back and lit a cigarette. He said curtly, 'Well?'

Blair shrugged. 'I'm here as requested.'

'You know why?'

'I can guess.'

Forla blew out a thin jet of smoke. He said, 'The Volpi break-up certainly started something. A lot has been coming out this last day or two. Every crook on

357

the waterfront is falling over himself to squeal.'

'That's good news.'

'Is it? We've picked up quite a few more things about you.'

Blair glanced at Forla sharply. 'What sort of things?'

Forla smiled humourlessly. His eyes were very cold. He sat back in his chair and looked at Blair. 'Enough to put you away for quite a while, if we were so inclined.'

Blair drew a deep breath. 'And are you?'

Forla didn't answer at once. He sat smoking impassively.

'No,' he said at last. 'We can't be bothered with you. You were never anything except a small-time crook, and not a very good one at that. And you have done us some service. So all we shall do is hold you as a witness as long as we need you, and then kick you out. As far as my country is concerned, you are still an undesirable.'

The insult was deliberate and calculated. But Blair took it without protest. He was even glad to. Somehow this more or less wiped the slate clean. And at the same time he was filled with a great sense of

358

relief. He was free at last, or very nearly free, of the life he had been living for the past two years.

There was something else he had to know. He said, 'What about Vic—Vittorio Massena, my boy on the boat. Is he in the clear too?'

'Him!' Forla shrugged. 'I forgot him long ago. He was of no importance. What could we charge him with anyway?' He gestured, irritably. 'Let's only hope he's learned enough sense to keep clear in the future of characters like you.'

Blair said quickly, 'I'm sure he has.'

'Good,' Forla said. 'Don't change your address without informing the police—we shall still want to know where we can find you.' He stood up. 'Now get out. I have other things to do.'

Blair got up too. He hesitated. He had not expected to be so summarily dismissed. Then he held out his hand. He said, 'Thanks. Thanks, Lieutenant, for what you've done for me.'

Forla gestured impatiently. Then, at the last moment, the man broke through. He took Blair's hand. 'Good luck.' For the first time Blair detected a faint warmth in his tone. 'You're a brave man. But stop being a damn fool.'

Blair said soberly, 'I have.'

'I think you have.'

Forla turned abruptly away and sat down at his desk again. He picked up a sheaf of papers and glanced through them. He already seemed to have forgotten that Blair existed ....

Blair went out. He walked out of the *questura* into the crowded streets. He was free!

He bought himself a drink and a sandwich for lunch. He idled over the snack, and then went out to stroll through the streets until it was time to go to the hospital. He was free! He smiled suddenly at the memory of some long-ago words of Meya's. *You look over your shoulder at people.* Well, he had no need to do that any more. From now on he need only look straight ahead.

When he reached the hospital, the whole of the Pieroni family was there gathered round Vic's bed. Little Tomaso too. Little Tommy seemed to be as much one of the family as any of the others. He no longer wistfully stood in the background.

Vic was propped up on pillows. His face lit up when he saw Blair. Grinning, Blair held out his hand. Vic reached out and grasped it in both of his. It was the first time they had met since the long swim, and it was a good moment.

'Nice to see you, pal,' Blair said. The boy looked pretty fit, he thought, and the grip on his hands was encouragingly strong.

'It is wonderful to see you, *capitano*,' Vic said. He went on wringing Blair's hand, grinning with delight.

'You're as good as mended now?'

'*Si*. As good as new. They are going to let me out soon.'

'Forla's talked to you, I suppose?'

Vic nodded. '*Si*. Many times. He's a tough one, that.'

'Did he tell you he's not going to prefer charges?'

Vic nodded again. '*Si*.'

'So it's all over.'

Vic's face fell for a moment. 'Yes. It is all over. I am sorry about our partnership.'

'Partnership? What partnership?' Papa burst in suddenly, waving his hands. 'How many times have I told you that you are now in partnership in the hotel, and nothing else?'

Vic said slyly, 'And how many times was it that you told me that I must buy my share?'

'It is bought!' Papa shouted. 'It is bought a thousand times over! I keep telling you too that you are a hero, my son. You and Signor Blair—you are both heroes! Gang smashers! Patriots! Italy is proud of you!'

Blair smiled. 'And am I right in thinking there is going to be a wedding very soon?'

Giannina blushed, and nodded, and came close to the bed to take Vic's hand ....

Blair took his leave as soon as he could, after promising to come again next day. He badly needed to see Meya.

She was waiting for him in the foyer of the hotel. He felt his heart beat faster, as it always did at the sight of her.

She got up and came to meet him, smiling but anxious. She said, 'You have seen the lieutenant?'

Blair said, 'Yes. And it's all right. They're not going to hang me or shoot me. They're not even going to put me in gaol.'

She closed her eyes with a sigh of relief. Blair took her arm and led her to a quiet corner of the foyer. They sat down together on a deep settee.

Meya turned to him and took his hands. '*Caro,* how long will it be?'

Blair said gently. 'Until what?'

'Until we can leave this country.'

Blair leaned forward and kissed her lightly. 'Does it matter—as long as we're together?'

She shivered a little. 'I shall be glad to go.'

'To Scotland? It's chilly and wet most of the year.'

'Anywhere, with you.'

'And you'll be living in the country—a sort of glorified farmer's wife. Won't you find it dull, after all this excitement?'

But she couldn't respond to his teasing mood. She could only repeat, simply, 'Anywhere with you.'

Blair looked at her. He thought of all they had been through together since their first meeting at La Goulette. They had both been very different people then, both disillusioned, both drifting, in mortal danger of losing their way in life for ever. He thought of the way they had fallen in love—it had happened that day on the beach below the villa; and of how their love had triumphed against the most terrible odds ....

Meya said anxiously, 'Caro, is anything wrong?'

Blair shook his head. Then he smiled at her. He couldn't do anything else. He wanted to tell her something of what he was feeling, but he couldn't. His heart was too full.

The publishers hope that this book has given you enjoyable reading. Large Print Books are especially designed to be as easy to see and hold as possible. If you wish a complete list of our books, please ask at your local library or write directly to: Dales Large Print Books, Long Preston, North Yorkshire, BD23 4ND, England.

This Large Print Book for the Partially
sighted, who cannot read normal print, is
published under the auspices of

THE ULVERSCROFT FOUNDATION

THE ULVERSCROFT FOUNDATION

. . . we hope that you have enjoyed this
Large Print Book. Please think for a
moment about those people who have
worse eyesight problems than you . . . and
are unable to even read or enjoy Large
Print, without great difficulty.

You can help them by sending a donation,
large or small to:

**The Ulverscroft Foundation,
1, The Green, Bradgate Road,
Anstey, Leicestershire, LE7 7FU,
England.**
or request a copy of our brochure for
more details.

The Foundation will use all your help to
assist those people who are handicapped
by various sight problems and need
special attention.

Thank you very much for your help.